Praise for Erin Claxton

"*The Supernatural Detective* is a sexy, supernatural thriller. A perfect read for the beach."—*Diva* Magazine.

"*Scarlet Thirst* is a book for those who like their erotica to be a little more subtle but still sexy—à la Anne Rice or Mary Renault. Surely a fangtastic read for fans of Buffy, Willow and Tara!"—*Gay Voice*

"Claxton manages to pull the disparate threads together with prose and plotting that is never over-written or superfluous. Claxton has created an entirely believable other world. *Scarlet Thirst* is a great big fun, sexy, smart novel. Look out for it."
—*Rainbow Network*

By the Author

Scarlet Thirst

The Supernatural Detective

Death's Doorway

Visit us at www.boldstrokesbooks.com

DEATH'S DOORWAY

by
Crin Claxton

2015

DEATH'S DOORWAY

ISBN 13: 978-1-62639-354-7

This Trade Paperback Original Is Published By
Bold Strokes Books, Inc.
P.O. Box 249
Valley Falls, NY 12185

First Edition: June 2015

CREDITS
EDITOR: CINDY CRESAP
PRODUCTION DESIGN: STACIA SEAMAN
COVER DESIGN BY SHERI (GRAPHICARTIST2020@HOTMAIL.COM)

Acknowledgments

Thanks to my beta readers Hiraani Himona, Katherine May, Chiara Williams, Semsem Kuherhi, and Shelley Francis. Thanks to my consultants Martina Laird and Louise Palfrey. Your feedback and advice are invaluable to me and have shaped *Death's Doorway*. Support and encouragement keep me writing, and I'd like to thank Campbell, Bill Claxton, and Victoria Villasenor in particular. Sandy Lowe from Bold Strokes Books is always helpful and charming. My editor, Cindy Cresap, deserves a special mention. Working with Cindy has made me a stronger writer with her tireless elimination of exclamation marks and fancy tagging. And, Deni Francis, you are both light and shade. You are the person who supports me most and longest. Without you, none of my books would exist.

For my sisters Susan, Shelley, Katherine, Sharon.
Your support is everything.

PROLOGUE

Felicia stared at the neat lines of pills on the pockmarked table next to the bed and felt nothing. She didn't remember lining them up. She couldn't remember checking into the dark and grubby motel room, but there she was. It stank of damp and alcohol. An upturned bottle of red wine formed a sticky, crimson pool on the mottled orange carpet. The image should have made Felicia nauseous. But she was empty.

Felicia was exhausted. Her body was drained and her mind dull. Her cheeks were still wet from crying. It was all she could do lately.

She lay back on the worn orange cover on top of the bed. She closed her eyes to sleep.

Nothing.

She opened her eyes again, and there were the pills. Perfect shiny white disks. They were soothing. Felicia counted four lines of ten. Beside them was a tall glass of water. A fluorescent light flickered overhead. Felicia searched for a rhyme. She should be busting words in this sordid scene. Her hand reached for the Tylenol with its bright blue edge.

"Pimp ma pill," she mumbled to herself trying to raise a smile, but she was spent. If she couldn't rhyme, she was nothing. All she'd ever had were words.

She held the little round pill between her thumb and forefinger. She stared at it thoughtfully and then placed it on her tongue. The fingers of her left hand closed around the glass of water. She took a sip and the pill was swept away.

She had a sense of doing the right thing as she worked her way along the lines. The analgesics slipped down her unresisting throat.

Dimly aware of the soft click of a door closing, Felicia let her head sink into the thin pillow and was peaceful. Her star had crashed and burned. Nearby, a bike purred like a panther watching and waiting. Felicia drifted on the sound, letting it take her.

CHAPTER ONE

Tony Carson followed the young female ghost down the stairwell. Her feet flew over the steps. The ghost ran ahead, peering back at intervals to check that Tony was still behind her. The ghost's olive face was taut with fear.

"Which floor did you say?" Tony gasped out. It felt like they'd been running down stairs forever.

"The second." The ghost wasn't out of breath at all. But then she didn't have any breath to be out of.

Tony cursed the faulty lift.

"Hurry," the ghost said. "It's starting to smoke."

Tony ignored her protesting lungs and ran faster.

Four flights down, the ghost peeled off. She sailed through glass doors that led onto the second floor. Panting heavily, Tony pushed through them and ran along a corridor that was identical to her own ninth floor one. Municipal pale green walls were broken up at intervals by dark green flat doors. The large, council-run block of high-rise flats was in a hotchpotch condition. People who hadn't bought their houses under the right-to-buy scheme waited a long time to get things fixed. People who owned their own homes often carried out their own repairs, ignoring the rule that they were supposed to use council contractors to maintain uniformity in the communal spaces.

"For God's sake hurry, or you'll be too late." The deceased woman came to an abrupt halt outside a freshly painted door. It was a different shade of green from the others.

Tony pushed the door. It was shut. She backed off and prayed the dead woman hadn't reinforced it.

Tony ran at the door. Her shoulder hit it first. The jolt went up into her neck. The crash resounded along the deserted corridor. The door held.

Tony backed off again.

"What are you doing?" a voice called sharply behind her.

Tony turned round. An old woman stood outside the flat opposite, hands on hips.

"I ain't scared of you. I'm sick of all the thieving round here. I've called the police," she said, glaring at Tony.

"Good. I have to break in. There's a baby in danger."

Tony didn't stop to reassure the ghost's neighbor. She ran at the door again.

It gave with a crack of splintering wood.

Tony followed the ghost inside. The neighbor trotted behind her.

Tony ran through a living room littered with toys and into the kitchen.

A baby girl crawled across the kitchen floor, toward the stove. Smoke poured out of a pan sitting on a glowing ring. An oven cloth next to it was crisp with heat.

The cloth burst into flames. Tony stepped over a body on the floor and ran to the stove.

Tony grabbed the baby. The baby yelled in surprise and then began to cry.

With no time to comfort her, Tony passed her quickly to the neighbor.

"Take her. Get out both of you. Call the fire brigade," Tony commanded.

"Pelin!" The old woman pointed to the ghost's body crumpled by the kitchen door.

"Get the baby to safety," Tony said with barely a glance to the body. She stepped over it again and ran to the gas stove. The oven cloth was burning fiercely. A cloud of smoke gushed toward her.

"Tea towels in the second drawer," Pelin's ghost cried.

Tony snatched tea towels out of the drawer next to the sink and soaked them.

She threw a wet towel over the burning oven cloth. Then another over the smoking pan. She turned the ring off under the pan.

A loud shhhhh hit the air as heat met wet cloth.

Choking on the smoke, Tony tried to open the window. It was locked.

"I was worried about the baby falling out the window. Then I lost the key," Pelin said. "My husband said he could get another. I didn't remind him. It didn't seem important."

Tony put another wet towel over her mouth and nose. Knowing it was too late if she was talking to Pelin's ghost, nevertheless, she bent down to feel the body's neck, searching for a pulse.

There was none.

"My chest hurt. Like someone hit me with a sledgehammer," Pelin said.

Driven out by the clawing smoke, Tony walked back along the hallway and onto the corridor. The old woman was standing in her own doorway, rocking the baby girl in her arms.

"It's a bit smoky in there, but the fire's out," Tony told her.

"What about Pelin?" she asked.

Tony bit her lip. "I couldn't find a pulse. I didn't want to move the body."

The old woman glanced down at the baby and then back to Tony. "Who are you, anyway? I've seen you in the lift," she said, like being in the lift was a crime. Tony didn't mind. She'd lived in the council block long enough to know that people were suspicious first, friendly last.

"I'm a friend of Pelin's." Tony made up on the spot. "I live on the ninth floor. She called me, said she was feeling faint."

"Did she call an ambulance?"

"I don't know," Tony lied. "She said she had a pan on the stove, then the line went dead. I came straight away."

"Well, I called an ambulance, and the police and the fire brigade. They'll be here any minute," the old woman said. Her voice was sharp with worry. She held the baby tightly.

Boots thundered along the corridor. Firefighters in black and yellow came toward them at a run, followed by green-jacketed paramedics, and finally the police in yellow high vis jackets.

Tony explained what had happened and left her details. After that, there was no reason to stay and she was late for work. She returned to the neighbor.

"I have to go. I hope she's all right," Tony said, looking at the baby.

"Don't you want to know how Pelin is?" the old woman said.

Tony's eyes flicked to Pelin. The ghost looked down at her daughter with sad eyes full of love.

"I'll call Newham General later," Tony said, setting off along the corridor.

❖

Tony stood at the counter in her kitchen making tea in a mug. She stirred the teabag with a spoon and then fished it out. She plonked it in the direction of the Provincetown teabag holder in the shape of a whale that sat next to her kettle. Drops of dark brown tea splattered onto her white counter.

Automatically, she reached for a non-scratch scouring cloth before remembering her girlfriend, Maya, was at her own flat. Tony sighed with relief. If Maya wasn't around to frantically scrub at it, the tea stain could remain on Tony's countertop for a few minutes.

Tony adored Maya. She was exhausting in all the right ways. She was thoughtful, political, and sexy. Her only faults were that she had to discuss everything about relationships in intimate detail, and she was completely obsessed with cleaning. Tony figured that was a small price to pay for having a gorgeous and talented herbalist for a girlfriend.

Maya had been very quiet about her own issues lately. Maya was a therapist as well as a herbalist. She liked to drill down into other people's emotional stories. She said she wanted to help them move on. But whenever Tony or Jade mentioned Provincetown, Maya clammed up and changed the subject. Maya didn't want to talk about the uncle that had tried to kill her. Tony shuddered. She didn't like to think about it either. Especially as he had tried to kill her too. Tony was quite happy to stuff all the feelings down and never refer to them again.

Tony was having a night to herself. It was a rare night when Tony wasn't at work in the theater, seeing Maya, or hanging out with her friend, Jade. Tony had got used to living by herself after her ex-girlfriend and child had moved out a year previously. Maya and Tony had fallen into spending the nights together, either at Tony's council flat, or Maya's Stoke Newington apartment. Part of Tony ached to call Maya so they could tumble into bed. But most of Tony was enjoying her space. She ignored her wanton body for once and listened to her head.

She poured milk into the mug, didn't bother putting the milk back in the fridge, glanced at the unwashed up washing up, and headed back to her living room.

She flopped down on her sofa, put her feet up on the coffee table, and switched the TV to a program about ice truckers.

"Holy Kamoly, from that angle you could scare small children." Tony's drag queen spirit guide, Deirdre, fizzed in out of nowhere and hovered above the coffee table. She looked down at Tony from underneath a huge curly wig, kept vaguely in place by a massive hair band. Deirdre had passed away in the 1980s, and the period seemed to inspire her extraordinary outfits. Tony sat up straight, blinking at Deirdre's Day-Glo pink leotard, topped with a tiny pair of matching pink shorts and fluorescent orange leg warmers. "I hardly like to ask, but what are you wearing, and why?"

"This is my homage to *Fame*," Deirdre said, patting her wig and coming to rest at floor level. She did a couple of vaguely high-kicks and sang a line from the theme song badly. Tony winced.

"I've decided to be a celebrity," Deirdre informed Tony, her New York accent as thick as cream cheese on a bagel. "I've heard it's all the rage in the world of the living, and I want to fit in."

Tony shuffled about on the sofa, pulling a big cushion under her back. Maya had turned up with a present of several cushions with Lichtenstein prints on them. Tony had never bothered with cushions before, but had to admit they were comfortable. "Why? It's only me you talk to. Except of course Jade can hear you. And I suspect my dad is still seeing ghosts, so maybe he can see you..." Tony trailed off, wondering if Jade had latent powers that would make her see ghosts one day, or whether she would always only be able to hear them.

"How arrogant! You think you're the only medium on my books." Deirdre pursed her lips.

"I thought you were a spirit guide not an agent," Tony said.

"Potatoes, po-ta-toes," Deirdre said brusquely.

"I'm glad you've dropped by actually," Tony said. "Is it all right for me to just follow any ghosts if they suddenly appear?"

Deirdre studied Tony through narrowed eyes. "You're referring to your little jaunt into a burning building."

"It wasn't a burning building. It was a smoking pan and a smoldering tea towel," Tony said. "But yes."

"Not my jurisdiction," Deirdre said. "I can't insist ghosts go through me. However, I can't be held responsible for any damage to persons or property that may result from people not going through a proper spirit guide."

"What does that mean? You can't be held responsible anyway, can you?"

"I have to answer to entities! Important entities. But that's none of your concern. What I will say is remember it's at your own risk. This is all very new to you and you haven't got an ounce of common sense. When they were doling out common sense, you were standing in the line for stupidness. Pelin was desperate and a good soul, but that doesn't mean another one will be. Now, I've brought someone to see you, so try and look relatively normal."

Tony was thinking what a damn cheek Deirdre had insinuating she didn't look normal, especially as she'd just noticed "foxy lady" spelled out in sequins on the back of Deirdre's leotard, when the air in front of Tony's windows shimmered.

A butch white lesbian materialized, in a plain white T-shirt and dark blue skinny jeans. The edge of a soft cigarette packet poked out from under one rolled up arm of her T-shirt. She looked about thirty-five. She was small and slight and taut rather than muscular. Her short brown hair was slicked back. She fixed green eyes on Tony and nodded quickly without smiling.

"This is Frankie. She died some years ago," Deirdre said.

Frankie stared at Tony. She didn't look impressed.

"I don't know. She's a novice, you said." Frankie turned to Deirdre.

"She's been around the block. Well, she's limped off in the direction of the block." Deirdre looked at Tony doubtfully. Tony felt like a used car. "She's not bad, considering she only discovered her powers a few months ago."

"Isn't there anybody—"

"No." Deirdre cut Frankie off. "Nobody else. Anyway, she's lesbian. That's got to be in her favor."

"Tell that to the bigots who huddle near gay marches with their 'not Adam and Steve' placards," Tony muttered.

"You want Rose to let go, don't you?" Deirdre sounded impatient.

Frankie nodded.

"Then quit stalling." Deirdre turned to Tony. "Frankie needs her girlfriend to move on. She's been mourning her since 1967." Deirdre came to sit beside Tony on the sofa.

"That is a long time."

Frankie pulled a comb out of her back pocket and drew it through hair glistening with hair cream. "She still thinks I was murdered."

"And were you?"

"She thinks I was murdered because I told her I was being hassled by a guard."

"A guard?"

Frankie sniffed. "I was inside. In prison. There was a screw who was always on my back."

"Screw?" Deirdre looked up from filing her nails.

"Guard! I just said, didn't I?" Frankie said. "I told Rose he was roughing me up and that I was worried for my safety. I made out I was more scared of him than I was. Rose was going to break up with me. I wouldn't have lasted five minutes in there without her visits."

"How did you die?" Tony asked.

"Fight with another prisoner." Frankie squared up. "She got lucky, that's all. I took a blow to the head. Bled out inside my brain in the night."

"Didn't anyone check on you?" Tony asked.

"They don't check on you during lockup, least they didn't then. They just look through the peephole a couple of times in the night. It would have looked like I was sleeping."

"That's sad." Tony hated the idea of someone just slipping away.

Frankie grimaced. "How do you know? You don't know me. Maybe I was horrible. Maybe it was a good thing."

Tony wondered why Frankie was so down on herself. She talked tough but clearly had issues. "What do you need from me?"

"Can you go see Rose? She's still campaigning to get justice for me all these years later."

Tony nodded. "Of course."

Frankie straightened her shoulders and nodded back.

"So how am I going to convince her you weren't murdered?"

"I don't know. That's your job, isn't it?" Frankie pushed the comb through her hair another time, replaced it in her back pocket, and disappeared.

Deirdre shrugged semi-apologetically and then also vanished, leaving Tony to ponder on the problem.

❖

Jade Rogers woke in a cold sweat. A lonely voice played at the edge of her consciousness. She patted her fingers across the smooth wood panels surrounding her bed, fumbling for the light switch.

Not sure if she had heard the voice in her dream or in real life, Jade looked round the familiar things in her houseboat bedroom. She needed to know there was no one hiding in the shadows. Her wardrobe doors and her bedroom door were all firmly shut. The giraffes, elephants, and African women carvings were in their usual places on the thick floating teak shelf opposite the bed. The photo of the Maracas lookout point in Trinidad was hanging on her wall. Her comb and her big, chunky quartz necklace were lying on top of her chest of drawers, in the same places she'd left them.

Jade lay still, controlling her breathing to slow down her heart rate. Water slurped rhythmically. There was the occasional creak and tap from the rest of the boat, but no unusual sounds, certainly nothing mournful. Jade shivered. She tucked the duvet around her as she tried to remember exactly what it was she'd heard. Dream or not, whatever it was had left Jade anxious and disturbed. Jade felt it in the cold beads of sweat on her forehead and the gnawing feeling in her stomach.

She sat up in bed, pulling the extra thick duvet with her, and reached for her e-reader. Unwilling to risk slipping back into a horrible dream, Jade was soon engrossed in the comforting, fictional world of Lyremouth.

❖

Tony walked into the lighting control room of the theater in London's West End, where she worked. She sat on her black swivel chair and powered up the lighting board.

Beth, the deputy stage manager, came through the door as Tony was flashing through channels. Jade trotted at her heels.

"Hey, Hot Stuff, look who's come to see you," Beth said, smiling broadly.

"Hey, Jade. What's up?" Tony said.

"I was in the area and thought I'd come check out the show… if that's okay, Beth?" Jade deferred to the stage manager. Beth was a stickler for rules.

"Fine by me. Always a pleasure to see you. Jade. You know that." Beth pulled down her black T-shirt till it stretched over her chest. Jade dipped her eyes. Tony didn't know if either of them were consciously flirting. They were both such outrageous flirts it was possible they couldn't help themselves.

"No visitors in the technical or backstage areas unless by prior arrangement," Tony muttered under her breath in an imitation of Beth's posh, often prissy voice.

Beth glared at Tony. "Jade's hardly a visitor. Seeing as she's in the Business, she's practically a cast member," she snapped.

"I wish…" Jade sighed.

"Not like that quack homeopath Miranda, always popping up in people's dressing rooms without proper clearance," Beth said in full prissy mode.

Tony took a deep breath. "*Maya* is a herbalist, not a homeopath, and she treats cast members' injuries in their place of work as a favor," she said, matching Beth's prissy and in danger of raising it to stick-up-the-butt priggish.

Beth narrowed her eyes at Tony and then inexplicably broke into a gracious smile. "Anyway, the LD passed by earlier and left you a note."

"Thanks." Tony took a folded sheet of A4 paper covered in the lighting designer's illegible scrawl. She wished the LD would email his modifications, but he was old school and liked to scribble notes while watching a run.

"The director's in tonight," Beth went on. "We may have to put in an extra rehearsal tomorrow if he doesn't like what he sees."

"Okay." A new musical meant lots of tech runs and rehearsals.

They were lucky that when *Cabaret* came off at the end of the previous year and *Little Shop of Horrors* came in, the company kept most of the stage management and crew. It was tiring, but Tony was used to long hours in production week. When a West End show ran for a long time there wasn't a lot for the lighting operators to do between shows except re-lamp and change lighting gel. It more than made up for the long days during production week.

"Don't forget, if anything comes up with my casting I'm resting right now," Jade called as Beth headed for the door.

"Got your digits on speed dial, babe," Beth said in a voice dripping with honey as the door closed behind her.

Jade bustled about trying to find a swivel chair she approved of. For some reason the lighting control box seemed to be where everyone dumped old chairs. Most were broken or dirty and should have been sent off to wherever old technical chairs go when they retire.

"So, you were just 'in the area,' huh?" Tony teased her.

Jade looked sheepish. "Nah. I come to see the show. Thought there might be casting agents in and I could tap them in the bar." Jade's day-to-day accent was RP—the standard British accent that most actors adopted. But every so many words, her natural Trinidadian voice broke through like a burst of sunlight.

Tony shrugged. "Fair enough. Seems you've got Beth wrapped round your little finger."

Jade pursed her lips. "Yeah, but I ain't going there again. Leh me tell you. She's very sweet and all that, but I like meh women a bit more…"

"Manly," Tony suggested.

"I was going to say dykey, but, yeah, butcher than Beth anyway. Though she was hot in bed," Jade added as an afterthought, dabbing her fingers tentatively at a brown stain on one of the chairs. "What is that?" she asked.

"How should I know?"

"Well, it looks like coffee or tea or…" Jade left the third possibility hanging as she pushed the stained chair away from her and swung another round for inspection.

Tony opened the script marked with all the lighting cues and checked her communication headset was plugged in. The clock above her said five minutes to go to the Half when she should put them on.

"Oh, I was going to tell you, Deirdre popped by last night with a 1960s butch."

Jade's head snapped round from sniffing what was hopefully a paint stain on another chair. "Ay, ay! What she look like?"

"White woman, green eyes, scowly. She combed her hair a lot."

"You real hopeless, yes! How can I drool over that description? Anyway, I glad you seeing dead people again. I need a job, I mean, we need a job." She sat on the chair and the seat crashed down about two foot.

"Oh yeah, I remember the thing that pumps up the seat is broken on that one."

"No shit, Sherlock," Jade hissed, rubbing her bottom.

"And I've also remembered, that isn't paint."

Jade narrowed her eyes. "What is it?"

"Strawberry ice cream milkshake. I was seeing if I could swivel round really fast at the same time as drinking a very thick milkshake from a bendy straw that doubled as a pair of glasses."

Jade looked unimpressed. She pulled a third chair toward her. Tony put her headset on and depressed the mic button. "Tony on cans," she announced.

"Thank you, Tony." Beth's crisp stage manager voice confirmed she had received Tony's comm call. "Ladies and gentlemen of the *Little Shop of Horrors* company, this is your half hour call," Beth continued.

The air in front of the control room window went wavy before materializing into Deirdre in leopard skin leggings, high-heeled ankle boots, and a tight pink, ripped T-shirt, topped with a pink and blond wig.

"Oh good, Sherlock Groan and Dr. Whatsit."

"Watson. Which would be Tony. I would be Sherlock Holmes, seeing as I is the one that actually does any detecting," Jade said.

"That's about right. Anyhoo, I've had an idea. We need a letter from Frankie saying she made up that stuff about being in danger from the guard. You'll have to forge one, and then pretend you found it." Deirdre twirled a blond ringlet around a finger.

"Easy for you to say!" Tony muttered.

"Lighting preset state Go please," Beth said into Tony's headset. "Two minutes till we open the house."

"Can we discuss this later? The audience are about to take their seats and I have to work." Tony switched off the overhead light in the control box and turned on the dim show lights directed onto the lighting desk and her script.

"There's still a letter from Frankie in her old flat. You should go get that and then you'll have something to compare with for your forgery," Deirdre said as loudly as if she were whispering on stage.

"Great! Got any more impossible instructions to impart before you GO!" Tony said pointedly.

Deirdre smiled sweetly before melting away.

CHAPTER TWO

Unusually warm April sun poured out of a seamless sky. Maya was stretched out on the deck of Jade's houseboat: a Dutch barge moored in Poplar Marina in the east of London, close to the financial heartland of Canary Wharf. She stretched lazily. A light breeze swept a fresh, river tang under her nostrils. The sparkling glass and chrome skyscrapers of Canary Wharf towered above the lines of barges and narrowboats that nestled quietly in the still, clear, green waters of the marina.

Maya took a big, happy breath and turned her eyes to Tony, who was propped up against the white boards of the cabin. Tony had her arms tucked up behind her head and had turned her face to the sun. Her tight fitting blue T-shirt and long stone shorts reminded Maya of how Tony had looked in Provincetown the previous summer. Maya had a huge crush on her then. Maya had mixed feelings when she thought about that trip home. She'd gotten together with Tony, but it was also when her uncle had died. Maya's stomach tightened. She still found it hard to believe her uncle had wanted to kill her. Maya moved closer to Tony, feeling a surge of love for her. Tony had been there at the right moment. As strange as they were to Maya, she was eternally grateful for Tony's psychic abilities.

Maya pushed the memories aside. She slipped a hand under Tony's T-shirt and ran her fingers over her stomach and chest. Tony pulled off her sunglasses and drew Maya in for a long kiss.

Through a sweet mist of lust, fresh spring air, and the scent of wood toasting in the sun, Maya heard Jade cough politely.

Reluctantly, she pulled away from Tony's delicious embrace.

Jade put a tray laden with croissants and coffee on the deck. Enticed away from Tony by the scent of Jamaican Blue Mountain, Maya stood up. Jade pressed a steaming mug of coffee into her hands.

"There is a bedroom downstairs, ya know, if allyuh need ya privacy," Jade joked. Her Trinidad accent was as vibrant in her throat as the laughter was in her eyes. Jade looked gorgeous in a white vest and white denim cutoffs.

Jade raised a glass of sparkling water. "Here's to PI," she said.

Tony crinkled up her forehead. "Pie? Are we having pie? I'd rather have a croissant."

"Paranormal Investigators. That's what I thought we should call ourselves." Jade laughed.

They were discussing Tony and Jade's detective agency. They'd formed an official company to cope with the requests from ghosts. Jade was especially keen on making the business work as she was out of an acting job.

"I thought we'd agreed on the Supernatural Detective Agency," Tony said.

"Yeah, but that's so boring, mon. If we're Paranormal Investigators, you can call yourself 'Tony Carson P.I.'"

"And why would I want to do that?"

"Because it's cool. And the ladies go love it." Jade winked.

"Really?" Tony raised an eyebrow.

Maya shot her a warning look.

"I have a lady," Tony said quickly. "You're very hot when you're stern," Tony muttered, grinning at Maya.

"Remind me about that later," Maya said, "when I can do something about it."

"Well, how about Paranormal Investigation Agency—PIA?" Jade said.

"Pee-er, Jade, really, are you having a laugh?" Tony said.

"How about the Unusual Detective Agency—UDA?" Maya suggested.

"Oh God!" Tony groaned. "Maya, please don't help Jade create a name out of pronounceable initials. Especially as neither of you seem to care how ridiculous the name sounds."

Jade laughed. "Okay, we'll stick with the Supernatural Detective

Agency for now. But you have to remember we're both in the agency. No more running into burning buildings to save babies on your own."

Tony looked sad. Pelin's neighbor had dropped a note through Tony's letter box saying Pelin had died. "It wasn't a burning building. More of a smoking pan on the stove. But what am I supposed to do if someone needs my help, Jade? I have to go straight away, don't I?"

Jade looked at her thoughtfully. "I guess it was an emergency. All the same, we need to think about some ground rules. I worry about you."

"Ground rules are a sensible idea," Maya said diplomatically. She didn't like the idea of Tony taking high risks either.

Tony smiled over at Jade. "Okay, if it makes you happy." She bit off a hunk of chocolate croissant and took a gulp of coffee "Now. We need to think about how we're going to get into Frankie's old flat. Rose still lives there. Can you believe that?"

Maya smiled affectionately. Tony had jumped to talking about their new case.

"I could play the part of someone calling on her, like a salesperson," Jade said thoughtfully.

"That's a great idea." Tony sat up. "Deirdre said that Rose loves anything to do with catalogs and household goods. What if you were one of those people that sell door to door?"

"But how could I distract her long enough to get the letter? You said it's tucked away behind a drawer in an old desk?" Jade asked.

"Hmm. I don't know. I don't want to be anywhere near the place, not if I'm going to go back and see her. I'll have a think about that later. Meantime, shall we go over your *Spotlight* details? That's why we came over." Tony shoved the last of her croissant into her mouth, and squinted at an A4 printout of the details Jade was sending to *Spotlight*, the online casting catalog for actors. "My God, are you really using that photograph again?"

Jade narrowed her eyes. "Yes, I was going to. Why?"

Maya looked over Tony's shoulder. The heavily contrasted black-and-white picture of Jade looked like a film noir shot. Her face was lifted from the hard shadows behind by soft backlighting.

"Because it's over five years old and it's not doing you any favors. Unless you were going up for femme fatale," Tony said.

Jade chewed her croissant thoughtfully. "It don't matter how old it is. I have a young face," she said through a mouthful of crumbs. Maya was astounded by how both Jade and Tony talked with their mouths full. It didn't seem to bother them at all that they displayed the half-chewed contents of their mouths to the rest of the world.

"But last week when you were going up for someone late forties you said you had an old face," Tony said.

"I said I could *play older*! Jesus Christ, Tony!" Jade snapped. "And I could play femme fatale."

"I didn't say you couldn't. Incidentally, you could *so* play femme fatale." Tony smiled.

"Thank you, Tony," Jade purred, her previous annoyance forgotten. Maya loved their relationship. Tony and Jade were tight. They'd known each other for years and had an easy, playful familiarity. They'd met on a show. Tony was a lighting technician, and Jade a musical theater actress. Tony said they were like family. Jade's last show had finished its run early, though, so she was looking hard for a new job.

"You need a new headshot. This is too specific, sweetheart. You need one that says you could play anything," Tony said, her eyes still fixed on the photograph.

"Yes," Jade said thoughtfully. "That *is* what I need."

Tony read down the page. "Circus skills!" She spluttered into her tea. "What circus skills do you have?"

Jade sniffed. "I can juggle!"

"Badly. I don't think dropping two oranges over and over constitutes juggling."

Jade frowned. "Oh yeah, I forget you came to the circus fundraiser for the Hackney Women's Football Club."

"What do they need money for anyway?" Tony asked. "Really short-shorts?"

"Do they wear really short-shorts?" Maya asked.

"Some of them," Jade said. "And actually, Tony, everyone's suffering with this recession. We need to look after our own."

"Very true," Tony said.

"I'm quite happy to look after our own," Maya said, helping herself to more of the fragrant coffee. "Particularly if they're cute sportswomen wearing short-shorts."

"Hmmph! You stay away from the Hackney Women's Football team." Tony narrowed her eyes.

"What, all of them?" Jade asked.

"Yes!" Tony replied.

"She might not be able to. Some of them might have sports injuries," Jade teased her.

"I can do circus skills," Maya said.

Tony and Jade stared at her.

"What circus skills? Lion taming?" Tony asked.

"Don't be ridiculous. That would be cruel. Why would I want to do that?" Maya glared at Tony.

"Yes, of course it would. Sorry," Tony said. "But can you ride one of those little bikes?"

"A unicycle? Yes, I can. I can ride it on the ground or on the high wire."

"No! High wire, for real?" Jade asked eagerly.

"Yes, I can even do it while juggling!"

"For goodness sake, where did you learn that? Can you do trapeze? Do you have any outfits?" Tony asked hopefully.

Maya laughed. "I learned at summer camp, of course, where all good American kids learn stuff."

"Awww. How sweet. Were there elephants there?" Tony asked.

"No!" Maya said. "What is it with you and circus animals?"

"I had this great story book when I was little. It was about a lion and an elephant, and there were monkeys and some clowns. One day the monkeys got into the clowns' caravan and—"

"Tony," Maya said gently. She never liked to trample on people's childhood memories. "That was a story. Keeping animals in a circus is wrong and must be stopped, as you well know."

"Yes, ma'am," Tony said in a charming attempt at a Southern accent. "You're a dark horse. What else can you secretly do? Brain surgery? Tree surgery? Cat burglary? I don't mean with real cats," she added hastily.

Maya bit off a small piece of croissant and chewed it properly, swallowing before replying. "I probably could do cat burglary, what with my climbing and lock picking skills."

"You know how to lock pick?" Jade raised her eyebrows.

"Sure, you had to be able to lock pick at Escapology Camp."

"Is there a summer camp for absolutely everything in the USA?" Tony asked.

"Pretty much," Maya said, biting off another small piece of the flaky French pastry. "I liked doing something different. And my parents encouraged it. My mother didn't believe in summer camp anyway, and my dad, well, he always liked it if I did something unconventional."

"Evidently. Well, I have some handcuffs if you'd like to demonstrate," Jade said suggestively over her tin mug.

"If she's going to demonstrate to anyone, it'll be to me," Tony said firmly.

"Honestly, Tony, you're so selfish. This could be the one thing I need to get my career started again," Jade said, winking subtly at Maya.

"Oh well, you could show us both, I suppose," Tony said grudgingly, gulping the last of her coffee.

"Oh, Tony, I thought you'd never ask." Jade squeezed Tony's knee lightly. "A threesome's just what we need to cement this new relationship of yours."

Tony choked. "That's not what I mean," she told Maya. "That's not what I mean at all!" She looked like she would have gone on protesting if Maya and Jade hadn't been laughing so hard. Tony's face turned thoughtful. "But you know what, Maya? That's perfect."

"What is?" Maya grinned.

"Your cat burgling skills. Fancy working for the Supernatural Detective Agency? You're just the person we need to get Frankie's letter."

❖

Jade sat bolt upright, her heart pounding.

A pitiful, crying noise rang in her ears. The face of a black woman swam in her mind: a storm of hair, strong, full lips, dark shadows under her eyes, and tears running down her cheeks.

Jade felt anxious as hell. Something awful was about to happen.

She fumbled for the light switch beside her bed and switched it on.

Her mouth was bone-dry. She reached for the glass of water on the cabinet next to her and drained it. The water was ice cold. Jade shivered. The air in her room was freezing. She pulled the duvet closer and tried to snuggle down under it.

Experimentally, Jade blew out a stream of air in front of her.

It was cold enough to see her breath.

What was going on? That was odd, even for England.

Jade cursed the UK's teasing weather. One minute it let a person believe it might actually give a little warmth, the next it threw a sheet of ice at her. Jade fancied a nice hot cup of tea. Laughing at how English that sounded, Jade stretched a toe out from under the covers. Then she remembered Tony and Maya were sleeping in the boat's living room next door. Noise really carried in the houseboat. She didn't want to wake them up by tripping past them to the kitchen. Jade had been pleased the previous night, when they had decided to stay over. With the weird dreams getting frequent, it had been comforting to know someone else was there. The frustrating thing was that Jade could never remember them when she woke.

She felt cold deep in her bones. She pulled the duvet even closer, trying to wrap it entirely round her body. If only she had a woman in bed with her to keep her warm and to take her mind off the haunting crying.

Jade glanced at her pic of Maracas lookout point and tried conjuring up Maracas Beach, where tall, green-fringed coconut palms swayed gracefully over white sand that shimmered in the midday sun. But even that didn't work. It seemed nothing could penetrate the cold that had seeped inside her body.

Shivering and tense, Jade padded over to the built-in wardrobe and put on a sweatshirt, and then a hoody on top of that. She pulled the hood over her head. Then she reached up to the top shelf for her batik bedspread and wrapped it around herself. She closed the wardrobe door, noting how cold the wood was under her palm. The icy temperature was freaking Jade out. She had never felt so cold in her bedroom, not even in the depths of winter.

The mournful crying played in her head like a tune that wouldn't leave her alone. Jade didn't like it at all. She was filled with a sense of hopelessness. Jade was a naturally upbeat person, so that must be from the dream as well.

She decided she was going to have to risk waking Tony and Maya and make some tea. Maybe she *should* wake Tony? *What if there was a ghost in the room right now? Not speaking. Just watching me.*

She was two steps from the bedroom door when there was a crash on the dockside.

Jade froze.

Something scrabbled about outside.

A loud, high-pitched, unnerving call pierced the silence. It sounded similar to a baby crying.

Jade let out a sigh of relief as she recognized the call of a vixen in heat.

"You foolish girl," she told herself. The sound of her own voice was comforting.

That must have been what she'd heard in her sleep.

Jade got back into bed, taking the bedspread with her. She snuggled under the covers. Her room felt warmer now that she knew what had been setting off the dreams. She chuckled at the power of her imagination.

The pillow was soft and familiar. Jade curled her relaxed body into the perfectly comfy, perfectly toasty bed and let sleep wash over her.

❖

Maya slipped through the side gate and into the backyard of the shop under Frankie's old apartment. She pressed herself into a dark corner, giving Jade time to ring the apartment's doorbell.

As soon as Tony confirmed through Maya's wireless earpiece that Rose had buzzed Jade in, Maya started to climb the drainpipe leading to Rose's bathroom. Her choice of black cycling shorts and neoprene jersey were perfect for the job. She prayed the wobbly fixing at the top of the pipe was going to hold.

When she was high enough to see the red Rawlplugs coming out of the wall, Maya reached into the open bathroom window and lifted it wide enough to get her head through. She quickly cleared some toiletries from the window ledge before climbing through the window and then used the sink to haul herself upright.

She cranked open the bathroom door and listened. There was a rumble of voices nearby. Maya crept onto the landing. Jade's voice drifted out from the sitting room.

"Look here, madam, in the recycling section of our catalog. These reasonably priced containers would enable you to neatly tidy away those piles of magazines. And look, with a quick flick of this long-handled static duster, you'd get rid of those cobwebs in a trice."

"Trice!" Tony's voice tweaked in Maya's earpiece as well as, she presumed, Jade's. "Ease back. You're not playing Cinders in panto."

Gratified, both that Jade was carrying off her role of door-to-door salesperson to distract Rose, and that the earpiece was working, Maya cautiously opened the door opposite the bathroom.

The door swung open into a small bedroom.

It was empty. Maya let out a breath. Even though Deirdre had assured Tony that the apartment was unoccupied apart from Rose, Maya liked to trust her own eyes and ears.

She went straight to an old school teacher's desk, sitting in front of a small window. She opened the middle drawer, carefully pulled it out, and then felt behind in the drawer cavity.

Her fingers touched paper.

She knelt and flipped on her head torch.

As she leaned in for a closer look, a floorboard under her knee creaked.

She froze.

"Did you hear that?" she said into the radio transmitter clipped around her ear.

"Yes," Tony grunted. "What did you do, kill a mouse?"

"What is it with you and animal cruelty?"

"I didn't really think you'd...anyway, we'll get into that later. Luckily, they're still rattling on about microfiber radiator brushes. Hurry up."

Maya tutted. She didn't want Tony barking orders in her ear, and she'd tell her so later.

She peered into the drawer cavity and saw a letter pressed flat against the wood at the back.

Pulling carefully so not to tear it, she pried it out.

"Got it," she said into her transmitter.

"Great. Oh no! Quick. You need to hide. Rose wants to show Jade her sock storage. They're coming to the bedroom. You can probably get to the bathroom if you go right now."

With fumbling fingers, Maya replaced the drawer.

She darted out of the room and across the hallway.

She was just closing the bathroom door behind her when the sitting room door opened.

She pushed her door shut softly.

Someone went past on the landing. Then the bedroom door opposite opened as Jade shouted from the sitting room, "But, madam, I really don't like to go into people's bedrooms."

A voice with a strong London accent answered her. "That's all right. I'll bring the sock drawer to you. Also, I want to show you my bathroom knickknacks."

Maya frantically scanned the bathroom for a hiding place.

There was nowhere.

More footsteps ran along the passage.

Maya was almost at the bathroom window when the door handle started to turn.

Even if she got out of the window in time, she hadn't replaced the toiletries. Maya scrambled onto the window ledge.

"Have you got a washday wonder?" Jade said desperately. Her voice was a good octave above her normal pitch. It sounded like she was just outside the bathroom door.

"Ooh. No. What is a washday wonder?" Rose asked.

"It will stop your windows from steaming up when using your tumble dryer," Jade said.

"But I don't have a tumble dryer." Rose sounded disappointed.

"Okay…but you have a shower, or a bath, don't you? And you must have steamy windows. Imagine…" Jade paused dramatically. "First the steam and then mold and mildew. Not only is it unsightly, but it leaves you prone to respiratory infections."

"Oh no, I don't want respiratory infections. I have to watch that colds don't go onto my chest."

"Good. I mean, of course you do. Come back into the sitting room. Bring your sock drawer. I'll show you the washday wonder in the catalog. It could cure your condensation problems forever."

Two sets of footsteps moved away.

Quickly, Maya eased back out onto the drainpipe and then moved the toiletries back into position.

She shimmied down to the bottom and then darted across the deserted yard.

As the gate clicked shut behind her, she had started to sprint down the street with Frankie's letter firmly tucked into the pocket of her cycling shorts.

❖

Tony sat next to Maya at the dining table. Maya's attention was firmly on the letter in front of her as she attempted to copy Frankie's handwriting. Tony watched her. Maya was very sexy when she was concentrating.

Tony sighed.

She tapped her fingers on the top of the dining table, making a rhythmic drumming sound.

Maya glared at her.

"I can't concentrate if you're going to make that noise," she said sharply.

Tony stopped. She really wanted Maya's attention on her, not on the piece of paper lying beneath Maya's fingers. "But you've been ages. This is my only night off, and I thought we might, you know…"

Maya's face softened. "Honey, I'd love to 'you know' with you, and Lord knows you 'you know' so well, but you said this letter from Frankie was urgent."

Tony ran her finger up Maya's bare arm. Maya's shoulders went up as she gave a little shiver. Tony dropped her voice. "I don't know if ghosts have a concept of urgency. Deirdre says time isn't the same for them as it is for us. I'm sure the letter can wait a few minutes." She nuzzled Maya's cheek, letting the words tumble over Maya's olive skin.

Maya's eyelids dipped as Tony came in for a kiss. Tony breathed in the citrus tang of Maya's perfume. She was soft and warm in Tony's arms. Sweet tension pulsed through Tony's body as Maya's tongue explored her mouth.

"Well, that trick will come in handy if you get caught underwater with only one oxygen tank between you."

Tony jerked her head away from Maya.

"What's the matter?" Maya said, alarmed.

"Oh, I'm sorry, darling. It's Deirdre." Tony frowned at Deirdre, willing her to take the hint and evaporate.

Maya's eyes darted round Tony's living room. Tony knew Maya couldn't see ghosts. She had to take Tony's word for it that Deirdre was there.

"Deirdre, can you go away please? We're busy." Tony reluctantly untangled her body from Maya's.

"But you're not busy." Deirdre perched herself on the edge of the sofa, folded her arms, and looked over at them sternly. "Maya should be busy, forging that letter. But you are seducing her, which is admirable, and some may have thought unlikely. I was as surprised as everybody else when Maya settled for you."

"What do you mean settled?" Tony asked, feeling annoyed.

"Hmm, how can I put this?" Deirdre peered down her nose at Tony. "If Maya was steak then you would be hamburger. Only hamburger's pushing it. You're more like soy protein dressed up to look like hamburger."

Tony glared at Deirdre. "As Maya is vegetarian, she would be the soy protein and I would be the steak."

"What are you talking about?" Only hearing half the conversation, Maya was clearly lost.

"You're not steak, honey. You do have certain charms, which are at their best in dim light. I presume that's why you work in that dark little room in the theater. Anyhoo, I wanted to pop in without that bad tempered butch frowning over my shoulder. She's carrying some heavy energy and an unfortunate haircut. I suppose she was cramped in a cell for a long time, clearly with no access to anything remotely stylish. All very sad, but I'm running out of sympathy. My life's been no fun at all since she showed up. She's a real party pooper."

"She probably had her hair cut in prison. I don't suppose they get much choice about styling," Tony said.

"You'd have to do something truly terrible to be punished with a haircut like that. She obviously pissed off Big Betty with the buzz clipper. And I don't think they liked her in the kitchen. Someone dumped half a ton of grease on her head." Deirdre sniffed.

"That was the style then, as you well know. Her hair's fine, a little short maybe. Your problem is you come from an era of huge hair. We like hair short again now."

"What *are* you talking about?" Maya sounded both confused and left out.

Tony stroked Maya's hand. "Sorry, darling. We're talking about Frankie's haircut."

"Why?" Maya said irritably.

Tony shrugged. "Sorry, baby." She had a hard time working Deirdre out. How much harder must it be for Maya? "What are you trying to say, Deirdre?"

Deirdre looked thoughtful. "Frankie's getting on my nerves. She's like a short, frowny raincloud following me around. She needs to pass over. She won't do that till you convince her girlfriend to let her go."

"We're working on it," Tony said. "But I'd be surprised if it's that easy. Rose must have loved Frankie very much to keep the campaign going all these years. What makes you think she'll stop now?"

Deirdre looked thoughtful. "Someone needs to tell her. It's cruel to let her keep wasting her time on that campaign. Who knows what she could have done with her life if she hadn't have been running around with a placard."

"I don't think it was that kind of campaign," Tony muttered. "I don't know, though, maybe they did go on marches."

Deirdre wasn't listening. "She could have been anybody, done anything. She could have been prime minister. Or a female wrestler."

Tony rubbed her eyes. There was no point in trying to make sense of Deirdre's tangents.

"Or the first female Mountie."

Tony frowned. "Wouldn't she have had to go to Canada?"

"Exactly! She could have gone to Canada. Instead she spent five decades of her life spearheading a doomed campaign. Only a lesbian would hang on to an ex for five decades, by the way."

Tony decided to ignore that. "You're saying that Frankie's annoying you and someone should tell Rose she's wrong about her ex?"

"See, that's why they call you the Supernatural Detective," Deirdre said sweetly. "Forge the letter saying that Frankie made it up about being in danger. Take it to the girlfriend. No doubt she'll be relieved to be able to let go. And voilà, you can go back to kissing and canoodling."

Tony glanced at Maya. She had resumed work on the letter. Tony wanted to talk more with Deirdre about Frankie. Something didn't sit right about the case. But it wasn't fair to Maya to carry on a conversation she couldn't be part of. Tony pushed the thought away.

❖

The photographer's studio was a loft room in Stoke Newington. Skylights in the sloping roof flooded the space with natural light. It bounced softly off cream walls onto blond wood floorboards. Jade had taken the plunge of getting new headshots done. She was perched on a stool, trying to compose her face into an expression that would make her stand out to casting agents—casting agents who scanned hundreds of actors' pictures every time they looked to fill a role.

Ambient trance music was playing at a low volume. Jade thought it was probably whale song. It wasn't to her taste, but it was innocuous enough. The photographer was a laid-back white guy. He had a neat brown beard and short wavy hair. He was stocky, rather than tall, dressed in jeans and a sky blue casual shirt, open at the neck. Jade felt comfortable with him but not completely relaxed. He didn't speak much, and when he did, he spoke to her through the camera lens. He was fiddling about with a big, round silver reflector that was reluctant to leave its case. Eventually, he got it out and clipped it to a stand.

Jade checked herself in the mirror set up behind the camera. She practiced an unsmiling, "Hire me, I'm fantastic, I can play any part," pose.

The photographer stepped back into position and started clicking away.

Jade tried looking fantastic and hirable in left profile and right profile. Then she was unsure if she looked good in profile at all. Jade hated trying to guess what casting agents were looking for. She needed to look attractive but not too much like a model. Some actors said you should look neutral, but then you ended up looking bland. *This is why I hate having my headshots done.*

"Excuse me; you're gritting your teeth. It's making you look severe. You might want to relax a little," the photographer said, bent over the camera.

Jade moistened her lips and leaned her head back, trying to relax her shoulders. The trance music had become annoying. There was a wailing sound that was getting on her nerves. Jade took a deep breath. *Head back, face to camera. That's always a good look for me.* She tried to project radiance.

The plinkety music faded into the background as shrieking sounds swelled. Jade tensed. *How is anybody supposed to look gorgeous with that god-awful noise in their ear?*

"Can ya turn the music down? Or better still, off," Jade said, trying to keep the irritation out of her voice.

"Music?" The photographer looked up from the camera. He cocked his ear, listening. "What music?"

Jade stared. How could he not hear it?

She took a breath.

A loud banging came out of nowhere.

The wailing swelled until she could hardly hear anything else. The photographer was looking at her strangely.

Suddenly, the silver reflector whipped off its stand and clattered to the floor.

"What's wrong with that thing?" he mumbled.

Halfway to retrieve the reflector, he stopped. "Hey, are you okay?" He looked at Jade with a worried expression.

Jade barely registered his concern. The banging noises and plinking music had stopped. All she could hear was the loud and terrible crying from her dreams.

CHAPTER THREE

Frankie's old girlfriend, Rose, buzzed Tony into her flat after only a minute of conversation through the intercom. Tony pondered on that as she mounted the stairs. Rose should be more careful. First, Jade had got into the flat on the strength of selling household products. Now, Tony had got through just by mentioning Frankie's name.

At the top of a dark hallway, a flimsy front door was ajar. Tony edged it open and called round, "Hello! It's the woman with the letter!"

"Come through, first door on the right." Rose had one of those female voices that Tony loved—confident and gravelly. She had a strong, white, working-class London accent.

Tony walked along a hallway covered in wood chip wallpaper, painted magnolia. It was a look popular in the 1980s. She passed clip frames full of photos of lesbians, mostly butches and femmes. There were shots of pride marches and feminist demonstrations, as well as groups posed at a party and on a day out at the beach.

In the sitting room, Rose was laid out on an Edwardian chaise longue with an iPad propped up on perched knees. She smiled, and Tony's heart skipped a beat. Rose's skin was etched with fine lines. She wore her silver hair long and tied back with a diamante clip. She had full lips, a long, straight nose, well-defined eyebrows, a haughty, determined chin, and startling eyes whose color was somewhere between green and light hazel. She was petite and elegant. Tony guessed that Rose must be in her eighties. She was beautiful.

"Are you going to stand there all day, love?" Rose's deliciously deep voice broke into Tony's thoughts.

"You shouldn't just let people in!" Tony blurted out.

Rose stared at her for a moment. "So people keep telling me. But didn't you say you had a letter? Why don't you sit down?"

Rose's chaise longue was spread out under a big sash window. Sunlight filtered into the room through net curtains. A floor-to-ceiling bookcase took up most of the wall opposite the door. It was filled with feminist books, lesbian novels, poetry, and classical English literature. Magazines were piled up by the chaise. A Victorian armchair sat next to a beautifully renovated fireplace with a black grate and pale mantelpiece. Photographs and posters covered the walls. Most of the photos were of Frankie.

The framed posters caught Tony's eye. They advertised fundraising club nights for the Justice For Frankie White campaign. From the lettering and entry prices, and the names of the singers and bands appearing, it was obvious the posters spanned several decades.

"I've heard of that campaign," Tony said. She had been reading up about it online, but, looking at one of the posters, she dimly recalled going to a fundraiser in the nineties.

Rose followed Tony's glance to the posters. "Justice for Frankie," she read aloud. "Well, love, we're still trying to get justice for her. We hadn't had a fundraiser for a long time, but funny enough we've decided to have a small event in the autumn. It's more of a get-together for all the supporters. I'm looking forward to it." Her eyes twinkled. "To be honest, it's a good excuse to catch up, and to keep Frankie's name out there. We'll make some noise about other prisoners' campaigns as well. I don't suppose we'll make a lot of money for ours. We rely on online donations these days. It's enough to keep us going. I still write my letters to the home office. They politely ignore me as always. But I'll carry on as long as the man that killed Frankie is alive."

With Rose in front of her, Tony wanted to hear her side of the story. "Do you mind telling me more about Frankie's case?" she asked.

"I don't mind at all. But only if you sit down. You're making the place untidy standing there." Rose tipped her head toward the armchair.

Tony settled into it.

"She died on the twenty-seventh of August, 1967, in Holloway prison. She was murdered by a prison guard, Ron Somers. The official line was that she hit her head fighting with another prisoner and bled out in the night, but I'm convinced that Somers was the one that hit her. He was always beating her up. The last time I saw Frankie she had two black eyes. She showed me her ribs too. Black and blue. She told me Somers was always on her back, and if he got the chance, he'd rough her up. He was a homophobe and he took a particular dislike to Frankie. It had to be serious for Frankie to tell me about it. She was tough, my Frankie." Rose swallowed.

"Even if, by some remote chance, they were right and she did get a brain injury from fighting a prisoner, then he was still to blame for her death. He was the guard on duty, and I know for a fact she never saw a doctor. He locked her up in her cell that night, and she was dead in the morning. They sent me a letter. That's how I found out that my girl had gone."

Tony shifted. "They didn't send anyone to see you?"

Rose shook her head. "No, love. They didn't come to see me, but I tried to see them. They wouldn't meet me because they didn't count me as a relative. I had so many questions I needed answering. I didn't even get her belongings. I would have liked that. She put me down as next of kin, but they didn't honor it.

"I went to the inquest, though. Frankie was fitted up, and nobody seemed to give a damn about a young, butch prisoner. That would have been the end of it for a lot of people. It's really hard taking on the system. But I've always been a fighter. I got my friends involved. At first it was just the queers: the butches, the femmes, and the queens. The feminists didn't want to know because Frankie was a butch and we admitted she'd been fighting, but they changed their minds and got on board later. It grew and grew. To be honest, the campaign kept me going in those awful first months after I lost her." Rose smiled softly at Tony. "I've met some wonderful people over the years, and we've had some triumphs. Because of us making a fuss about Frankie they started looking in on prisoners through the night. We're very involved with prisoners' rights groups, especially ones that look into deaths in prisons. But, oh goodness, listen to me rattling on. Didn't you have a letter for me?"

Tony smiled. "Yes." She got up. "It sounds like you've done a lot of good."

"Well, we're not going to stop anytime soon. I have a feeling in my bones, we'll get justice for Frankie one day." Rose's voice had a quiet determination in it.

Tony handed the letter to Rose and then returned to the armchair.

Rose stared at the envelope. "You haven't opened this?"

Tony shook her head. She truthfully hadn't.

"Oh. I wasn't expecting...I haven't seen that writing in a long time," Rose said. She pulled open a drawer in the small table next to the chaise. She took out a silver letter opener and used it to slice open the envelope. There was a tremor in her fingers as Rose pulled the letter out. Rose picked up a pair of glasses from the table.

Rose unfolded the letter and read it through. Tony knew what Maya had written: a description of how Frankie had been passing the time in prison, and some words of endearment, both copied exactly from the letter Maya had taken from Rose's desk. Then a short paragraph saying that Frankie had been lying about the prison guard harassing her.

Rose's mouth dropped open as she got to the bottom of the second page. Her breathing quickened. She read both sides of the letter and then turned it over and read the second side again.

Eventually, she laid the letter in her lap. She lifted the glasses from her nose and placed them beside her.

"Where did you find this?" she asked. The blood had drained from her face.

Tony took a breath. Jade and Maya had taken care to find a genuine 1960s stamp for the letter. Tony had carefully aged the paper and envelope by soaking in tea. "My uncle has just died, and we're clearing out his house."

"Oh, I'm sorry," Rose murmured.

"Thank you," Tony said. "The letter was in a handbag that must have belonged to my aunt. She's also dead, unfortunately," Tony said.

"I see. What was her name?"

"Martha Jones."

Rose shook her head. "I don't think I knew her."

Tony was absolutely certain Rose hadn't known her, as Tony had made her up.

"Did she work in the prison service?" Rose asked.

"No. She worked for the Royal Mail, in a sorting office. The letter was stuck to a paperback that was in her handbag. I can only guess that she was reading at work and accidentally picked up your letter. She would have been mortified to know she'd been responsible for a letter not getting delivered. She died a long time ago, 1967."

"The same year Frankie died." Rose's voice was flat.

"Yes."

Rose's eyes dropped to the letter, still in her hand. "So, this letter has been sitting in a dead woman's handbag all these years." She glanced up at Tony. "I don't mean to be callous, dear."

"That's okay. You look like you've had a shock." Tony didn't know what to do. This wasn't the scene she'd imagined.

"Sorry, love. This letter's from Frankie." Rose ran a finger over the words on the page tenderly. "But it looks like I've wasted a lot of people's time. Frankie wasn't the woman I thought she was."

Rose sank back onto the chaise. Her shoulders drooped.

Tony followed Rose's eyes to a silver-framed, black-and-white photo of Frankie on a Triumph motorbike. She was wearing the jeans and leather jacket Tony had seen her in. Her arms were folded and she smiled rakishly at the camera.

Tony coughed.

Rose blinked. "I'm feeling tired, dear. Can you let yourself out?"

As Tony stood, Rose looked up and mouthed, "Thanks." Her eyes didn't say thank you at all. Her eyes were filled with despair.

❖

Jade reached for her mobile as it sang the first bars of "Indian Gyal." She didn't know the number, but as soon as he started to speak, she recognized the photographer's voice.

"Ms. Rogers, I'm very sorry to say that something has corrupted your jpeg files."

Jade hoped that wasn't as unpleasant as it sounded.

"I'm afraid we'll have to arrange another shoot."

Jade sighed.

"Obviously, at no cost to you," the photographer rushed on. He sounded stressed. "I've sent you the thumbnail files anyway, even though some weird double exposure thing's happened. That isn't possible with digital images so I can't begin to understand it. Anyway, there are a few great shots of you, at least they would be great without the distortion. So have a look, and if you like them we can re-create, hmm?"

"Okay." Jade stretched, willing a knot of tension to melt away. She didn't like photo shoots at the best of times, and now it looked like she would have to do that one again.

"Let me know what you think, and email me some times and dates you can come back to the studio."

"Sure. Bye." Jade booted up her tablet, hit the email icon, and scanned the bold subject titles. "Thumbnails, Jade Rogers" caught her eye. She opened the compressed folder and extracted the contents.

The first three images were fine. Unfortunately, they were awful of Jade. The next few images had a distorted area next to Jade's right shoulder. It was impossible to make out what it was. It looked like a stain or like an image that had been magnified to the point of just seeing pixilation.

As Jade clicked through the images one by one, the bleary area began to form a shape. First the dark mass near Jade's head resolved into a shock of natural African hair. Then the obscure area by Jade's shoulder began to look like a face.

Jade clicked quickly from image to image with fear growing in her belly.

She froze as she stared at the twentieth image. On the right-hand side of the photo was an attractive, dark-skinned, young black woman in a tight red T-shirt. Her mouth was wide open, and the tendons of her neck taut and prominent, as she screamed, in profile, her lips inches away from Jade's face.

❖

Between two appointments, Maya made up some repeat prescriptions. When people came to see her, she prepared their scripts at the end of their consultation so that they could take the herbal medicine away with them. However, there were always postal prescriptions for regular patients between visits that needed to be mixed.

Maya had moved most of her herbal tinctures and supplies to the alternative health center when she had rented a consulting room there, six months previously. The room suited her fine. It had three chairs and a examination couch. She didn't feel safe seeing clients at home anymore. Maya had practiced at home for seven years, ever since she had qualified as a medical herbalist. Unfortunately, it had only taken one bad experience to change that. Maya tensed as she remembered Sheila, the client who had attacked her in her own garden, and then followed her to attack her again. Sheila was in prison, but that hadn't helped Maya feel safe, certainly not safe enough to see patients in her house.

Maya buttoned up the white coat the health practice insisted she wore. Maya wasn't sure if her values suited the clinic's. She hated the white coat for a start. But, she had to admit, it did give her more distance, and considering how nervous Maya now felt around her clients, that was a good thing.

Maya concentrated on measuring out the restricted herb ephedra. The hay fever season had started with the spring blossom. It was important to measure out the quantity of ephedra sinica exactly.

When the repeat script of hay fever mix was made up, Maya placed the bottle on the white countertop in front of her. She stared at the label, comforted by her own neat writing. She loved herbal medicine and working as a healer. Sheila had spoiled that for her. Now Maya was jumpy with new clients. Occasionally, she got distracted when taking case histories and had to ask clients to repeat themselves. Some days she was surprised anyone wanted to see her. Thankfully, most of the time Maya went automatically into healer mode, a place where her own feelings didn't matter and her only concerns were listening, taking notes, and finding the best herbs to help.

Maya took a deep breath and shoved Sheila down into the dark recesses of her psyche. That reminded her—Maya needed to make an appointment with her counselor. Following the crazy events of the previous summer, Maya had decided to study for her postgraduate diploma in psychology. Her undergraduate qualification was American, which meant she couldn't automatically work as a psychotherapist in the UK. Maya didn't know if she wanted to work as a counselor, but it was comforting to delve into that world again. Being in counseling herself was essential to the process. It was also helping her heal, or at least to understand how much the events had impacted on her.

Maya pulled another plastic travel bottle off the shelf and began making up a prescription for colitis. She didn't want to talk about her feelings with Tony or Jade, even though both knew what had happened, and both had even been there when her uncle had tried to kill her. Maya was embarrassed and ashamed. She hated being made into a victim.

And she'd been made a victim not once but twice. She was furious really. That's when she wasn't jumpy and terrified. She adored Tony, but she had a nagging fear she might be clinging to her because Tony made her feel safe. It was certainly time to make an appointment with her counselor.

Her thoughts were interrupted by a sharp rap on the treatment room door. Maya glanced at the big clock on the wall and frowned. There was still half an hour before her next appointment. Maybe the client was early.

"Come in," she said, replacing the lid on the tincture bottle she had been measuring into the glass vial. She quickly poured the completed mix from the vial into the travel bottle so that none of the volatile components would evaporate.

Maya looked up as a slim, brown-skinned woman with short jet-black hair walked confidently into the room. She had a strong, slightly prominent nose, large oval eyes, thin eyebrows, and firm, dark lips. She had a white coat draped over one arm.

"Sorry to interrupt. I wanted to say hi. My name is Sunita. Most people call me Suni. I'm an acupuncturist, and I'm going to be working here four days a week."

Maya smiled, taking the acupuncturist in. She was good-looking with a strong magnetic quality.

"Welcome. I'm Maya. I'm a medical herbalist. I've only been here a few months myself. Everyone seems very nice," Maya said.

"You're American!"

"Yes. So are you, by the sound of it."

Suni nodded. "By way of India. Well, actually by way of India, then East Africa, and then America, Florida to be exact."

"Ah, I was trying to place the accent, thank you."

"And you." Suni studied Maya. "You have that gorgeous East Coast thing going on. New England?"

"You're good at accents."

"I love New England. What's your home town?"

"Provincetown."

"No way! How did you manage that? Lucky you," Suni said and then pulled herself up. "Sorry, what a presumption. I mean, I think that's wonderful because I'm gay. Ptown's my favorite place after Key West."

Maya grinned. "People say that a lot. Especially Americans. I'm gay too. Though you know, when I was growing up, Provincetown wasn't as gay as it is now."

"I see. But hey, any time you want to go home you've got it made, no?"

Maya flinched. "I guess. I've got no plans to go home just now."

"Well, here we are, two Americans, far from home. Two gay Americans and we stumbled into the same clinic. How weird is that?" Suni smiled.

"It's a strange coincidence, isn't it? So, you're an acupuncturist. Are you a Chinese herbalist as well?"

"Yes." Suni nodded. "And I'm an Ayurvedic practitioner, plus I do acupressure and Ayurvedic massage."

"Right. Ayurvedic, that's Indian herbal medicine?"

"Yep. Traditional medicine from the Indian subcontinent. One of the oldest forms of medicine in the world. So what's the deal with this white coat?" Suni pulled the draped coat off her arm and flapped it at Maya.

Maya laughed. She smoothed her own coat down where it had wrinkled some.

"The practice manager likes us to appear professional. He said that people in the UK associate medical people with white coats. I didn't want to wear one, but he insisted it was non-negotiable." Maya shrugged. "I could have looked for another practice, but this has a good reputation, and it's near where I live." As soon as the words were out of Maya's mouth, she regretted them. She didn't want anyone to know where she lived. She realized her hand was clenched into a fist. Self-consciously, she relaxed it.

"Aha." Suni was looking at Maya curiously. "So, where does a gay girl go to have fun in this city?"

Maya smiled. "The bars and clubs are mostly central. You can find all the details online."

"Do you have any recommendations? Where do all the hot girls hang out?" Suni grinned.

"I couldn't really say." Maya smiled back. "I haven't been to a club in months. The Candy Store's popular. I go to a champagne bar with my girlfriend, but it's straight."

"Your girlfriend or the bar? Just joking. Champagne bar. Jeez, your girlfriend must be rich." Suni's eyes twinkled.

Maya shook her head. "Not at all. It's not as expensive as it sounds. You can get champagne more reasonably here. Not that it's cheap. You have to go to Paris for that."

"Wow! Sounds like you've got a lot to teach me." Suni leaned in, still grinning.

Maya pulled back, flicking her eyes to the clock on the wall. "Sorry, Suni, I've got a client in a few minutes." She felt anxious and wasn't sure why. Suni was being perfectly nice. Maybe she was flirting a little, but not inappropriately so.

Suni shrugged. She didn't look in any way offended. She walked to the door and then turned. "If you think of any places it would be good for me to go, let me know." With a smile, she opened the door and was gone.

Maya grabbed her client's case note file for a quick once-over. She skim-read the notes to the previous appointment, her mind still on Suni. Maya's instincts were all messed up. It looked like anybody new made her nervous now, not just new clients. Maya took a deep breath. This wasn't good. As soon as the next appointment was done, Maya decided to call and book in with her counselor.

❖

Jade sat propped up in bed with her tablet resting against her knees. She tapped the touch screen keypad as she replied to her agent. Jade didn't know how hard her agent pushed directors and casting companies to open their ideas of what parts a black actor was suitable for. She'd been lucky with the casting agents for *Oklahoma*, her most recent show. Things were changing, but not as quickly as Jade would like. She couldn't sit around waiting for a part in *Carmen Jones* or *Sister Act*. She needed people to consider her for any available part within her casting range.

The wind picked up outside, making the boat rock. Jade pulled the duvet up around her. She was glad the nights were getting shorter and the days vaguely warmer. She had been on edge since the photo incident.

The wind started to whistle. Jade stopped typing and listened. The boat rocked rhythmically from side to side. It would have been soothing if Jade wasn't so tense.

A wailing began, distinct from the wind. Jade willed it to be foxes calling.

The crying sound built until it filled the room.

The room temperature dropped.

Jade jumped out of bed, turned the lights on full, grabbed her dressing gown, and pulled it tightly around her.

"Shut up!" she shouted to the bright, empty bedroom.

The noise stopped.

Jade scanned the room. She knew she wasn't able to see ghosts, but she looked anyway.

"Who are you? What do you want?" she said.

The room was quiet.

Jade felt foolish. She was sure she was imagining things.

"About time. You're the worst psychic ever." An American voice, female, low, and sinister growled into Jade's ear.

Jade gasped.

"What do you want?" Jade made her voice as tough as she could.

No one answered.

Jade waited. She shivered in the freezing room.

Still nothing.

Jade got back into bed.

She pressed her tablet and pulled up the image of the screaming woman.

"Is this you?" Jade asked.

"Yes." Again, the voice was right next to her ear.

Jade spun her head round, but of course, there was no one there. No one she could see.

"I can hear you, but I can't see you," Jade said.

"Yeah, I know. What's up with that?" The voice had a Southern twang to it. Jade usually liked Southern accents, but she wasn't feeling very warm to this one. "Wow, I'm really screaming in that one, aren't I? You should see your face."

"I can see my face!" Jade snapped. "I can see *your* face in the photo. I just can't see you now."

"Why?"

"I ain't know!" Jade felt frustrated. She didn't deal with ghosts on her own. Tony was always there. "You should go see my friend. She'll be able to see you, and she's got a spirit guide who can probably help you as well."

"She white?" the woman asked.

"Yes."

"Don't want to talk to her. I want to talk to you, sister. You're from the Caribbean. I can hear that when you let your accent slip."

Jade softened. Maybe there was a reason the ghost only trusted black people. Maybe she'd been the victim of racism.

"What do you need from me?" Jade asked.

The woman took a breath. "I don't know what happened to me. I was in a motel room. I took some pills. I can remember that, but I can't remember why."

"Do you need me to investigate?"

"No. I don't care." The woman's voice was sharp. "I was surrounded by haters and players. The only one I trusted was my girlfriend. Don't remember saying good-bye to her. I need you to."

"Where is she?" There was no way Jade had the money to fly to the States.

"She's here. She moved here. Maybe because she was grieving, I don't know. My name's Felicia. She's called Suni. You find her, I'll leave you alone."

"What's her last name? Where does she work?" Jade called out.

The room was silent. Jade didn't know how she knew it, but she was certain Felicia had gone.

The boat was as solid as if it sat on dry land. There wasn't a breath of wind.

Jade's eyes fell back onto the photo of Felicia screaming into her face, and she shivered.

❖

Tony took a long gulp of beer and crammed a handful of peanuts into her mouth. "How long till dinner?" she called through to Maya, who was cooking up a storm in Tony's galley kitchen. Jade had come round for a meal and a catch-up on the old-school butch case.

Maya appeared in the doorway. She had a dab of tomato sauce on her nose. Tony thought it was fetching.

"What was that? I can't understand a word you say when you speak with your mouth full," Maya said sharply.

Tony grinned, not minding in the least being told off. "Jade and me just wanted to know when the food will be ready. We're starving." She grabbed another handful of nuts and managed to stuff three olives into her mouth as well.

Maya winced. "There are some benefits to you not having an eat-in kitchen. I don't have to watch you doing that."

Jade laughed.

"Eat-in kitchen? What's that? A kitchen-diner?" Tony asked.

Maya nodded. "My spaghetti alla puttanesca will be another twenty minutes."

"You made that sauce sound very rude," Tony said, giving Maya a long look up and down.

Maya bit her lip. "It is rude. It's spaghetti alla lady of the night." She dipped her eyes at Tony.

"Why do working girls get a special sauce?" Tony asked.

Maya shrugged. "Don't know. Olives and capers are obviously too risqué for some."

"Make mine a large portion then." Tony smiled. Maya gave a cute little swallow.

"It's like I've stumbled across a late night channel watching the two of allyuh." Jade cleared her throat before putting a handful of nuts into her mouth.

"What do you know about late night channels?" Maya asked with a teasing expression.

Jade studiously ignored her. "Tony, why there not any openings in *Little Shop of Horrors*? It's been on a month. Someone usually fall ill by now, or break thcy leg."

Tony pulled her eyes away from Maya's body. She made a mental note to ask Maya not to wear such tight tops when they had company. It was too deliciously distracting.

"Earth to Tony!"

"Sorry, Jade. Actually, there is a spot in the chorus. I was going to mention it, but we've got a new choreographer."

"That's okay. I'm good at dance," Jade said.

"Yes, I know you are. Usually. But, Jade, it's Matt Baker."

"Oh no! Why they change choreographer and why it had to be him?"

Maya perched on the edge of the couch. "What's wrong with Matt Baker?"

"Matt Baker was the choreographer on *Arabian Nights, the Musical*. They contacted my agent because I had it on *Spotlight* that I was a Raqs sharqi expert."

"That's Egyptian dance, what most people call belly dancing," Tony explained.

"I didn't know you were a belly dancer. Go on then, do some! What sort of music do you need?" Maya said. Her voice squeaked with excitement.

"I will never dance that dance again. The memory still haunting me." Jade put the back of her hand up to her brow.

Tony laughed. "It's your own fault. You shouldn't have gone to the audition. And you shouldn't say you can do things when you can't."

"You can't belly dance?" Maya looked disappointed.

"I can. Sort of. I've had training."

"You did a taster day. When you were thirteen," Tony said, "and you went to the audition letting them think you were an expert."

"Well, I'd done it before, albeit some time ago, and I thought how hard can it be? I'm a good dancer, after all, and brilliant at picking up steps. How was I to know Matt Baker lived in Cairo for five years and studied with the best of the best?"

"Do you think he'll remember you? What if you auditioned under a different name?" Tony asked. It was a real shame. It would perk Jade up to get a part in the show.

"Oh, I think he'll remember me. He'll remember me as the one getting behind in the moves, and then breaking into an entirely different dance routine."

"Why did you do that?" Maya asked. Tony collapsed with laughter on the sofa.

Jade winced. "I didn't mean to. I was getting all flustered, trying to keep up and then I don't know, it was like a body memory or something. Suddenly, I was doing the dance break sequence from 'Hey, Big Spender.' Our version of *Sweet Charity* had an Arabic twist, well, 'Big Spender' did anyway. There was some belly rolling, and a lot of high kicks, and a bit with a feather boa. I didn't have a feather boa at the audition so I improvised."

Tony laughed so hard a peanut came out her nose.

"It's a shame Matt Baker was so appalled. The director wanted me."

"Everybody wanted you when you did that routine. I loved it when you were in *Sweet Charity*. When 'Big Spender' came on, I wanted to marry you, and that was before it was legal," Tony said.

"Oh, you are a love." Jade patted Tony's hand.

"Before what was legal?" Maya asked.

"Gay marriage. Jade's dance moves still aren't legal in many countries and several American states," Tony said.

Maya got up. "Well, as entertaining as you two are, I need to put the spaghetti on if we're going to eat my *Pretty Woman* pasta." She sashayed all the way to the kitchen. Tony's eyes were riveted to her bottom until it disappeared beyond the doorway.

"I can see what you did there, with the film reference, very good!" Jade called after her. Then she lowered her voice. "Are you going to tell her she has tomato sauce on her nose?"

Tony shook her head. "No. Someone's got to help her with her cleanliness obsession," she said, deliberately spilling a couple of peanuts out of the bowl and scattering them across the glass coffee table. She decided against crushing one under foot because that would be tacky and going too far.

"I love how sexy it is between yawl." Jade grinned at Tony.

"Yeah, it's great. We don't talk about anything, but we are having a huge amount of sex."

"That's good, isn't it? You don't like talking."

"Normally I don't." Tony wondered how to explain the nagging feeling inside her that something wasn't right with Maya. She turned the volume on the TV up. "But don't people need to talk, when things have happened to them?" She moved closer to Jade and spoke quietly so Maya wouldn't hear. "Maya's always saying it's wrong to bottle stuff up. You'd think she'd want to talk about her uncle trying to kill her. You'd think she'd want to, what's it called, progress it."

"Process it," Jade said.

"Yes, that as well. She's only mentioned it once, and she couldn't really get any words out, just cried a lot."

"Maybe she just needs some time."

"Maybe." Tony tapped her fingers against the cold glass of her beer bottle.

"Anyway"—Jade took a swig from her own bottle—"are you going to fill me in on the case? How did Rose take it? Is the cute butch resting in peace?"

"You only think she's cute because you haven't met her."

"She's cute in my imagination."

Tony leaned forward. "It was sad, actually. Rose looked like the fight had been knocked out of her. I expected her to be relieved to find out Frankie wasn't murdered. She just looked defeated. She's spent her whole life trying to get justice."

"What a shame," Jade said. "You said she was gorgeous?"

"Who?" Maya walked to the dining table with steaming plates of spaghetti. She placed them squarely on each place mat. "Get it while it's hot," she said, beckoning them over with a finger and a wink.

"Rose," Tony said, walking to the table. "Yes, my God, such a beautiful woman! I bet she had some admirers in her day."

"Listen to yourself. I bet she's got lots of admirers now." Jade grabbed a chair.

"Didn't you say she was in her eighties?" Maya asked.

Tony and Jade nodded.

Maya stared at them.

"So?" Tony shrugged.

"Well, she's twice your ages," Maya said.

"She's not twice both our ages. Anyway, that, Maya, is ageism. When a woman's gorgeous, she's gorgeous whatever her age, surely?" Tony said.

"True, I guess," Maya said. She caught sight of herself in the mirror above the table and grimaced. "Why didn't you tell me I had tomato sauce on my nose!" She marched back into the kitchen. Shortly afterward came the sound of running water and brisk scrubbing.

Tony pushed all thoughts out of her mind while she savored mouthfuls of Maya's tasty, tangy, and utterly moreish pasta. She had almost cleared her plate and was thinking of second helpings when Jade put down her fork.

"I've had a visit from a ghost," she said, studying Tony's face.

"*You* have?" Tony asked. That hadn't happened before.

"Who?" Maya asked.

"A woman called Felicia. She's American. From Florida. Her girlfriend's over here, and she wants to say good-bye to her."

"Oh, that's sad." Maya looked at Jade sympathetically. "It's nice she came to you."

"Is it?" Tony said.

Maya frowned at her. "Yes. Why wouldn't it be?"

Tony was trying not to, but she felt childishly put out the ghost had gone to Jade.

"I don't know why this woman come to me." Jade swallowed, glancing at Tony. "I don't like her. She's whiny and annoying, and she scared the life out of me for several nights pretending to be a fox."

"What do you mean, pretending to be a fox?" Maya asked.

"She made a crying noise like a fox in heat. I kept waking up thinking there were foxes outside the boat." Jade thought for a moment. "Or maybe there were foxes outside the boat. But she was definitely talking to me in my sleep, giving me nightmares."

"Do ghosts do that a lot?" Maya looked horrified.

"They can be disturbed," Tony said quietly. She'd thought Jade looked tired. How long had this been going on? Why hadn't Jade said anything before? "Is she hostile?" she asked Jade.

Jade took a breath. "Not now. Well, she's talking to me at least, rather than just screaming in my face."

"Can you see her?" Tony asked.

Jade shook her head.

"So how do you know she was screaming in your face?" Tony remembered Deirdre's warning about not going through spirit guides.

"Let me show you." Jade got up and picked her tablet off the coffee table.

Tony and Maya followed as Jade moved to the sofa.

Jade pulled up an image. It was a strong head and shoulders shot of Jade with a faint, distorted image beside her. Tony's stomach tightened as she made out an angry woman in profile, her mouth frozen in a scream. The distorted image looked like it had been superimposed. If Tony hadn't known Jade, she would have been sure it had been created by image software.

Maya shuddered. "Is she here right now?" she whispered.

Tony double-checked. "No," she said.

"Well, thank God for that. She looks horrible." Maya grabbed Tony's hand. "To be honest, I don't like the idea of her talking to you," she said to Jade.

"Neither do I," Tony said. She was worried. "Is there anything I can do to help?"

Jade smiled weakly. "I don't know. I don't think so. She would have come to you, wouldn't she, if she'd wanted to? This woman's been freaking me out."

"Oh no. I don't want you getting freaked out, Jade. Why don't you talk to Deirdre about it?" Tony said.

"I might. I'm glad I've told you. I didn't say anything because I didn't know what was going on for ages. I just got the photos back yesterday. I think Felicia's come to me because she doesn't trust white people."

"That's not very nice," Maya said.

"Sure, but you don't know what her background is. Maybe she has good reason." Jade rubbed her eyes.

"You can't write off a whole group of people." Maya looked indignant.

"Of course not," Jade said in the calm voice that Tony knew Jade used when she was getting annoyed herself. "I can understand it sometimes, though. Felicia said she wanted to speak to a sister. I said she should talk to Tony. When she found out Tony's white, she didn't want to."

Tony shrugged. "I appreciate that, but I have to say she doesn't look very sisterly in that photograph. You should do what you think best, Jade. I'm here if you need me, that's all I'm saying."

Jade smiled. "Thank you. I thought that, as Felicia has come to me, I will go and see the girlfriend. She's an acupuncturist."

"The horrible ghost woman is an acupuncturist? She doesn't look like a healer. But then I suppose healers can be disturbed," Maya said.

Tony waited for her to finish asking and answering her own questions.

"The girlfriend, Suni, is an acupuncturist," Jade clarified.

Maya stared at her. "Suni? A new Ayurvedic healer has just started at my practice. She's an acupuncturist."

"Ah," Tony said, "that's why she's come to you."

Maya and Jade were both looking at her.

"Why?" Maya asked.

"Well, there must be a connection. Maybe Jade is the nearest black medium. Maybe that's how these things work." Tony plucked an answer out of the air.

"You really haven't got a clue, have you?" Maya asked.

"Not so much," Tony admitted.

Maya took a sip of her white wine. Tony liked the way she ran the tip of her tongue over her lips after tasting it. "Well, meeting her will be easy enough."

"Will it?" Jade asked. "Oh, yes, of course! I could hook up with you after work." She broke into a strong Trini accent. "I could be yuh Trini cousin!"

"Why?" Tony asked.

"Or we could do the sales rep thing again. I could be selling herbal supplies. Of course I'd have to gen up on Ayurvedic medicine and acupuntery."

"I think it's called acupuncture," Tony muttered.

"Or, seeing as she's an alternative practitioner," Maya said, "you could just make an appointment."

CHAPTER FOUR

Jade was unprepared for the utter gorgeousness of Felicia's ex-girlfriend. As she sat across from Suni in the minimalist practice room, Jade's heart was beating fast as she looked into Suni's dark chocolate eyes. Her mid-brown skin glowed as if she'd just come in from lying in the sun. Suni's jet-black, dead-straight hair was cropped short at the sides and back but left a little longer at the front, and swept to one side. She was making Jade's breath shallow and her body tingle in a way it hadn't in the longest time. All thoughts, except how stunning the woman in front of her was, promptly vanished from Jade's head, including whatever question Suni had just asked her.

"So, can you remember when the neck pain started?" Suni leaned her head to one side. Her closed lips formed a smile.

Jade rubbed her neck. Her mouth was dry. She reached for the glass of water on the little white table between her and Suni. "A few months ago." Her voice was husky.

"Are you taking any medication?"

"No."

"That's good. So you've described the pain as starting here..." Suni leaned across the table, reached under Jade's hair, and touched the nape of her neck. Jade shivered and then bit her lip as heat flushed through her. The feeling was intense and absolutely indecent. "And you said it runs as far as here."

Suni ran her finger down the outside of Jade's T-shirt along her spine to the small of her back. Jade closed her eyes. "Um-hmm," she murmured.

"You would clearly benefit from Abhyangam massage. I have a

suitable oil for you, but I need to warm it. Could you take off your T-shirt and jump up on the couch? I'll be with you in a minute."

Jade was relieved when Suni turned away from her and poured oil into a bowl set on a small electrical burner. Jade began to take her clothes off. It was hard to do when she was attracted to the masseuse. Fortunately, there wasn't a peep from Felicia. Jade prayed the ghost was nowhere near the practice room.

Suni glanced over when Jade was sitting self-consciously on the couch in her bra.

"Would you be upset if oil got on your underwear?"

Jade swallowed. "No, that's fine," she said quickly. She wouldn't be able to focus if she took any more clothes off.

"Then lie on your front and think pleasant thoughts. I'll be right over."

Jade had imagined the meeting differently. She'd watched several episodes of *Ghost Whisperer* and knew better than to blurt out that she had a message from beyond. She'd thought she would suss Suni out, getting a massage as a bonus. Then, once she knew Suni a little, she'd imagined she would find a way to gently pass the message on. She hadn't anticipated finding Suni so attractive.

Ask her something about herself. Get her to open up. Jade didn't want to think about Felicia, let alone talk about her, but that was why she was there. Maybe she could steer the conversation to ex-girlfriends.

"Have you got family, friends, anyone back in the States?" Jade mumbled into the couch.

"You will get more benefit from the massage if you don't talk. Just relax." Suni's voice was calm and persuasive.

Suni's warm, wet fingers found her back. Jade sighed under Suni's touch, and she felt herself drifting. She relaxed as knots evaporated and a pulse began to beat in her most primal self. Nothing mattered except the fingers on her body kneading all her tension away. Her skin was warm, oiled, looked after. The muscles around her neck and shoulders dissolved until she lost all sense of her bones and her joints, until she was a pool of warm liquid floating on air. Her breath was deep and even. Jade was calm and secure. Nothing outside the moment mattered. She was suspended in a pure, spiritual place.

"We will stop there for now."

A towel was laid over Jade's shoulders. The magic touch was

gone, but Jade was okay with that. She was calm to her core. She didn't think she had ever felt as relaxed as she did in that moment. Tentatively, she stretched, and then turned over.

"Most of the oil has been absorbed into your body, but there may still be some on your skin. Do you want me to wipe it off with the towel before you put your clothes on?" Suni's voice was as sweet as her touch. Jade felt taken care of. The intense desire had lifted to leave Jade feeling something deeper. She shook her head. Her body felt wonderful. She had been making it up about the neck pain, but she now realized how full of tension her body had been. She slipped her T-shirt over her shoulders.

"I think you would benefit from another session," Suni said.

"Absolutely," Jade said straight away. She wanted to come the next day, but she forced herself to make an appointment for several days' time.

At one with her body, she walked to the door.

"It's been lovely to meet you, Jade." Suni held Jade's eyes for a moment before Jade pulled herself away.

❖

Tony rushed into the lighting box determined not to be late. Maya had come home early from the clinic, having splashed tincture on her top. She'd taken it off to wash out the stain just as Tony had come out of the shower. One naked body had led to another. When the steam was cooling off the bathroom mirror, Tony had noticed she was an hour later than she wanted to be. It had been worth it, as long as she didn't incur the wrath of the deputy stage manager.

Tony stopped short at the sight of Beth standing in front of the control board in dim lighting.

"Why are you in the lighting box in show light?" Tony asked suspiciously.

Beth arched one eyebrow and pushed a strand of hair off her forehead with the end of a pencil. She had a hand on her hip and her body leaned toward Tony. She glanced pointedly at the clock positioned over the lighting desk. "Because it's practically the Half," she said. "And I wanted to be sure to see you."

"Well, you would be sure to see me, as that's where I sit all the way through the show." Tony thought Beth had got the message that she was with Maya. Anyway, it was well known that Tony didn't like going out with anyone she worked with. Of course, there was that trapeze artist, but that was a one-off, and trapeze artists were hard to resist. They were so very bendy.

Beth narrowed her eyes. "I haven't got time to dally words with you. Is your fit friend Jade still looking for work?"

Tony nodded.

"Then be sure to tell her about the auditions for Mary's part."

"Sadly, that's a no go. She had a disastrous previous audition for the new choreographer."

"Oh no. I was relying on her being the new 'woman on skid row.'" Beth's face fell.

"Yeah, Jade would make a good 'woman on skid row' or a great 'wino number two,'" Tony said. She dropped her bag and switched on the lighting board. A fuzzy movement by the door caught her eye. Deirdre materialized in a bright pink nineteen eighties sweatshirt and tiny pink shorts. Beside her stood a teenage white boy in a black hooded top and baggy dark blue jeans. He was skinny, with a drawn face. He had the hood pulled up over his head. He scowled at Tony.

"I said, I'd better get down to the stage manager's desk!" Beth stepped in front of Tony, looking at her crossly.

"Of course, of course." Tony bustled about getting the lighting cues loaded.

When Beth had gone, Tony glowered at Deirdre. "How many times have I asked you not to come when I'm at work?" she said.

"You may have mentioned it once or twice, but quite frankly, Tony, I don't see what the problem is. You just sit there pressing a button. You don't even have to listen for your coos or whatever they're called," Deirdre said.

"Cues! Obviously, they're called cues. Why would they be called coos?"

"Why's a green room a green room? Why is laughing on stage called corpsing? Why are you going out with a stunning Portuguese lady? There's a lot of mystery in theater."

Tony glared at Deirdre. "Don't start comparing me to hamburger again. And she's not from Portugal. Her people are, way back. She's from Provincetown."

"Yes, I know," Deirdre said. "I was there, remember, in your last adventure." She turned to the boy beside her. "She's not the sharpest penknife in the scout toolbox. Anyway, as I was saying, you just press a button and don't have to concentrate because that Sappho-come-lately is always whispering in your ear, telling you when to press."

"I suppose you mean Beth, and yes, she hasn't been out long, but really. And I do have to concentrate, so whatever you want you'd better be quick," Tony snapped. Honestly. Deirdre could try the patience of a saint. Tony glanced at the boy. He looked like he was having a bad day. "What can I do for you?" she asked more softly.

The boy folded his arms. "It ain't easy for me to ask outside my fam, but I need bare help."

Tony glanced at Deirdre, who was smiling encouragingly, or she could have been wincing; the pink shorts looked sardine-can tight. Deirdre turned to Tony. "Translate?"

"He's saying he needs a lot of help and he doesn't like to ask me."

The boy nodded. His lips were pressed together and his eyes narrowed. Tony guessed he was sizing her up. "You think she can handle it? She don't look that street smart," he said to Deirdre.

Tony tried not to bristle. She also tried not to react to the boy's hostile attitude. She'd misinterpreted youth energy on a previous case, and that boy had turned out to be scared rather than scary.

"Tony, are you in preset?" Beth voice came over Tony's headset.

"Sure am," she replied. She glanced over at the ghosts. "Look, I don't want to be rude, but you're going to have to go."

The boy scowled. "What about the other one?"

"What other one?" Tony asked.

Deirdre averted her eyes. "They work together. Anyway, she's smarter than she looks. I was joking earlier."

"You mean Jade. I thought you were *my* spirit guide." Tony wondered if she sounded as childish as she felt. There was no reason Deirdre couldn't go to Jade, she supposed.

"Oh, you want to talk to me now," Deirdre said with more than a hint of smugness. "Suddenly, the big singing plant can go whistle for her lighting changes."

"It's not Audrey Two you want to worry about. It's Sappho-come-lately who'll have my guts for garters if I don't get the cues right. And Beth isn't someone you'd want to mess around with."

"I'm pleased to hear you say that, because she would most certainly like to mess around with you. I'm constantly amazed at how many women find you attractive."

"Again, why? Not that they do, but if they did."

"Cast and crew of *Little Shop of Horrors*, this is your beginners call." Beth's voice pulled Tony back to the job at hand.

"Whatever you need from me will have to wait," she said firmly, going into preview and double-checking the cue stacks.

She thought she heard a bit of whispering and something that sounded like "bag of blow," but when she glanced toward the doorway again, the ghosts had gone.

❖

Jade's body hummed with pleasure on Suni's couch. She was soothed by the slippery warmth of the oil; the sweet, heavy scent of the herbs; and the firm pressure of Suni's fingers as she swept from Jade's neck down her back to the base of her spine.

The towel landed gently on her back. She felt a moment of sadness as she realized the second session was coming to an end.

Jade stretched and yawned and then got back into her jeans and shirt. Suni was wiping her hands on another towel. She smiled and arched an eyebrow.

"Please don't think me forward. Could you recommend a gay bar or club? Somewhere friendly. I'm still pretty new in town, and I'd prefer to go on a recommendation." Suni looked as relaxed as Jade felt.

Jade took a quick breath. She had been downplaying the attraction, but whatever it was about Suni that got Jade's pulse racing, it was up and running again.

"There's a nice bar in the center of town, in Old Compton Street. Do you know Compton Street, the so-called Gay Village?" Jade kept her voice measured.

"I don't suppose…well, I'll just come out with it. Would you come with me? It's so much nicer to explore a place with a local in tow." Suni gave a cheeky smile, but her voice was shy. Jade found the combination hard to resist.

She hesitated. Yes, she fancied Suni, but she was committed

to passing on Felicia's message. She didn't feel she knew Suni well enough to blurt out something like that.

So I should go with her to the bar. It's important I get her to trust me.

Jade reasoned that she was just doing her job. "Yeah, why not," she answered Suni. "I'm free tomorrow night."

Suni grinned. "Me too. Write down the address. We can meet there."

Jade jotted down the details, grabbed her coat, and left the practice room. She wondered if Maya was at the clinic, but then wasn't sure if they should reveal they knew each other.

I'm sort of undercover, but it's not like we've got Suni under surveillance. I should ring Maya and Tony and check.

As Jade stepped up to reception to pay, someone cleared their throat right by her left ear.

She jerked her head round.

There was no one there.

The guy on reception looked at her strangely, but was quickly absorbed in getting some change.

"What are you doing?" Felicia's voice had an angry, sinister edge.

Jade tensed. She couldn't respond; the reception guy was coming back.

"You haven't even mentioned me, have you?"

Jade took her change and got out of the clinic as quickly as she could. She walked down a side street.

"I can't talk here," she said under her breath, looking up and down the street to check no one was watching.

There was a heavy silence.

Jade sensed Felicia to her left.

"You can keep your hands off her."

Part of Jade felt guilty, but she was annoyed at the way Felicia spoke to her. "I will pass your message on, as soon as it seems appropriate. That's all I've promised you to do."

"You don't want to make an enemy out of me," Felicia said sharply.

Jade was scared, but she squared her shoulders. "I don't respond to threats."

"Don't cross me, girl." Felicia's normally long tones were clipped. "That's one hot mess you don't want to dive into."

Jade swallowed. She sensed Felicia had gone. She hung back in the side street, waiting to see if Felicia said something else.

She feared the ghost was still around. Watching.

❖

Maya tutted with annoyance. The computer in her practice room had completely frozen. She had tried rebooting it, but now it wouldn't start up. Thank God all her information was on the cloud server, so one individual PC going down wouldn't mess up access to her files. She had a client in half an hour. She could take session notes the old-fashioned way with pen and paper, but she needed to read the previous notes.

Danny at reception picked up on the first ring.

"I'm having a nightmare with my computer. Can I get on yours for twenty minutes?"

"Oh hi, Maya, well, maybe you don't need to. Practice room three is empty today. Just log on there."

Neat. Practice room three was just down the hall.

As Maya walked into the room that Suni, the new Ayurvedic healer, used she wondered how Jade was getting on. She'd been quiet for a couple of days. Maya hoped the nasty-sounding ghost wasn't still giving Jade a hard time. She wondered what Jade made of Suni.

Maya sat at the desk and picked up the mouse. As she moved it, the screen sprang to life. Maya made a mental note to send an email around. Everyone needed to do their bit to save energy, and that included switching off computers when they weren't being used.

She looked at the start menu. Suni was logged on. Well, she would have hoped Suni would be more energy conscious. Maya hit Internet Explorer to go onto the cloud server. It had been minimized.

Maya glanced at the website as Internet Explorer resumed. It was an article on psychotropic drugs used for interrogation purposes. Maya read down the page, interested in the proposition that mind-altering drugs like LSD could be used to distort reality, confuse prisoners, and give interrogators greater control. Perhaps Suni had a client who had experienced something like that. Maya was aware that people sought political asylum in the UK who had experienced horrific regimes in their own country.

She glanced at the clock over the desk. Hell! She had allowed herself to become distracted and now only had fifteen minutes before her client's visit. Quickly, she logged on to the cloud server and brought up her patient's notes.

❖

Tony stole a glance at Jade, who was watching a basketball game on TV, and relished a rare moment alone with her best friend. Maya was off at a herbal talk, and Jade was round for dinner. Tony was over the moon to be in the new and very sexy relationship with Maya. But she had to admit, she missed special time with Jade. They had seen each other through several relationships. Jade loved her, in the way that friends do, not because they fancy you but because they really like who you are.

The TV was blaring. Crisps, nuts, and popcorn were strewed across the coffee table, still in their bags and definitely not in the little bowls that Maya loved to put them in. The teensy bowls were ridiculously impractical. You had two handfuls and needed to fill them up again. Tony couldn't see the point of traipsing to and from the kitchen all night. Jade agreed with her, in private. But when Maya had brought the snacks in and said, "See how nice it is to use these lovely bowls, I bought you, Tony," Jade had nodded wisely.

"They are lovely bowls," she'd muttered, avoiding Tony's eyes.

Tony pushed the sixteen-inch pizza, still in its box, toward Jade. "More super-stuff-your-face-meat-feast pizza?"

"You know it's not really called that." Jade's hand hovered over the pizza, drifted to one of Maya's tiny bowls filled with salad leaf, and then returned to the pizza box. She took a slice.

One eye on the basketball game, Tony grabbed another slice herself before tossing the box back onto the coffee table. Her only real interest in sport was the occasional foray into women's tennis at Wimbledon; however, now that she was with Maya, she was familiarizing herself with all things American. Unfortunately, she didn't think she could sustain an interest in tall blokes bouncing a ball around a court for forty-eight minutes, no matter how many dribbling spins and tricks the players did. "They could call it super-weight-gain-meat-n-cheese pizza, but that might be seen as insensitive," Tony said wryly.

"Yes, it might."

"Could be called cardiac arrest pizza."

"Again. Might not be the best selling point ever."

"This is nice, though, yeah?"

Jade pulled her eyes from the TV screen and held Tony's. "What?"

"Us. Like old times. Eating what we like, talking rubbish."

"Watching basketball…"

"Okay, so we wouldn't have been doing that, but the rest of it is like what we used to do."

"Tony, it's only been a few months. And before that you weren't single that long. You were with Amy for ages, remember? We weathered that storm."

"Ah, yeah." Tony fondly remembered how Jade had been there all the times her ex, Amy, had broken her heart. After a brief attempt to get back together, Amy had retreated back to Manchester, taking their three-year-old daughter Louise with her. Tony swallowed. She tried hard not to think about Louise, especially when she was drinking. She took a swig of beer.

"So what's happening with Louise? Have you made proper arrangements yet?"

Sometimes Tony swore that Jade was the psychic one. It was like she was reading Tony's mind. Tony clenched her teeth. "No." It hurt like hell to think how much she was missing out on Louise growing up.

"Maybe you need to see a lawyer."

"God, really? Won't that antagonize Amy? Surely it will cost a fortune?"

"Tony, it's not going to cost that much to get some advice. I'll help you if you need it."

"You can't afford to help me out. You're not even working."

"Yeah, but I've got a bit put by, and this is important. Tony, I don't get on your case, because I love you, but, hon, you need to fight for your daughter."

Tony stared at her. She realized she had been pushing down her anguish about not seeing Louise, and burying herself in the exciting new relationship with Maya.

"You just need to make regular arrangements to see her.

Manchester's not that far."

Tony nodded. "I know. I'll call Amy tomorrow; see if she will agree to something. My God, she used to love drawing up schedules and rotas. Maybe she'll get a kick out of it. It wasn't like we left on bad terms."

"You need to push, and not do what you normally do: run away from anything uncomfortable."

Tony smiled and then spontaneously reached across to hug her.

The air to the right of the couch went fuzzy, like air did in front of a heater.

Seconds later, Deirdre materialized in a tight polyester top with a matching pink and white pleated miniskirt. Her hair was in high pigtails, and she wore pink tennis shoes with fluffy balls stuck on them. The teenage boy stood beside her, looking exactly the same as when he had appeared in the lighting box.

"Perhaps you can grace us with an audience now, your royal lowness," Deirdre said. "Hello, Jade, shame you can't see my pompoms."

Jade opened her mouth to say something but clearly thought the better of it and just smiled weakly.

Deirdre studied the seven-foot, fit, mainly African-American men in shorts and tight vinyl tops. "Am I interrupting something? You two appeared to be fondling when we dropped in."

"It was a platonic hug," Tony said. "I don't suppose you know what that is."

"What an assumption!" Deirdre huffed back her shoulders. "Just because I'm a gay man you think I don't know what a platonic hug is. Well, you're right. What the hell is it, what a waste of a second, and why would anyone with a feeling bone in their body want to have one?"

The boy puffed his chest out. He looked like he was struggling with something. "Who's that?" He tipped his head in Jade's direction.

"That's the assistant," Deirdre said.

Jade's head snapped in her direction. "Why am I the assistant?" she said.

"Someone's got to be the sidekick. You're like Watson, or Robin, or Trigger," Tony said, thinking being a character might pacify Jade.

"Are you comparing me to a horse?" Jade's voice shot up an octave.

"No. Yes. Well, it's just that I'm the one with the spirit guide aren't I?" Tony wasn't even sure why she was trying to justify Jade being a sidekick. It wasn't her that had brought it up.

"That's a good point. Deirdre, why don't I have a spirit guide? I'm seeing ghosts on my own now, after all."

Deirdre picked a bit of fluff out of an extremely long and obviously false, fluorescent orange nail. "Haven't a clue, much like you two most of the time." She yawned. "I don't get to decide these things. And you should be careful seeing ghosts without proper representation. As I said recently to Tony, that kind of thing can bite you. And not the nice kind of biting neither."

"You never said she was black." The boy balled his hands into fists.

Tony frowned. "So what if she is?"

His eyes darted to hers. He was furious. He glanced warily at Jade but didn't say anything.

Tony was about to say, "If it's a problem, you can go find someone else," but Deirdre spoke before Tony could.

"Scott needs you to help his friend," she said.

Jade switched off the TV. "Who's Scott?"

"The young white boy standing next to Deirdre," Tony said.

"Young white racist, you mean." Jade was bristling, and Tony didn't blame her.

"So what if I am racist?" Scott said. "No one black's ever helped me, and I don't expect you to. The Jamestown Massive Crew are racist too. Being white's all you need to get shanked, if they catch you in their territory."

"What's he talking about?" Deirdre asked.

"Being shanked is being stabbed. Are you in a gang?" Jade tilted her head in his direction.

"Yes. I'm in the Stepney Walk Boys, or I was, before the JMC took me out."

Jade frowned at Tony. "I don't want to get involved with any gang stuff," she said. She looked anxious.

Scott pulled on Deirdre's arm. "Take me somewhere else, man. I ain't got time for this."

"Girls, please listen. Scott needs your help." Deirdre's voice was soft. Her eyes pleaded with Tony.

Jade folded her arms and leaned back on the sofa, shaking her head. Tony was apprehensive too, but there was something about the boy. He looked very young, only fifteen or so, and he was clearly scared. His body was rigid with tension. Tony noticed a pool of dried blood in the chest area of his black top.

"I moved the stash. It seemed like a good idea at the time, but that was before I got shanked. It's a K of blow, and we're supposed to sell it on. It belongs to some bad men."

Deirdre sighed long and hard. "Why do I keep being sent these cases? What does all that gibberish mean?" She threw her hands up in despair.

"He's moved a kilo of cocaine somewhere that belongs to some big drug players," Jade said. She spoke quietly, but the disgust in her voice was clear.

"Repo, Repo's my blood. He's a dead man if he can't find that blow."

"His best friend, someone called Repo, is in trouble if he can't find the drugs," Jade told Deirdre. "You realize you're talking black?" she threw at Scott. "Blood, bad men, shanked?"

Scott looked confused. "It's all the same. Everyone says them words."

"He's right, you know," Tony said to Jade. "I did that community show last year. *Lawds of de Manor* it was called. Everybody ended up dead at the end of the show. Very Shakespearian. All the kids spoke like him. Black, white, whatever. It's not like when you were young."

Jade glared at her.

"You need to tell Repo where the stash is." Scott's voice was clipped, like it was hard for him to get the words out. Tony suspected he didn't ask for help much.

"I don't think this is the right case for us," Jade said firmly.

Tony knew from experience, Jade wasn't going to change her mind. Jade was easygoing ninety-nine point nine percent of the time, but when she fixed on something, there was no shifting her. Tony also knew that Jade had no time for gangs, whatever part of the world they came from.

"What if we sent a text to your, what did you call him, your blood?" Tony asked.

Scott shook his head. "No good. He's always on a burner phone.

Chucks it away and gets a new one every week. I've no idea what the number would be."

"Well, you must know where he lives. We could send him a letter," Tony said.

Scott laughed long and loud. "What century are you in? No one sends letters. He would just rip it up. He'd think it was the feds."

"Feds! What are you now, African-American?" Jade said sarcastically.

"Email then," Tony said.

Scott shook his head.

"Facebook? Twitter?"

Scott carried on shaking his head. "We change accounts every week. Security. I ran a tight ship." He sounded proud.

"You ran it? You were the gang leader?" Jade asked.

"Yep," Scott said. "Repo is now."

"Did you kill anybody?" Jade asked.

Scott dropped his head.

"What about this Repo? Has he killed anyone?" Jade asked into the silence.

Scott didn't answer.

"I'll take that as a yes. That's why I don't want to help you, harsh as it may sound. Anyway, it wouldn't be safe. We'd have to go and see Repo. Tensions will be running high, seeing as you've just been killed," Jade said.

Tony looked at her. Jade would normally help anybody. If she felt that strongly, Tony wouldn't go against her. "Deirdre, I think you'd better take Scott to someone else."

"I knew this was a waste of time." Scott turned away. His shoulders slumped, then he disappeared.

Deirdre raised her palms upward, as if she didn't know what to do, and then she vanished too.

Tony studied Jade's troubled face. "You don't think we could—"

"Tony." Jade rested her hand on Tony's arm. "Don't you remember me telling you about Martin? I had to put up with boys in gangs at my school, remember? Some of them had tough lives, and I even understood why they wanted to be in a gang, but they were horrible people. They terrorized everyone else. Those boys killed Martin."

Tony had forgotten. Martin was pretty much the only school

friend Jade had had when she'd first come to England. He'd been white. People at Jade's school had thought them weird hanging out with each other.

"They killed him because they thought he was in another gang. He wasn't. They took his life anyway." Jade swallowed. "I don't want us to take gang cases. I don't want those people in our lives."

Tony pulled Jade in for a hug. "Okay," she said softly into Jade's neck.

❖

Jade sat on a bench in St. James's Park with Suni, watching ducks and pelicans swim in the lake. Bushes heavy with new green leaves surrounded the water in clumps. The Shell Tower, the Shard, and the top semicircle of the London Eye rose above trees in the distance. The cries of waterfowl interrupted the gentle splash of water from a fountain set in the middle of the lake.

It was eight o'clock in the evening, and dusky twilight was just beginning to settle around them. Jade liked the extra daylight in summertime in England. It was early May, and the days were getting longer and longer. Jade felt the excitement of good things to come. Day and night were equal all year round in the Caribbean, so there was no feeling of long summer days. Wintertime in the Caribbean, though, now there was somewhere to be.

She snuck a look at Suni.

Talking of good things to come.

Suni's long eyelashes fluttered as she blinked. A buzz of attraction shot through Jade. She felt tingly and restless. She could hardly sit still.

Breathe, girl.

She hadn't remembered Suni's eyelashes being quite so long and luscious. It must have been something to do with the light. Not that Suni needed any help being attractive.

Suni turned. "Are you warm enough?"

Jade nodded.

"I'm just comfortable. I'm used to warmer climates."

Jade smiled. "Yeah, I get that. It took me several years to get used to the freezing, damp winters here."

Suni grimaced. "I hate the cold. It's nice being outside, though. I feel like I've been cooped up since I arrived." She stretched her arms out. Her fingers brushed against Jade's leg. Jade jumped at the touch. At this rate, it was going to be hard to concentrate on her reason for meeting up with Suni. Jade let her eyes drift back to the lake. A mallard bent his head and touched beaks with his mate. It had been a long time since she'd felt loved like that. She pushed away the small ache in her heart and tried to think of a way of bringing Suni's ex into the conversation.

"You're reflective." Suni touched Jade's knee gently.

Jade swallowed. She was sure Suni must see how the touch affected her. She opened her mouth to speak.

"When did you wash up on these shores like the treasure of outstanding natural beauty that you are?" Suni spoke first.

Jade closed her mouth abruptly. She wanted to giggle. Suni's way of putting things bordered on corny, but Jade's heart lifted at being compared to a beautiful shell or something like that. She had a flash of herself lying across white sand with wet clothes clinging to her body and warm waters lapping over her. Suni would be in the picture, of course, bending down to lie beside her.

Jade pulled her mind back to St. James's Park, admonishing herself for the naughty thoughts.

"Is it that long ago you're still trying to remember? I don't need the exact date." Suni laughed. Her eyes twinkled with reflected light from the deepening sunset.

"I came here when I was fourteen. That's over twenty years ago." Out of habit, Jade didn't say it was more like thirty years ago. The theater industry was notoriously ageist when it came to casting women.

"My, a young girl. That must have been some cultural change."

"It was harsh, leh me tell you." Jade broke into Trinidadian for a moment.

"Now you sound Caribbean," Suni said.

"Yeah." Jade smiled. "I've mostly lost my accent now. I'll get seen for more parts if I have a standard British accent. When I'm offstage, I forget myself every now and then and my real voice bursts out."

"You seem so comfortable here now. What was that journey like?" Suni settled back on the bench. Jade was touched at how interested in her Suni was.

"The first couple of years weren't easy. I came from a large and loving family in Matura. My mum cried all the way to the airport. She was crying so hard, I didn't, if that makes sense."

Suni nodded.

"I was scared. I was coming to live with my aunt. I knew her quite well because she came out most winters to visit us in Trinidad. We always got on. I was her favorite. It was her idea I came to the UK. I didn't want to leave my school or my friends and family, but I was excited to come. Everyone said it would change my life, give me opportunities I'd never get in Trinidad, and that's true, it did."

"So, what happened when you got here? Was it very different to what you were used to?"

"The biggest shock was the miserable faces. I came from a little coastal town. It sounds like a stereotype, but no one had much of anything, and still they were laid back and happy. Or at least they looked happy. People know how to laugh in Trinidad. They ain't afraid to smile. I know the UK well now, and I know that everyone in the UK isn't miserable. Londoners are not the smiliest of people, that's for sure. I thought it was because it was so damned cold."

"Well, it probably doesn't help," Suni said, laughing.

"I was real quiet when I got here. My aunt was the only person I knew in the whole country. Most kids weren't welcoming at my school. If my mum had known what it was going to be like, sending me to Wilsden, she wouldn't have sent me. Some of the black kids liked me, though. I was far posher than them, but they thought I was dope, because I was straight from the Caribbean. Not Jamaica, mind. Most of them spoke with Jamaican accents even if they'd never been there. But once they found out I wasn't a bashment singing gangsta they didn't want to know me. A lot of them didn't even know soca tunes, unless they'd heard them at the Notting Hill Carnival. My aunt said, 'keep yourself to yourself, child,' and that's pretty much what I did. But just after I turned seventeen, she died." Jade stopped talking. First, the gang boy had made her think of Martin, and now Suni's innocent question had conjured up another painful memory. That time had been the loneliest and most vulnerable point of Jade's life.

Suni didn't say anything. She shifted closer on the bench. The early evening air was starting to cool. Suni's body warmth was welcome. After a minute, Suni gently picked up Jade's hand and rested it in her own. Jade took a moment to compose herself.

"I was alone in England then. It wasn't easy, but I threw myself into studying and going to youth theater sessions. I did everything I could to make sure I got into the stage school LAMDA." Jade smiled, remembering how elated she'd felt when the acceptance letter had come.

"So, you've been through some tough times." Suni's voice was kind. She lifted Jade's hand to her lips and gently kissed it. Jade's eyes dipped as the warmth of Suni's lips lit a trail to her loins.

Suni's lips found Jade's. Suni was salty and soft and tantalizing. Jade opened her mouth and kissed her back. Everything faded except the kiss.

Slowly, a series of whistles diverted Jade's attention. She pulled back and looked around, feeling dazed. A park keeper stood a few meters away.

"The park's closing, girls," she said, grinning broadly.

As the park keeper walked off, blowing her whistle again, Suni took Jade's hand and pulled her to her feet.

"Would you like to go get some dinner?" she asked.

Jade nodded. Her head was full of their kiss, but in the back of her mind she knew she was supposed to speak to Suni about Felicia. She had a horrible feeling she'd just complicated matters. But then, she couldn't feel anything was horrible at that moment. She followed Suni with a light heart.

CHAPTER FIVE

Jade had come to Tony's for advice. She'd turned up with takeaway from her favorite restaurant. Not only was it Caribbean, it was Trinidadian.

Jade finished her goat curry roti in four bites. She was buzzing about the hot masseuse at Maya's clinic. Even though Tony secretly thought getting involved with the woman might complicate the case, she hadn't said a word. Jade had been down lately. Tony wanted her to be happy more than she wanted the case solved.

Unfortunately, Felicia had stepped up her haunting. Jade was being woken in the middle of the night. Jade didn't function well without sleep. She had deep shadows under her eyes.

"Come on, Deirdre, we need to talk to you," Tony said impatiently. She turned to Jade. "I've no idea how to summon a ghost. Have you?"

Jade shook her head. "I want to know how to make them go away."

Tony closed her eyes and screwed her face up. *Deirdre!* She focused all her attention on psychically calling Deirdre to them.

"Well, for goodness sake. What's the emergency?" Deirdre was standing on the other side of the coffee table with her hands on her hips. She had a black lacy slip over a ruffled miniskirt. Her black stockings were ripped. Her lipstick was a smudge running up one side of her mouth.

"It's not exactly an emergency. But Jade badly needs to talk to you. Thanks for rushing here so quickly. I can see you weren't dressed."

"What do you mean? This look is intentional. It was all the rage in 1986. I was at a delightful retro party when you drilled a hole upside my head with that banshee shriek of yours. You need to tone that down, girlfriend, boyfriend, thing friend. Whatever you are."

Tony ignored the jibes about her gender.

"What's up, Jade? Can I fetch you a porter for the bags under your eyes? You could use some sleep, lady."

Jade scowled in the direction of Deirdre. "I've got an annoying ghost."

"So've I," Tony muttered under her breath. "Annoying, and rude."

Deirdre narrowed her eyes but kept them fixed on Jade. "Felicia."

Jade perked up. "Oh, you know her name. She's hounding me. What am I supposed to do?"

"I don't know," Deirdre said. "She hasn't gone through the proper channels. Hasn't she told you what she wants from you?"

Jade pursed her lips. "She wants me to say good-bye to her girlfriend."

"Well, then. Pass on the message and hopefully Felicia will flit off into the happily-ever-afterlife."

Jade looked thoughtful.

Tony looked at Deirdre in her laddered stockings, the underwear as outerwear, the smudged makeup, and the back-combed wig and felt a surge of fondness. Deirdre had looked after her. Tony couldn't imagine coping without her often annoying, but ultimately thoughtful, spirit guide.

"Why hasn't Jade got a spirit guide? If she's talking to ghosts direct, doesn't she need one?" Tony asked.

Deirdre looked sideways at Jade. "It doesn't work like that. I don't make those kind of decisions. We just get assigned. That's all I know. If Jade's supposed to get a guide, she'll get one."

"But shouldn't ghosts go through people like you?"

"Shouldn't the most talented people rise to the top? Shouldn't good people have good things happen to them? Shouldn't I have been assigned to a steamy, tropical paradise instead of this rainy, slang-infested, stupidly stylish city?"

Tony stared at her.

"Yes, they should, but we can't make them." Deirdre studied Jade for a moment. "Jade, honey, be careful. Felicia may be disturbed. She's found you without assistance, which means she has a powerful need. I can see Tony's point. I'm not sure you should be dealing with this all on your own. I'll put a suggestion in the suggestion box."

"Is there really a suggestion box?" Tony asked.

Deirdre snorted. "Oh, the fun I could have with you, if only I had the time. Jade, pass on the message, and with any luck that will be that."

Jade looked down at her plate. It didn't look like that was the answer she'd been hoping for.

❖

"You haven't said anything yet, have you? You haven't said anything yet!"

Jade woke with a start. Felicia's whining, nasal voice droned on. Jade had a headache. She turned stiffly. Tony's sofa bed had never been comfortable. Jade swore it was getting worse.

Jade's whole body was tense. She'd been dreaming about something horrible. The dream slipped away, but she thought it had been about Martin.

The pain of losing him twisted inside her. It was dull now, compared to what it had been like once. Her late teenage years had been hard. She'd had to deal with two deaths, both sudden. She'd had to cope on her own.

Oh well, that was a long time ago. No point in dragging up the past.

"Don't pretend you don't hear me, girl," Felicia grumbled into Jade's right ear. Jade clenched her jaw and sat up, trying to ease out her cramped limbs. She stood and stretched. She'd love to hear from Martin or her aunt. Instead, she was stuck with high-maintenance Felicia.

"Answer me, damn it."

When Felicia got going, it was torture. Jade was worn down with it. Felicia annoyed her, but she also unnerved Jade. She never knew when Felicia would launch a tirade. And there was a menacing quality to the way she spoke right into Jade's ear, or came up behind her.

Apart from Felicia's incessant nagging, the flat was quiet. Jade clicked on her phone. It was four a.m.

She padded to the bathroom. She was shattered. She needed a way to block out Felicia until she could broach the subject with Suni. Jade wanted to pursue something with Suni once the message was passed on, so she had to go carefully. She didn't want Suni thinking she was delusional.

"You need to pee a lot. You should see a doctor. Maybe you have diabetes. A lot of black people get diabetes."

Jade groaned. "Get lost, woman. I need my privacy, dammit."

"You so self-conscious, girl. Have you told Suni? Have you slept with her yet? I bet you haven't told Suni. In fact, I know you haven't told Suni. You haven't, have you?" Felicia kicked off.

Jade heaved a sigh.

Felicia trailed behind her, moaning all the way to the bathroom.

Jade sat on the toilet and peed, not caring if the ghost was watching. She washed her hands slowly and carefully, using both the hand wash and hand cream that Maya had put in Tony's bathroom. Jade's hands smelled of oranges and rosemary.

"You shouldn't sleep with her. For a start, she hasn't gotten over me yet. Why would you want to open up that can of worms? And there's no point in waiting. I don't think she'll ever be over me. And then it's not professional, sleeping with your clients. Except she's not your client. I am. So you shouldn't sleep with your client's girlfriends. That's not right, is it? And anyway, you're her client. So you shouldn't sleep with her because *she* shouldn't sleep with her clients."

Jade knew from previous experience there was no point in saying anything. It just inflamed Felicia. She hadn't found any way of shutting her up. Jade had tried responding. That drove Felicia to new heights of ranting. Jade had tried ignoring her. Sometimes that worked, like now when Felicia didn't need anyone to acknowledge her. But sometimes that made Felicia get right up into Jade's face until she said something.

Jade glanced at herself in the mirror above the sink. She looked tired. Her head was pounding. She opened Tony's bathroom cabinet, looking for paracetamol. The prescription bottle next to it caught her eye.

"Pills. Pimp ma pills."

Jade shut her eyes.

Felicia had gone quiet. Jade breathed in and out silently for several breaths, enjoying the absence of noise.

"They were all in lines. I don't do lines."

Jade opened her eyes, flicking them to the mirrored inside of the cabinet. She half expected to see Felicia over her right shoulder. There was no one there.

"So where do you get off, coming on to my girlfriend? I came to a sister for help. Sister! You're a joke, girl. You so funny you should get yourself a routine and hit the comedy battles."

Jade's gaze returned to the prescription bottle. It looked familiar. She picked it up and read the label: diazepam. She recalled Tony getting them from her doctor a year previously when she'd needed a break from a difficult spirit. Tony's father had said they would make Tony stop seeing ghosts. Jade stared at the label thoughtfully. Mr. Carson had said the tranquilizers didn't work for Tony because she didn't get the dose right.

"Bad things shouldn't happen when you die. People should listen to you after you die. You should listen to me. That's your problem. You don't listen."

Jade walked out of the bathroom, taking the tranquilizers with her.

❖

Tony was almost out the door on her way to Jade's, when Deirdre materialized with Scott Brooks, the young gang member. He looked more wired than ever.

"This is serious. We're running out of time," Deirdre said.

"Deirdre, I thought you were going to ask someone else," Tony said. "Jade's my best friend. She's also co-owner of the agency. I respect her wishes, and anyway, I have to say I agree with her."

"Things have moved quicker than expected. Repo is in serious danger if you don't come right now. There's no one else to ask, only you and Jade," Deirdre said.

"I'm expected at Jade's. Maya's still away so we're having dinner," Tony said.

"That's perfect. Convince Jade, and then you can go together. It's only a few blocks from Jade's boat to Scott's housing project. That's where Repo is."

Tony didn't know what to do. Jade was right. Getting involved with gangs was dangerous stuff. She didn't want to help people that terrorized others. She'd never heard anything good about gangs. On the other hand, she didn't know that much about them either.

"Why do you care about this guy, this Repo?" Tony asked Scott. He stood next to Deirdre with hunched shoulders, hood up, and his hands in the pockets of his jeans. He turned to her and pushed the hood slightly back to reveal a blond crew cut. His eyes were sockets in a pinched, thin face, with skin stretched taut over cheeks and jaw.

"Repo's my brother." Scott took his hands out of his pockets and clasped them. "He's the only fam I ever had. Never knew my dad. Never even knew who was my dad. My mum's a crackhead. They'd have taken me into care if anyone had ever noticed me. Mum said they'd take me away from her if I wasn't dressed right at school. So I knew how to wash and iron by the time I was nine. I didn't make trouble. I wasn't smart. I was the quiet boy in the back of the class. Even when I joined the Stepney Walk Boys I kept my head down."

"Did they make you join the gang?" Tony asked.

Scott shook his head.

"So you could have chosen not to?" Tony didn't understand why anyone would join a gang.

"There ain't no choice. Not where I live. If you ain't in a firm, you're no one. You're fair game for everyone then. You just need to walk down the wrong street. They don't care that you're not in a gang. They treat you as the enemy anyway. It happened to me. I got this." Scott pushed up his hooded top and T-shirt. On his skinny abdomen, ribs stood proud of a thin layer of flesh. Scrawled across his belly was the pale outline of a scar about ten centimeters wide. It looked like three badly written letters: JMC.

Scott pushed his top down. "I was eight. I never went down that street again. Ever." His eyes glistened. "You don't understand what it's like. Outside of the gang, all I was, was scared. Who was going to protect me? Not my mum. Then when I was in the SWB, everyone was fired up with anger all the time. The JMC done this. The Poplar Boys done that. Now I'm dead, none of it matters. All the anger's gone. I'm not scared anymore, just sad."

"But you've killed people." Tony couldn't get past that.

Scott smiled sadly. "No, I didn't, and Repo neither. I couldn't admit it before." He glanced at Deirdre. "She told me off, after. Told me I was stupid. I was still worried about my rep. But I'm beyond all that now."

"You're racist." Tony wanted to help, but it stuck in her throat to help a racist. Jade was family to her, same as this boy's Repo. And it wasn't just about Jade. It was something that ran to the very core of Tony's personal code of honor.

"I wasn't once." Scott cradled his right thumb in his left hand. "After the JMC carved their name into my belly, everyone told me on the estate, they told me it was because I was white. All my life, that's all I've heard. White look after their own. Black look after theirs. You know what? That attitude don't help no one. I can see that now. All of it, even how much I hate the JMC seems stupid.

"Someone came to my school once. She stood up at assembly, talking about gangs. I was in the SWB by then, so really I wasn't paying her no mind, but I remember this. She said more boys were killed in the UK than forces in Afghanistan. It didn't mean nothing to me then. But it does now. It's a waste. I miss Repo. I don't care if that makes me a faggot. I miss him with all my heart, but I don't want him here, dead like me. I want him to have kids, to be a rapper, whatever, to have some kind of chance to do something." He looked deep into Tony's eyes and bit his lip. "You need to go now, if you're going to keep Repo alive."

❖

It was getting dark by the time Tony reached the council estate where Scott used to live. The entrance from the main road was a small, poorly lit alleyway. Three men hanging out by a BMW stopped talking and stared at her as she passed.

She turned into the alleyway and walked quickly through into the internal courtyard.

Blocks of flats rose on all four sides of the enclosed cobbled area. The estate was built in a square with a hollowed-out center. Each block was five stories high. Restored, the brick-faced, red tile-topped buildings could be beautiful, but these were scrawled with tags and graffiti, while the doors and windows ironically cried out for paint. Washing was strung outside individual flats, providing a splash of color behind the black railings of each walkway. Cooking smells combined with cannabis, tobacco, and urine. Music drifted through open windows. Far off, a baby cried.

"I don't like this. Ring Jade," Deirdre hissed in Tony's ear, making her jump.

Tony looked around, trying to see into the shadows. The place looked deserted. "I can handle it," she said tersely. "Jade will be angry. This will take me five minutes. Jade never needs to know."

Deirdre vanished. That took the biscuit. Tony couldn't believe Deirdre would go on and on about coming to the place and then bail out on her.

Scott was still beside her. He stared up at the buildings. He looked like he was searching the walkways.

Following his gaze, Tony felt exposed out in the middle of the courtyard. She walked over to a set of railings on one side. A couple of bicycle skeletons were still secured to railings by thick bike locks, long after their wheels had been stolen. Tony had always wondered why people didn't remove the bike frames when that happened. Had they been visiting friends and couldn't be bothered to come back? Or were they leaving the skeletons there as a warning to other bike owners?

There was a clatter and a screech to her right.

A black cat tore out of another entrance to the estate and sped off across the gray cobbles into the shadows of the block opposite.

Then Tony saw what had disturbed the cat. A group of hooded figures strolled out of the entrance, fists clenched, shoulders back, eyes fixed in her direction. They came straight for her.

"Be back in a minute," Scott muttered.

"What?" Tony said, but he was gone.

There were four young men. Tony guessed they were somewhere between fifteen and twenty. None were very tall. All were white. One looked like he worked out. Two were slight. The fourth was fat.

"What you doing here?" The fat boy walked up to her. The others flanked her on both sides and behind till she was surrounded. The fat boy leaned his face in till he was a breath away from hers, and dropped his voice. "This is my manor."

Tony forced herself not to pull her face away or step backward. She'd grown up on a smaller but similar estate. She knew the rules. "I'm looking for someone."

"Fed. I told you," the worked-out guy said.

The fat boy narrowed his eyes at her. "Shit. It's a bitch," he said.

"I'm not a bitch. I'm a woman," Tony said before she thought better of it.

"Same thing," the fat boy said.

"She's one of them community police. They're the only ones stupid enough to come here on their own," the worked out guy said.

The others laughed. Tony didn't think it was the moment to tell them she wasn't police, community or otherwise.

"What phone you got?" The fat boy pulled Tony's jacket open. She stepped back and walked into the youth behind her. He shoved her forward. She felt his hand slip into her back pocket.

"IPhone five. Nice," he said.

Tony turned. "Give me my phone back," she snarled.

"Give me my phone back." The fat boy did a whining imitation of her voice.

Tony shut her mouth.

With no phone and no one coming to help her, Tony was in serious trouble.

❖

Jade tore through the south side entrance of the estate. She saw Tony, surrounded by youths in hoods. Anger pushed her fear aside.

"Don't go to them. They won't take no notice of you. Especially as you're a…a black person." Scott spoke quickly, close to Jade on her right side. "Turn left, go up the stairs. Repo's on the third floor."

Jade hesitated. "Tony needs help now."

Scott shook his head. "You can't do nothing. They're tooled up. Repo's the only one who can make them stand down."

Against her instincts, Jade trusted Scott and headed for the stairs. She ran up them. She was terrified for Tony. She was also furious with her. Tony had gone back on her word.

"It was my fault," Deirdre said for the third time. It was like she was reading Jade's mind. "Tony didn't want to come. I persuaded her."

"You shouldn't have been able to persuade her," Jade muttered. "And this is exactly why."

Jade stepped onto the third floor walkway. She stood panting and looked along the length of it. It was empty.

In the courtyard below, a fat boy held a phone in front of Tony's face and then pocketed it. A slight youth standing behind Tony stepped up to her and put her arms around her, pressing himself against her.

To hell with it. She was calling the police. Jade took her phone out and got one nine dialed.

"That's a pretty phone," a voice said quietly in the shadows.

Jade started.

"That's Repo," Scott said.

A sweet-faced boy stepped through a black security gate enclosing one of the apartments.

"Pretty phone for a pretty little lady." Repo stopped in front of her. He was about a head taller than her, and handsome, with blond hair allowed to grow past the crew cut of the other gang members. He had an angelic, rosebud mouth and blue eyes that sparkled, even in the dim yellow light of the walkway. A wooden-handled knife with a four-inch blade glinted in his right hand. He gestured it toward Jade's phone.

"Why don't you just give that to me?" he said pleasantly.

Jade calculated whether she could tap the numbers before Repo could grab her phone. She didn't think so. She put her phone in the inside pocket of her jacket and zipped it up.

Repo gave a soft chuckle. "Brave? Or stupid? Which is it?"

Jade ignored the question. She kept the blade in her peripheral vision. "Call your dogs off," she said.

Repo laughed openly. His smile was warm. "You got to be Old Bill." He looked up her and down. "Though you're bare short. I thought the police had standards. They getting desperate?"

Jade didn't say anything. She wanted to check Tony was all right, but she didn't dare take her eyes off the knife.

"Only Old Bill would be arrogant enough to come in here. Undercover are you? That why you got no radio?"

"I've got a message for you," Jade said.

"This is a white-only estate. You got no business coming here. We don't speak to the filth anyway, but if we did, we'd only speak to the white ones." Repo spoke as pleasantly as he had before, but there was disgust in his eyes.

"I've got a message from Scott."

The smile disappeared from Repo's lips. "Liar. No one calls him Scott except teachers and the filth."

"A. My name's A. They call me Straight A because I can't lie," Scott said.

"Straight A is standing next to me."

Repo glanced to either side of Jade. "What you chatting about, you crazy bitch?"

"He told me he moved the stash. You can't find it, can you?"

A tic pulsed across Repo's cheek. "You're talking shit. I don't know nothing about any stash. What is a stash anyway?" He was messing with Jade even though he was clearly rattled.

"I'm not the police. Neither is Tony, my girl, there." Jade tossed her head in Tony's direction, still keeping the knife in view. "We're psychics. Scott came to us. I didn't want to help him. Tony did. I didn't think you were worth saving."

Repo raised his eyebrows. She had his attention.

"Apparently, you'll die tonight if I don't tell you where the drugs are."

Repo stared at her.

"Call your boys off, or I won't tell you anything." Jade stared as hard back.

Repo glanced over at the gang.

He thought for a moment then put thumb and first finger to his lips. He gave two short whistles. The boys on the ground floor froze.

Repo pulled out a phone. The fat boy's phone rang. He accepted the call.

"Stand down. Peel back. Tell the bitch to stay where she is. You step back to the railings. Keep your eyes on her."

"Tell them to give her back her phone."

Repo shook his head sharply, once. "Where's the stash?"

"Oh no." The knife was still a swipe away from her chest. "I'm not telling you till Tony gets her phone back and we're both outside on the main road."

Repo laughed. "Well, then, we've got a problem. You don't trust me. And I sure as fuck don't trust you. You shouldn't even be standing there. It's a disgrace."

He went quiet, thinking. "You're to do with them, ain't you? You're with the JMC. You trying to trap me? Get me out onto the main road?" His grip tightened on the knife. He took a step nearer.

The knife was close enough to touch her skin.

"Do I look like a gang member?" Jade said indignantly. Her eyes never left the tip of the blade.

"No, you're too old," Repo said quickly. He thought for a second. "Maybe you ain't with the JMC, but we still got a problem."

"He can never let something go," Scott muttered beside her. "Tell him he's being as stupid as the time he stood up to Mr. McGonigal."

Jade told him.

Repo narrowed his eyes.

Scott spoke into Jade's ear. "McGonigal thought he was the big man of the school. We was only nine, both just joined the gang—little Stepney Walkers. We were playing at it, really. Tell him, this ain't worth getting the belt for."

Jade was horrified. "Scott says this isn't worth getting the belt for." She turned in the direction of Scott's voice. "What do you mean, the belt? Corporal punishment in schools was outlawed a long time ago in this country."

"So what? McGonigal knew my mum wouldn't notice, and he was sleeping with Repo's old lady. He knew she wouldn't care. Repo stood up to him in front of the whole class. At Repo's house later, McGonigal whipped us both good, but Repo had his moment, even if it took his back three weeks to heal. Tell him I said to give your phones back and let you go."

Jade passed on the message. Repo listened. His eyes darted left and right of Jade as if he was trying to see Scott.

After a while, he pointed the knife down. "I don't believe A's here. He's gone. But maybe he had time to call you and tell you all that shit before he died. No one knows about that, so it must have been him. Whatever. If A wanted me to trust you, all right then. I got nothing to lose. Something's going down tonight, anyway, so let's have it." Repo said the last words cockily, as if going into a fight.

He put his fingers to his lips again and gave a long whistle that cut through the air. He pocketed his knife.

Most of the gang padded away. The fat boy handed Tony back her phone before he turned into the alley too.

Jade made Repo walk in front of her down the stairs to Tony. Tony stared like she was shocked to see her.

Repo scanned the area carefully before they stepped off the estate. Even then, on the main road, he hung back, keeping just within earshot.

"Scott bought his mum a new freezer. Under the bottom drawer is a secret drawer for ice and stuff. You have to take the whole drawer out to see it. That's where it is," Jade said.

Repo nodded. He held her eye for a moment. Then he disappeared, back into the darkness of the estate.

❖

As Maya turned the key in Tony's door, she heard raised voices inside. She dropped her bag in the hall and went straight into the living room.

The coffee table was covered with foil takeaway containers dumped straight on the surface, with no mats or kitchen paper to protect it. Tony and Jade were sitting on Tony's couch next to the food. Jade had a heaped plate and was looking crossly at Tony. Tony was piling spoonfuls of rice onto her plate, with no regard to how much she was spilling onto the couch. From the delicious spicy aromas, Maya guessed the food was from Tony's favorite Bengali restaurant.

"I've never been this angry with you, Tony," Jade said. She looked up, saw Maya, and smiled. "Oh, thank God. Now that's the first good thing that's happened this evening."

Tony's eyes lit up. "Maya. I thought you were coming back tomorrow."

"I left early. The lectures tomorrow are mostly about Chinese herbal medicine. Anyway, I missed you." She bent and gave Tony a smooch. Tony tasted of spinach and potato curry. "Mmmm, you taste even better than I remember," she said.

"There's plenty of veggie stuff here, if you're hungry." Tony waved a hand toward the food. Maya tore her eyes from the spots of sauce on the table. The yellow turmeric stains would set if they were left too long.

"Sit down. Let me grab you a plate." Tony plonked her meal down. She was half out of her seat.

"No, no. I can get it myself, honey. You're in the middle of eating." Maya decided to grab some kitchen paper at the same time as a plate, and minimize the damage.

The atmosphere was decidedly strained when Maya returned. She filled her plate with sag-aloo, tarka dal, and pilau rice without saying anything. She mopped all the spills, sat carefully on the armchair next to the couch, and began to eat her dinner, waiting for someone to tell her what was going on. It was puzzling. She had spoken to Tony at lunchtime, before she'd decided on the spot to come back. Everything had been fine at one o'clock. Tony had been looking forward to having dinner with Jade on Jade's houseboat.

After ten awkward minutes, she asked, "What's wrong?"

Tony gave her look as if to say, "Don't ask."

"Tony put us both in danger tonight. She went steaming into a council estate on her own and got into trouble with a gang. Deirdre had to come get me," Jade said.

"That doesn't sound good, Tony. What's a council estate?" Maya asked.

"Oh, sorry. It's social housing, public housing. This was one of those big old blocks that are built around an open courtyard. Basically, once you go onto the estate you're pretty much surrounded by the apartment blocks with only a couple of ways out," Jade said. She turned to Tony. "I was terrified for you when those boys had you cornered."

Maya's stomach tensed. Recklessness was a part of Tony's character. It was admirable, to a point. Maya realized she would have to accept it now that they were in a relationship, but she didn't like the idea of Tony in danger.

"What happened?" she asked.

Jade related the night's events. Tony sat stony quiet, eating her dinner slowly.

"Thank God you got there in time, Jade," Maya said. "Tony, you need to start thinking about your own safety."

Tony looked at her but didn't unclench her jaw to reply.

"You promised me we wouldn't have anything to do with the case." Jade's normally calm voice was tight with anger.

"I didn't promise anything," Tony said quietly. "I agreed not to take the case, but I didn't promise."

"You went back on your word."

"He came to see me. He was desperate. I thought I could quickly go see Repo and get out of there."

Maya put her plate down. "What made you put this ghost's needs over your friends?" she asked Tony.

Tony narrowed her eyes at her. Maya realized Tony was feeling cornered. She backed off.

"Repo was going to die," Tony said sullenly.

"Oh. You didn't mention that, Jade," Maya said.

Jade cleared her throat. "I didn't mention a lot of things. Like how racist the ghost was. The whole gang is racist. I didn't want to help racist, murdering gang members."

"He didn't murder anyone. Neither has Repo. Scott told me when he came back again. I didn't want to help racists, but what you don't know is the other gang are just as horrible." Tony put her plate down on the coffee table. It was still half full.

"I'm sure they are," Jade said. "I didn't want to help any gang members. You really let me down tonight, Tony."

"I let *you* down?" Tony's voice was cold with anger.

"Yes," Jade spat back.

They glared at each other.

"How are we going to run this agency together if I can't trust you?" Jade asked.

"Well, maybe we should think about that," Tony said quickly. "Like you say, if we can't trust each other. If we can't rely on each other."

Maya frowned. Tony was trying to say something, but Jade either didn't pick up on it or was too upset and angry to care. Jade was on her feet.

"It was lovely to see you, Maya, but I'm going to get off now." Jade looked at Tony and shook her head. Maya could see the hurt in her eyes.

Tony shrugged but didn't look up.

Jade grabbed her jacket and bag, and within a few strides was out the door.

The front door opened and shut. Tony switched on the TV and then picked up her plate and started eating.

"Tony…" Maya watched Tony as she stared blankly at the TV. "Do you want to talk about—"

Tony pointed the remote at the screen and hit the volume plus button till the noise of a sitcom filled the room.

❖

Jade lay on Suni's massage couch, stripped down to her bra and panties trying not to be so turned on that she could hardly breathe. When they'd met for coffee, Suni had noticed straight away that something was wrong with Jade. Suni was so observant. Under Suni's gentle questioning, Jade had revealed that she was taking Valium. The combined effect of falling out with Tony and Felicia's unrelenting verbal abuse had driven Jade to the diazepam bottle. She didn't tell Suni that. She just told Suni she'd been feeling anxious. Suni had insisted that they go immediately to Suni's clinic for an acupuncture session. Jade thought of the concern in Suni's eyes when she'd said, "Honey, you can't take those horrible drugs. They'll kill your spirit. Let me reduce your anxiety."

The room was warm and dark. Candles flickered on a ledge. Jade watched the dancing light through heavy eyelids. There was a sweet, relaxing scent in the air. It smelled like a spa. Like a sexy spa.

Stop it.

Jade tried to push an image of Suni massaging her intimately out of her head.

"Try not to move," Suni said as she stepped back from slipping a long, slim needle into a point just above Jade's elbow.

"What would happen if we do? I mean, if I do?" Jade was barely stopping herself from kissing Suni. "Could I injure myself?"

"Unlikely, but you would spoil the treatment. It's best you just lie there, very still, for the moment." A smile spread slowly from Suni's eyes to her lips.

Jade swallowed. A shiver went through her. She didn't think she could lie still. Her fingers itched to dash the needles from her body and pull Suni on top of her.

She shut her eyes. She hadn't a hope if she kept looking up at Suni.

The sweet, floral smell filled Jade's head.

Music started. Something ambient and electro. It wasn't Jade's kind of tune, but it was soothing. She drifted along on the female vocalist's resonant tone. After the acupuncture session, she was determined to get Suni back to the houseboat.

Her thighs felt tingly and warm. Half in a dream, she opened her eyes to find Suni's hands hovering a couple of inches above her body, one hand over each inner thigh. Jade gasped.

Suni's head turned toward her. She looked completely calm.

Holding Jade's gaze, she lowered her hands almost imperceptibly slowly until the tips of her fingers made contact with Jade's skin. Jade arched.

She felt a slight pressure on her abdomen as one of Suni's hands gently pressed her back onto the couch. She opened her mouth to speak. Suni's fingers left her abdomen and then one of them rested lightly against Jade's lips.

"Shh." The sound escaping Suni's mouth was like waves over shingle. Suni grazed Jade's ankle with one hand, moving upward along Jade's inner thigh. With her other hand she traced circles around Jade's breasts and snaked a line down the center of her belly. As Jade's eyelids fluttered open and shut, she saw Suni taking out some of the needles.

Jade let out a sigh as the hand running up her thigh and the hand inching down her belly met. Suni's hands rested on top of Jade's panties. Jade began to arch again, and this time Suni answered by slipping her fingers inside the waistband and leg of the underwear.

"You still have needles in, so move cautiously." Suni's voice was full of desire.

Jade reached for Suni's fingers. Keeping most of her body still, she flexed the center of herself, finding a rhythm with Suni.

"I will guide you. I won't let you come to harm." Suni's voice blended with the music, the perfume, and with the pleasure building between Jade's legs.

She moved on Suni's thumbs until the ride carried her smoothly over the edge into an orgasm that pulsed through her.

Jade lay quietly on the massage couch. She let the sounds and smells of the room meld with the glow in her body.

Her eyes drifted open. She watched Suni take out the rest of the needles.

"I told you I'd take your anxiety away." Suni popped the last needle into a sharps container.

Jade grasped Suni's shoulder and pulled her gently but firmly onto the couch.

CHAPTER SIX

Jade snuggled up to Suni, drifting in and out of a dream. The houseboat rocked gently beneath her. Something had woken her, but she wanted to stay warm and dreamy, wrapped up against Suni's soft and sexy back.

A faint crying noise tugged at her consciousness. Her eyes fluttered open.

"I'm not angry at you anymore."

Jade sat up.

She got out of bed, grabbed her robe, and padded over to the door leading to her living room.

She switched on the table lamp and sat on the sofa.

"Why won't you help me? I don't understand." Felicia sounded depressed. Jade turned in the direction of her voice.

"I'm sorry. I don't think I can help you. I'm involved with Suni now. I didn't mean it to happen like this. I'm still working up to passing on your message. But to be honest, it would be quicker and cleaner if you went through Tony."

There was silence. For a hopeful minute, Jade wondered if Felicia had indeed gone to see Tony.

"She's white, isn't she?"

"Yes." Jade's heart sank.

"I don't want to chat my business with a white woman. I came to a sister. We're supposed to help each other."

"This help is a one-way street. You're not helping me. You want me to help you," Jade pointed out. "And right now, I'm not the best person for that, sister." Jade tried to say the word "sister" neutrally.

She felt solidarity with most black women. Felicia was using that to manipulate her. Jade felt sorry for her when she was being sad and reasonable. But Felicia could turn at any moment.

"What's the point in me talking to your friend? You already know Suni. She's in the other room. Why don't you just go tell her?"

Jade could see the sense of Felicia's words, but she didn't want to talk to Suni about her dead ex. Suni hadn't even mentioned it. She was probably too traumatized. Felicia said she had killed herself. What would that do to a person? Jade didn't know what to do. She wanted to talk to Tony. She hadn't made it right with her, and she needed to.

"Go tell Suni now, for God's sake." Felicia's voice had the sinister edge in it that frayed Jade's nerves.

Jade went to her bathroom. She pulled the little bottle of Valium off the top shelf and uncapped the lid.

There was a step behind her.

"What are you doing with that? I don't want you to take it. Give it to me." Suni stretched her hand out, bending in for a kiss at the same time. The bottle left her hand as Jade lost herself in the smooch.

Suni pulled her back into the living room and sat them down on the sofa.

"Now. Why are you feeling anxious? Do you want to talk about it?"

Jade thought for a moment. Obviously, she didn't want to tell Suni about her ghost of an ex.

"Couldn't you sleep?"

Jade shook her head.

"Why didn't you wake me? I would have taken your mind off whatever's troubling you." Suni smiled a sultry smile that completely distracted Jade. She put her hands on Suni's shoulders, pushing her down. Jade didn't even care if Felicia was still around; she had to have Suni. But Suni pushed back.

"What's wrong, honey? Surely you can tell me?" Suni asked.

Jade frowned. She'd rather lose herself in sex, but it was nice Suni cared. She decided to talk about the other thing that was bothering her. "I miss my friend Tony. You know, I told you we had a row."

"Because she betrayed you."

"Um, yes. Betrayed is a bit strong."

"Oh, I'm sorry. I was just repeating the word you used the other day when you told me about the trouble with those gang members."

Jade swallowed. It was true she had said she'd felt betrayed. Her friendship with Tony was deep, and she trusted her completely.

"And because she pretty much controls your detective agency." Suni sat back, linked her fingers behind her head, and stretched.

"Did I say that? I'm not sure she controls it exactly." Apart from Felicia, all the ghosts went to Tony. It did feel like Tony was in charge sometimes.

"I suppose it's how you view consultation then. It's a very strange detective agency anyway. You don't seem to do a lot, the pair of you."

"We just finished a case."

Suni didn't say anything.

Jade realized she couldn't tell Suni much about the agency. "Most of our cases are private."

"Oh, I see. That makes sense. I don't mean to pry. How on earth did an actor and a stage manager become detectives?"

"Quite by chance. A friend needed help. We have a good success rate, considering we're new at this."

"Do you liaise with the police?" Suni asked.

Jade shook her head. "We don't need to."

Suni raised her eyebrows. "It's a dangerous business, especially for amateurs."

Jade was piqued. "Most of our cases are perfectly safe." Suni was right, though. Tony hadn't a clue what she was doing. Neither of them did. That was why Jade wanted to take things slowly. She needed to know Tony would consult her. They could have both been seriously hurt.

"I'm not meaning to get into your affairs. It's just, I don't want anything to happen to you. I'm getting fond of you." Suni looked deep into Jade's eyes, and all Jade's angst melted away. Suni was laid back and a little bit shy, but boy, was she intense. Jade bit her lip.

"I just need to go see Tony. We'll work it out. We always do."

Suni smiled reassuringly. "It's nice you have such a strong friendship. I'm sure the friendship's just as important to Tony. She probably just needs some space."

Jade frowned. "Tony likes to give people space. I don't think…

Oh, I see what you mean. If she likes to give people space, maybe she likes it herself. Yeah, that would make sense." She squeezed Suni's hand. "God, I've known Tony all these years, and I've only just made that connection."

"Happy to help any way I can." Suni ran her fingers along Jade's arm making all the little hairs stand up. "It's all part of the service, ma'am."

Jade shivered. She pushed her lips against Suni's, closing her eyes. Suni opened her mouth, quickening Jade's heartbeat. Jade felt better about Tony than she had in days. Suni was right. Jade didn't need to be so hard on her. Tony probably just needed a couple more days' space.

I'll drop in on her at the theater on Monday.

Suni kissed Jade hard, and her only thought was where Suni's hands were on her body.

❖

Tony called Jade again. The number rang, but Jade didn't pick up. There was no voice mail facility, as Jade had to pay for voice mail on her new pay-as-you-go plan, and Jade was feeling the pinch. Tony thought about sending a text but didn't trust herself not to send an angry one. It had been nearly a week since the row. Jade hadn't responded to Tony's calls or her emails.

Tony had to force herself to make contact with Jade. She'd been feeling weird about her since the night they'd helped Scott and Repo. Tony hadn't told anyone the things the boys had threatened to do to her when she'd been surrounded by them.

Tony shuddered. She felt the boy's body pressed up against her again and clenched her fists till the nails bit into her palms. She could smell his aftershave.

On the way to the theater, she'd walked behind someone with the same scent. As the smell hit her, a wave of nausea had engulfed her, and she retched in the gutter.

Tony blinked away tears. She felt stupid. Nothing had really happened. Not really. Not compared to what some people went through.

The boy had put his hands all over her. She hadn't been able to stop him. She kept thinking about it. Part of her wanted to go back to the estate, get him on his own, and beat him until he was out cold.

She was furious with Jade. She didn't want to be. Tony knew it was her own fault she'd been on the council estate. She guessed the bad stuff would have happened anyway, but she couldn't get over the fact that Jade had seen her surrounded by the boys and left her there. Jade had been talking to Repo when Tony had been groped.

Jade was angry with Tony for going against her wishes. Tony understood that. She had even texted *sorry*. Jade hadn't replied. That hurt a bit, but then, Tony didn't want to talk to Jade, so maybe it was for the best.

Tony pushed all thoughts of that night down into the deep recesses of her psyche and shut the door on them. She was good at that.

The show was ticking over nicely, and Tony didn't have a lot to do apart from press the go button when Beth, the deputy stage manager, called the lighting cues. The only setting up to do was powering up the lighting board, but Tony arrived at work early anyway. She liked the peace and quiet of the lighting box before the show.

Since the incident, she'd been relishing her solitary pre-show time.

She'd made a cup of tea in the green room on the way up. It was sitting on the desk in front of her, next to her currant bun. Tony unfolded her newspaper, leaned back in her swivel chair, and breathed a peaceful sigh.

The door opened with a thump. Beth strode in and stood in front of the broken chair Tony had been meaning to dump backstage.

"Hi, handsome. See you're in early as usual. I looked for you in the green room, but you weren't there."

"Do you need something?" Tony said as politely as she could. She wasn't happy her solitude had been disturbed.

"No, I just came for a moan. I've had it up to here with those fly men. Well, that's their problem, isn't it?"

"Huh? You're not making sense. Oh wait, don't—" Tony put her hand up to try to stop Beth sitting in the faulty chair.

"That's their problem, they're men. Ahh!" The back of the chair flipped outward and then recoiled like a bucking bronco, throwing Beth onto the floor.

"Yeah, it's been doing that a lot. I've been meaning to throw that chair out." Tony reached down to help Beth up.

Beth glared at her. Then she accepted Tony's extended hand. She rubbed her rump and sat down gingerly, being careful not to lean back.

"I am so off men," she said, grimacing. Tony wasn't sure if she was grimacing at her sore butt or at half the human race. She didn't ask.

"Men are such a pain," Beth said a little louder.

Beth had come out some months previously. Before that, she had been very into men. Was she now saying she was bisexual? "So, are you back on men, again?" Tony asked cautiously.

"No. That's just it. I'm completely off them; that's why they annoy me so. You know how it is when you're a hundred percent lesbian. Men must annoy you all the time."

Tony wasn't following Beth's logic. "Erm. Not so much."

"This macho, masculinity thing isn't doing it for me anymore. You're a bit too butch for me, to be honest."

"Good to know." Tony wondered if she'd ever be able to get back to the crossword.

"But of course, you're not actually a man. And you'll always have a special place in my heart."

"Well, that's true. That I'm not actually a man," Tony added hastily. "Of course I have a special place in Maya's heart."

Beth heaved a sigh. "You don't have to mention the quack homeopath every time I pay you a compliment. Well, I can't sit here talking to you all day. We should go out some time. You, me, and your fit friend Jade. You can bring the homeopath if you must."

"Oh, I think Jade…" Tony had been about to say Jade had a girlfriend, but she caught a sadness in Beth's eye. There was no reason to crush her hopes. "I think Jade's got a job in the provinces starting soon," she amended.

Beth just shrugged and left. Tony looked at her watch. She only had five minutes before show call.

"I can't see it myself. You and the newbie fruit of the loon."

Deirdre materialized. She sat elegantly in the broken swivel chair. As she was a ghost, it didn't spit her out. She was wearing a shiny, gold metallic body suit, topped with a pink rah-rah skirt.

"What have you got on now? And do you mean fruit of the loom? You said loon."

Deirdre ran her fingers through the long blond wig that sat on top of a shiny gold mask covering her face. "You're in the future, right?"

"I'm in the present actually."

"You're in the future from when I died, which makes you futuristic, so of course I've come as C3PO. Haven't you seen *Star Wars?*"

"I haven't seen anything that looked like that in any *Star Wars* film."

"Well, I wasn't going to come in just the bodysuit. I felt practically naked. And there was no way I was going to appear bald."

"Of course not. So you're that robot thing?"

"C3PO. But a female version."

"And moving swiftly on, what do you need? The show's starting soon and, as I keep telling you, I can't talk at work." Tony plonked on her comms headset and opened her script.

"The frowny 1960s butch with the bad haircut. She's still hanging round, cramping my style. It's ruining my Tupperware parties with the angels."

"Seriously?"

"Angels are very sensitive. They have this positive vibe thing going on. They can't function in negative atmospheres. And yes, they do like tidy boxes. Don't go there." Deirdre raised a hand in Tony's direction as Tony opened her mouth. "I'm fond of angels. They're pretty, and yet muscular," Deirdre said, panting slightly. "I need pretty muscles around me. I don't think it's too much to ask."

Tony had stopped listening. "I keep thinking about Frankie."

"Really? With that haircut? She looks like she was attacked by sheep shearers. And then dressed by them. I thought you liked your women a bit more like women."

"I do. I mean, I don't fancy Frankie. I keep thinking about the case."

"I suppose it's a sad story. Maybe she's gotten used to being pulled back to the living by Rose and misses it. I may have to bring her to you, to help her move on."

"Why me?"

"She won't listen to me. Okay, see you later, Terminator, gotta fly. Angels are calling."

Deirdre's visit gave Tony food for thought. It was good to think about something other than the incident. She opened her script, feeling lighter than she had for days.

❖

Jade picked all the cushions off the sofa and threw them to the floor. It was getting ridiculous. She wanted to go to the gym, and half of her possessions had taken a walk in the night. She was searching for her iPod. She'd had it the previous day when she'd jogged into Docklands. It wasn't like there were many places things could disappear to on a houseboat.

She squeezed herself under the sofa, wrinkling her face against the dust and bits of fluff living under there. She stretched her arm as far as she possibly could into the far reaches. Her fingers curled around something vaguely iPod like, but as she pulled it out, she realized it was too thick and large to be her MP3 player.

In the light streaming in through the windows, Jade stared at a phone that looked just like her own. She clicked it on. It was her phone. Well, that was one thing found. Jade had been searching for it since Saturday. It was switched off. That explained why it didn't ring when she was looking for it. Jade had looked under the sofa several times.

"Felicia!" Jade called the ghost's name. She had started to think of Felicia as "the ghost." She knew she was depersonalizing her, but she couldn't help herself. She hadn't talked to her for several days. Every time Felicia went quiet, Jade hoped that was the last of her.

"I told you, go see Tony. And leave my damn stuff alone."

It must be the ghost moving her stuff around. Two days previously, Jade had spent half the morning looking for her tablet. She'd found it under the mattress. That wasn't the kind of place something fell to by accident.

Jade needed to talk to Tony. She hadn't spoken to Suni about Felicia and had no intention of doing so. Maybe Felicia knew that somehow and was messing with Jade's stuff to punish her.

Jade had planned to drop in on Tony that evening, but Suni had booked a table at Plateau, an expensive restaurant with stunning views over Canary Wharf. She pulled up Tony's name from her contacts.

The call went straight to voice mail. It was the standard greeting, though, rather than Tony's personalized one.

Jade left a message anyway.

"Tony, call me back as soon as you can, will you? This ghost of mine is getting out of hand. Honey, let's get together and talk. I'm out tonight, but I'm around tomorrow. We've been friends too long to let stuff get in the way. I miss you. And, babe, I need your help. Call me."

❖

Maya stood at the gate to Jade's marina, her finger poised over Jade's buzzer. She remembered standing in the same spot, over a year previously, on a late spring evening. That was the night she'd met Tony properly. Maya smiled. Tony had been funny and sweet and very, very sexy. She still was for that matter, but she'd been distant for days. Maya put it down to the row with Jade. Someone had to get those two to see sense.

"Hello." Jade's voice came out of the intercom.

"Hi, Jade," Maya said brightly.

There was a pause.

"It's Maya," Maya said quickly. She hoped Jade wasn't upset with her as well as Tony.

"Fantastic. Come in, come in."

Maya pushed through the released gate and walked along the quayside until she reached Jade's boat. Jade had pots of daffodils on either side of her steps. They cheered up the dull scene. Some days Maya really missed the hazy, open skies of Provincetown. She loved London, but it could be gray for days on end, making her long for the beaches crashing with surf and misty skies that she'd grown up with.

Jade opened the door as Maya got to it, and pulled her inside. She hugged Maya tightly.

"So what brings you here, girl?"

"I wanted to see you. I miss you," Maya said, glancing around. Cushions were strewn everywhere, and the couch was pulled away from the wall. Jade was in her sweatpants and top. Strange clothes to be cleaning in, if that was what Jade was doing. Jade looked tired and drawn, with dark circles under her eyes.

"Sit down, sit down." Jade bustled about, throwing cushions back onto the couch. With a forceful movement, she flattened the couch back against the wall. "I'll make some tea."

"How are you?" Maya followed Jade up into the tiny galley kitchen. Jade filled the kettle and got out two cups.

Jade opened her mouth. Then shut it again and thought for a moment. "Okay, I guess. I feel tired."

Maya raised her eyebrows and smiled.

"Well, yes, partly because of lots of fantastic sex. But also because I haven't been sleeping too good. Do you want herb tea or ordinary?"

"Mint if you have it. Why aren't you sleeping?" Maya slipped into herbalist mode.

"I think it's the ghost." Jade poured hot water into the cups, handed one to Maya, and then walked back down the boat to the sitting room. They both sat on the couch. "Felicia's not speaking to me at the moment. I told her to go and see Tony. Has she, do you know?"

Maya shook her head. "I don't think so. Tony hasn't mentioned it, anyway."

"And I don't have an appetite."

"That's odd." Maya smiled. Jade had the appetite of a horse usually.

"Food tastes funny. I've got a salty taste in my mouth, and my mouth feels dry a lot of the time."

"Have you seen your orthodontist?"

"I haven't got money to see a dentist. But I have a healer. She's given me some powder to clean my teeth with." Jade wrinkled up her face.

"Neem?"

"Sounds about right. It tastes horrible. I'm not using it," Jade said in a stage whisper.

Maya tutted. "She can't help, you know, if you don't let her."

Jade grinned. "I miss you guys."

"I miss you too. I was hoping you and Tony would have sorted it out by now. Do your rows always go on this long?"

"Never. I just left her a message, actually. Do you know why she hasn't answered my texts and calls?"

Maya stared at Jade. "No." She didn't know what to say. She was sure Tony thought Jade was ignoring her attempts to communicate.

"Maybe the three of us can meet up. After I've touched base with Tony and made things right with her."

Maya nodded. She was happy to hear Jade wasn't still angry at Tony.

"I'll go to the theater. And I want you guys to meet Suni. Well, I know you've already met her, but I mean hang out." Jade dipped her eyes shyly.

Maya smiled. "It's going all right then?"

Jade nodded enthusiastically. "Yeah, girl, it's going great. The sex is incredible."

Maya smiled. Jade was looking tired, but she also had a glow that was lovely to see. Jade caught Maya's eye and grinned from ear to ear.

"Have you ever done it while having acupuncture?" she blurted out.

Maya swallowed in surprise. "Er, no. Have you?"

"Yes. We did it on her massage couch. It was intense."

Maya blinked. Suni was sharing her practice room, so Suni's couch was Maya's couch. Maya felt that healers should never blur the lines between professional and personal during a healing session. She tried not to let her disapproval show.

Jade didn't seem to notice. "Suni's been helpful. Made me see sense about Tony. I was annoyed." Jade sighed, then smiled. "But Tony means well. She's got a big heart."

"She sure has. She's been quiet lately. I think she's missing you." Maya cast an eye round the room. "Were you in the middle of clearing out stuff or something?"

Jade followed her gaze. "No. I was looking for my iPod. God, Maya, I don't know what's wrong with me. I keep losing things." She lowered her voice. "Actually, it might be the ghost."

"What things have you lost?"

"I just found my phone this morning. That went missing on Saturday. My tablet disappeared for nearly a week and turned up under the mattress in my bedroom."

"That's an odd place to lose something."

"That's what I thought. Oh, and my old address book is still missing."

"So is this ghost like a poltergeist then?"

Jade shrugged. "No idea. That's another reason I called Tony."

Maya cleared her throat. "There's no chance you could be misplacing the stuff yourself?"

Jade frowned at her. "Why do you ask that?"

"Well, you're sleep deprived, and Tony mentioned you've borrowed her diazepam."

Jade raised her eyebrows. "Ah. I see your reasoning. I am sleep deprived, but Suni has confiscated the Valium."

Maya laughed at the way Jade said it. "Has she? Good for her. Sorry, you know I hate tranquilizers. I mean, unless people really need them. Have you told Suni about the ghosts then?"

Jade shook her head furiously. "I like her, Maya. I don't want her running a mile."

"So, what does she think you were taking the tranqs for, just in case I bump into her at the practice?"

"That was easy. I told her it was anxiety. I was treated for anxiety when my aunt died."

"Oh, I'm sorry to hear that."

"No, it's okay. She died years ago. I was only seventeen. Hasn't Tony told you?"

"No. You know Tony. She's far too honorable. She wouldn't tell me something that personal about you."

"Well, it was a terrible shock. My aunt was my only family here. I didn't have friends then either. After the funeral, I stayed on, in my aunt's house. Fortunately, she owned it and left it to my mum. I was desperately lonely, and for a short while, I was anxious that everyone I loved would die. I wrote home all the time. This was the eighties so my family didn't have emails. Every morning, I rushed down to check the post, hoping for a letter, just because I wanted to be sure no one had died. When my hair started to fall out, I knew I had to get help. I saw a therapist for a couple of months, but as soon as I started at LAMDA I was fine."

Maya sipped her tea, letting Jade's words settle. Jade left her cup of tea on the coffee table, untouched. She scratched at her arm, lost in thought.

"Thank you for trusting me with that," Maya murmured.

"Well, you know that Tony's family to me. You're starting to feel like that too." Jade pulled Maya to her for a hug. Jade felt thinner.

"You've got my number, haven't you?" Maya asked.

Jade nodded.

"You can talk to me anytime."

Jade shifted on the sofa. "I'm okay, you know. Just tired." She stood up.

Jade looked uncomfortable. She was probably feeling vulnerable at having revealed personal information.

Jade started walking to the houseboat door. "Tell Tony to call me, will you?" she said.

"Of course." Maya grabbed her bag and followed Jade.

"I'll buzz you out," Jade said, catching Maya's eyes for a moment before she let the door swing slowly shut.

❖

Tony stood at the kitchen sink washing up. She glanced out the kitchen window, down nine stories to the busy street below. Tiny people scurried about, some going into shops and others heading for the Tube. There was a constant stream of cars with white lights from the front, and red from the rear as they sat bumper to bumper in rush hour traffic on the main road.

"Changes" by David Bowie drifted in from the living room. Maya had put it on. They shared a love of Bowie. In Tony's mind, he was still the coolest songwriting dude in the music industry.

Tony sighed contentedly. Maya was a marvel in the kitchen. She had spent the afternoon making pumpkin ravioli from scratch. Tony could still taste the buttery sweetness on her tongue. Tony knew she was a lucky woman. Maya made her feel warm and cozy inside.

Tony was starting to put the gang incident behind her, but she had pulled back from Maya sexually.

It was a shame. In bed, she connected with Maya on a deep level. Maya took Tony to places she'd never gone with anyone else.

Tony swallowed. Well, it was just a matter of time. Tony was starting to get sparks of desire again. She exhaled and closed her eyes. Maya was absolutely gorgeous, and she had a beautiful personality as well. She was kind, political, and thoughtful. Her only real fault was her cleanliness obsession. Maya put it down to having to clean up after her father when she was a kid. When Maya's late father had had his mental health crisis he'd been very messy. Maya's mother had abandoned them several times, leaving a very young child in dirty surroundings, with a disturbed adult. Even though she lived in England, Tony had never met Maya's mother. Tony had some things saved up to say to her, if she did.

Tony hated thinking about what Maya had been through. So she was a neat freak. So what? Tony could help out by being extra clean. She took her time with the washing up. Then she dried the pots and put them away, something she'd never have done pre-Maya. They would have been left, stacked higgledy-piggledy on top of each other to drain.

"Are you ever coming in?"

Tony looked up from scrubbing away at a tomato stain on her counter. Maya was standing in the doorway, a half-empty glass of red wine in her hand.

"I'm feeling lonely," Maya said with a sultry smile.

"Just trying to make the place look nice," Tony said, smiling back.

Maya glanced at the countertop. "Well, you're using the wrong scourer. You'll scratch the counter if you use that one." She stopped. "I suppose it doesn't matter. It's your countertop."

Tony could see Maya was making an effort not to wrench the sponge out of Tony's hand. She abandoned the stain and followed Maya into the sitting room.

"I'll do it later," Maya whispered into Tony's ear, before handing her a beer.

"Tony, I wanted to talk to you about Jade." Maya broke into her thoughts, sounding hesitant.

"Yeah?" At the mention of Jade's name, Tony's stomach tensed. "She's still not answering my calls." Tony dropped her head. "She probably just wants some space with her new girlfriend."

"No, it's not that. She misses you. She says she hasn't had any texts or calls from you."

"That's crazy. Look." Tony picked her phone off the arm of the sofa. "See all the texts I've sent? She hasn't answered a single one." She scrolled down a list. Maya read them, frowning. "Jade can go out of communicado, you know, when she's got a new woman."

"Jade is positive she hasn't had any texts or calls from you."

"Why would she say that?"

"I don't know. Has Jade had any history of confusion, or, well, not quite seeing things as they are?"

Tony tensed. She didn't want to talk about Jade. She knew it was ridiculous, but she associated Jade with that night, with what had happened and with the things the boys threatened to do. She knew it would all settle down with a little time, but not if Maya picked at it.

"Are you listening to me, Tony?" Maya said sharply. Tony knew one fast way to irritate Maya was if she felt ignored.

Tony looked Maya in the eye. "Yes. Why do you think something's wrong with Jade? I'm sure she's fine."

"I went to see her today. She doesn't look good. She's not sleeping. She's misplacing things. And I noticed she was scratching her skin a lot."

Tony bit back a laugh. "Oh my God, that must mean she's completely crazy, Maya." Tony shook her head. Maya's habit of analyzing everyone was annoying. Her father had had real mental health problems, but that didn't mean everyone in the world did. "Look, Maya, I know you know a lot about these things, and you've done a counseling course—"

"Yeah, I'm thinking of taking my MSC," Maya interrupted.

"Oh, I don't think that's a good idea," Tony said quickly. She shut her mouth when Maya glared at her.

"Why?" Maya said.

Tony took a moment to think. She didn't want to be insensitive. Maya couldn't help the fact that she saw mental health issues everywhere. "Well, never mind about that now. Back to Jade. Maybe she's mistaken about the texts, but you can't jump to her having some kind of episode. She doesn't have any mental health problems."

"She has a history of anxiety."

"Why do you say that?" Tony put her beer bottle down.

"She told me. She was treated for anxiety when she was seventeen."

"For God's sake, that was years ago. And completely understandable. Her aunt, her only family in this country, died. That's enough to make anyone anxious."

"You didn't see her. Something's not right." Maya narrowed her eyes.

Tony stared at Maya, not liking her attitude at all.

"I'm just saying." Maya took a sip of wine.

"Well, don't. You need to back off people. You get too much in people's faces." Tony couldn't believe how one-track minded Maya was sometimes.

"By people you mean you. We're not talking about Jade now, are we? Why do you feel so vulnerable?"

"I don't," Tony said, feeling vulnerable as hell.

"You've been real quiet since I got back from the herbal conference. What's going on?"

Tony felt backed into a corner. "Nothing," she lied. "I know Jade, okay. I know her a lot better than you. I am upset she hasn't called me, but I'm going to give her the space that I think she needs."

"She doesn't want space from you, or me. Why don't you go and see her?"

"Okay, but I'm not going to just barge round there. I'll text her and get a date to go round."

Maya sighed. "That's your stuff. You learned from your father to take space when you can't handle things."

Tony really wanted some space at that moment, from Maya. "God help me, Maya, stop analyzing me."

"Why are you so resistant, Tony? If you don't face these things you'll never move on."

"You're behaving like a therapist, except not a very good one because you're really not subtle at all."

"I'm not meaning to be subtle. I'm not acting as a therapist. I'm your girlfriend, and I'm being open and transparent with you. I want to improve our communication. I happen to have counseling training, and I'm using it to try to make our relationship better. At least I'm trying," Maya said, her prissy voice bursting past the forced calm tone that set Tony's teeth on edge.

"Well, here's something for you to stick in your counseling pipe: you're behaving exactly like my therapist mother did to my ghost-seeing father. So what do you make of that, Sigmund Freud?" Tony spat the words out more angrily than she meant to.

Maya flinched. Tony wished she hadn't said anything.

"Okay. Well, you're being honest. That's good." Maya went back into calm-voiced counselor mode.

Tony slowly counted to ten.

"Maya, you spent most of last year convinced I was mad."

"I would never have used that term," Maya said.

"I know. But nevertheless, you thought I was mad when I was in fact seeing ghosts."

"You know how that sounds, right?" Maya giggled.

Tony cracked a smile.

"Yes, you have a point," Maya admitted. "But then a lot of why I believed you was because Jade could hear ghosts…" Maya tailed off.

"Seriously? Seriously, you're going to tell me you don't believe me anymore. We're going back to you thinking I'm hallucinating." Tony was half off the sofa. Maya's disbelief in her had been painful. Tony's feelings were about to burst out of her, and that was the last thing she wanted. She hated exposing her feelings.

Maya reached for Tony's hand. "No. No. I don't think that. Come on, baby, sit back down."

Tony sat down. She was all churned up. Maya picked up her hand and nestled it between both of hers.

"I saw my dad, remember?" Maya's eyes searched Tony's. "In the middle of that storm, on the boat. I saw him. And even if I tell myself I hallucinated for a moment, I know for a fact my uncle saw him. So, Tony, I do believe you can see and talk to ghosts. It's good for us to clear the air about some of this stuff, but I don't want to argue with you."

"I don't want to argue either." Tony pulled Maya into her arms. She smelled of tomato, herbs, and red wine, with a faint whiff of cleaning fluid. Tony stayed snuggled up to Maya's neck. "I'll call Jade again," she said, prepared to do anything, anything at all except talk.

CHAPTER SEVEN

Maya was halfway through an online order. With an hour between clients, she had decided to check the levels of her herbal tinctures, dried herbs, and ointment bases, and to replenish the stock.

It was a beautiful day. Sunshine poured through the large window that overlooked the practice garden. Maya had the blind up and the window open to air the room. The sunshine showed up every speck of dust on the glossy white surfaces. Maya stopped her stock check for the fourth time in ten minutes to wipe dust away. She wasn't sure whether to clean Suni's half of the cupboard. She wrinkled her nose at the dust gathering around Suni's Ayurvedic tablets, teas, oils, and tinctures.

Ten minutes later, Suni's half of the cupboard was sparkling, and Maya felt her stomach muscles begin to relax. She was getting used to sharing a practice room with Suni. The downside was that Maya never saw her, as they worked on different days. Maya would have liked the chance to get to know Suni. The clinic manager had rented out Suni's old room to a Reiki practitioner. The manager had pointed out that it made sense for the two *herbalists*, as he called them, to share the locked tincture cupboard, as they both used tinctures, oils, and dried herbs in their work.

Maya had found a way to deal with Suni's bright yellow sharps disposal box. On her days, Maya propped a picture of a purple lavender field in Provence in front of it. The only thing that had really bothered her was the thought of Jade and Suni having sex on the examination couch. Maya had scrubbed the couch as soon as she'd had the chance, and then rubbed it down with tea tree and geranium oils. Maya didn't have a problem with people making out in unusual places, but she was absolutely clear that sex had no place in her practice room. Tony had come on to her a couple of times when she'd picked her up after work. Maya had firmly turned her down. Maya needed to draw a clear line when she was in work mode. Being a healer was a pure thing for Maya. She needed to keep her sexual energy separate from her healing energy. She realized everyone didn't feel the same. Suni clearly didn't.

What if Suni and Jade regularly had sex on the couch? Maya grabbed the bottle of tea tree oil, poured some onto a cotton wool pad, and gave the couch a good once-over, just in case.

Maya sighed. She needed to get that order done before her next client arrived. She walked over to the computer, the list of items in her hand. The little desk in the corner of the room was the only area that was hard to share. There wasn't enough space to leave anything on the desk surface. Maya tidied her stuff away into the top drawer beneath the desk at the end of every day, but Suni regularly left a small pile of papers on top of it. Maya had to admit that Suni was generally tidy. This was the only area where she was messy.

Maya picked up the pile to straighten it out of habit. There was a piece of folded paper that wouldn't allow Maya to create a neat line. Maya unfolded it. It was an advert cut out of a magazine. Maya glanced over the picture of a log cabin in the middle of woodland. It was a rental cabin up in Scotland. The advert promised total seclusion in natural surroundings. Maya smiled. Suni must be planning a romantic trip away.

Maya glanced at the clock on the wall in front of her. Goodness! Her client was due in the next five minutes. Maya quickly stuffed Suni's pile of papers into the second drawer. She didn't like to move Suni's stuff, but it wouldn't be hard for her to find them. If it annoyed Suni, maybe it would encourage her to file her own papers. Maya realized that she was being passive aggressive. Maybe she'd have a think about that later, but for the moment she needed to concentrate on finishing the order.

She shut the drawer and got her head into the online order form.

❖

Beth called out to Tony as she walked past the stage management office on her way up to the lighting box.

"A card came for you, Tony."

Tony stuck her head round the door that was wedged open with a red travel case from *Cabaret*, the musical. Beth was brandishing a white envelope with Tony's name and the address of the theater on it.

"Did you read last night's show report?" Beth asked.

Tony shook her head. "I was going to check it out while I powered up and flashed through."

"Oh, I love it when you talk lighting," Beth said suggestively.

Tony smiled weakly.

"Well, the director popped in and he thought that Audrey wasn't in light during 'Skid Row,'" Beth said.

"She's in a follow spot. You should talk to the operators. They've been sloppy lately. I saw Seymour's follow spot bobbing up and down all the way through 'Suddenly Seymour' the other night. When I ran down to the auditorium left spot box, the guy was opping one-handed while playing a game on his phone with the other. He wasn't even looking at the stage."

"That's appalling. Why didn't you tell me before? I'm going to have a word with management right away." Beth was up and out of her chair before she'd even finished her sentence. "Oh." She stopped midway through squeezing past Tony in the narrow corridor. "While I remember, you never got back to me with dates to go out clubbing."

Tony vaguely remembered Beth suggesting they all go out. Beth was pressed up against her and looking hopeful. "Maya's very busy at the moment," Tony said, even though she'd forgotten all about it and never even mentioned it to Maya.

"That's okay. It's you I wanted to go out with anyway. You're my friend, and a good dancer. God knows what Maya's like on the dance floor. Those quack healers are notoriously wafty." Tony couldn't even begin to get inside Beth's mind. She didn't try.

"Er, I'll have to consult my diary," Tony said.

"You can let me know after the show," Beth said in the same commanding tone she used to give Tony the lighting cues. "It'll be fun. You can help me find a girlfriend. You can be my wingman, or beard, or whatever."

Tony was tempted to correct Beth's terminology but didn't want to prolong the time they were pressed up together in the corridor. Fortunately, Beth took off, presumably to harangue management about inattentive follow spot operators.

Tony climbed the stairs to the lighting box. Beth talking about Maya made Tony think about their conversation. Maybe Tony should have confided in Maya. She felt so stupid. It wasn't as if anything had really happened. Tony knew it wasn't rational, but she felt sick at the thought of talking about it to anyone.

While the lighting board powered up, she opened the card that Beth had given her. On the front was a picture of a bunch of flowers and the words "thank you" in multicolored block lettering. Inside was a note from Frankie White's girlfriend Rose.

Dear Tony,

Thank you so much for bringing me the letter from my partner, Frankie. Inside was some important information. Finding out that information has allowed me to finally let go of the past. Unfortunately, I've been acting on false information for the past fifty years. I'm very thankful to find the truth out now. I've shut down the Justice for Frankie campaign. I'm not surprised now that the home office never listened to me. I only wish the letter had been delivered all those years ago so that I could have done something different with my life.

I will always be grateful that you took the time to track me down.

Kind regards,
Rose Henderson

As Tony read the card, an uneasy feeling in her gut grew stronger and stronger. She'd had premonitions all her life. She hadn't always known exactly what the warning meant, but something always went wrong soon after. This time she didn't feel any danger but she was sure Rose was being led up the garden path. She hadn't a clue how or why.

Tony glanced at the clock above the lighting board. She still had half an hour before show call.

"Deirdre," she said quietly. A few seconds ticked by. "Deirdre," she said again, a little louder.

Tony tried to summon her spirit guide without shrieking at her. She shut her eyes and visualized Deirdre. For a second, she wondered what Deirdre would look like without a wig and not in female clothing. It seemed indecent to think of her that way. Almost as bad as imagining herself in a dress with long hair. Tony winced at the thought.

"If it's that bad, take a Dulcolax."

Tony opened her eyes to find Deirdre perched on the edge of the long workbench that the lighting desk sat on. She was wearing bright pink tights under a leopard print leotard, six-inch leopard print stilettos, and a bright pink headband. "I was relaxing at home. Whaddaya want?" Deirdre ran her words together when she was annoyed.

"Relaxing? Seriously? Haven't you heard of onesies?"

"Whoseys? Whatseys?" Deirdre creased her brow. "Who careseys? What is it?"

"I got a card from Rose. She's moving on."

"Great. Glad someone is. You could have just sent me an email."

"Could I?" Tony had never thought of that possibility. "Where would I send it?"

"It doesn't matter." Deirdre shifted on the workbench. "It's like a letter to Santa Claus. I'll get it anyway."

"Will you?"

Deirdre thought for a moment. "Actually, I don't know. I'll go away. You send me an email. Let's see if I get it." She made a move to get up.

"Wait. What's the hurry? You weren't really relaxing at home, were you?"

Deirdre pouted. "I might have been. With an angel."

"Oh, I see. Well, I won't keep you long. I have a strong premonition that there's more to the Frankie White case. Something isn't right. I feel it in my waters."

"Are you sure it's not gas?"

Tony grunted in annoyance.

"Okay. Leave it with me. You're probably right. The short, scowling one is still hanging around like a bad smell. I'll start a few lines of inquiry of my own."

"Will you?" Tony sat up, full of interest. "How will you do that? What will you do? Who will you ask?"

Deirdre glowered at her. "I'm busy. B to the U to the S to the Y, girlfriend. I came to see you because you called so loudly, but you have taken up enough of my time. See you later, investigator."

"Oh, I like that. That's clever. In a while—"

But Deirdre disappeared before Tony could even begin to think of something witty and funny that rhymed with while.

❖

The secluded cabin advert had got Maya thinking. She had promised Jade that she would talk to Tony, and somehow that had turned into an argument. That was common when people didn't own their stuff. Maya found that part of Tony frustrating. The harder she pushed, the more Tony closed down. Maya was prepared to give Tony some leeway. After all, Tony wasn't familiar with the concepts that Maya was. Maya had spent years studying psychology and counseling. She couldn't expect Tony to embrace the kind of changes and emotional honesty that Maya was used to demanding of herself.

Maya couldn't understand Tony's attitude. If it was one of her friends, Maya would never have left it so long to make things right. Not unless she didn't want to, and she was sure Tony was missing Jade just as much as Jade had said she was missing Tony. Tony didn't tackle things head on. That was Tony's father all over. He had apparently pretended for years that he didn't see ghosts. So much so, that it was a real shock to Tony when she'd started to see them herself.

It wasn't that far out of the way to Tony's to take the detour to Jade's marina. It was a nice evening, and Tony wouldn't be home till after the show. Maya wasn't sure what she would say to Jade. She was sure that Jade wanted to hear from Tony, not her. But she couldn't sit by and do nothing to try to resolve things.

Although Maya hadn't liked what Tony had said about her seeing mental health issues everywhere, she was prepared to consider it. After all, if the suggestion made her that uncomfortable, it was a good idea that she have a good look at it. By visiting Jade, Maya could reassure herself that Jade was okay.

The sun was starting to drop behind the gleaming skyscrapers of Canary Wharf as Maya walked from Blackwall DLR station to the marina gate. Maya pressed the button with Jade's name on it.

Nobody answered. Maya gave it a minute and pressed again. She tried calling Jade's mobile, but it just rang out.

Maya had turned to go when Jade's voice came out of the little speaker on the panel.

"Who is it?"

Jade sounded croaky and confused. Maybe she'd just woken up.

"It's Maya," Maya said brightly, pleased that Jade was in. "I was just passing. Have you got time for a coffee?"

"I don't like coffee."

"Oh. Oh yes, I remember, you've gone off coffee. Well, it doesn't have to be coffee. Have you got five minutes?"

"I'm busy."

Jade's voice was matter-of-fact. She hardly sounded like Jade at all.

"Well, maybe we could meet tomorrow?"

Jade didn't answer. Maya didn't know what to do.

Maya thought she heard another voice. It was more in the background.

"Come away, honey. Give me the phone."

It sounded like Suni, but not like Suni. Maybe the intercom was making everyone sound strange. Maya wanted to see Jade even more than ever, but she couldn't force her way in. Jade could be in the middle of anything. She could be having a hot scene with Suni. Or they could be having a row. There were lots of potential reasons why Jade might not want a visitor. Maya pressed the buzzer again.

This time there was no reply.

Maya waited another five minutes, pressing the buzzer twice more, but no one spoke.

Maya began walking back to the Tube. Something didn't feel right to her, but she remembered what Tony had said. Maybe Tony was right that Jade just wanted to be left alone, and Maya was looking for problems. After all, Maya didn't know Jade that well. Perhaps Tony could throw some light on it all.

❖

Jade's skin itched. It felt like something was under her skin. The buzzer went again. Jade shut her eyes against the noise.

"Come away from it. If it's bothering you so." Suni's voice was soothing. She took Jade's hand and pulled her away from the door, back into the living area.

"It never stops," Jade said.

"I know." Suni was comforting and kind. "Drink this."

Jade took the cup of herb tea. She couldn't stand coffee or ordinary tea anymore. They tasted bitter. She'd gone off milk, and meat, and bread tasted like cardboard, even the good bread. Jade's tongue felt thick and like it was coated with something horrible. Suni said she was dehydrated. She wanted Jade to drink lots of water.

The buzzer went again.

"Why don't they leave me alone?" Jade half sobbed. It had been the same with her phone. They had been ringing her all the time, whoever they were. She didn't know them. They were unknown contacts. The texts had begged her to call them. Jade shook her head, trying to clear her mind. Why would she call someone she didn't even know? Didn't they know they were unknown?

"Don't worry. Lie down." Suni was the only one Jade could rely on. Everyone else was back home, and they never wrote anymore. Jade had a horrible feeling they were all dead. Somebody had died. Jade struggled to remember.

"Tony…" Was it Tony?

"Don't think about that now. You'll only upset yourself."

Suni was real. But she changed sometimes. Jade couldn't trust her own senses. Things moved about. Her stuff moved all the time. It got lost and then it reappeared. The cup of tea in her hand, she didn't dare put it down because it might not be there when she went to pick it up.

"You are a real mess, girlfriend."

Jade could see Suni, and touch her and feel her. She was definitely real. Jade had a voice going on and on in her head, and that scared her. Sometimes the voice didn't talk for ages and then it wouldn't stop talking.

"You're losing it, girl."

That was her now. It wasn't Suni because Suni's lips weren't moving.

"You've got more in common with me than I thought. What Suni sees in crazy black women, I don't know. Must be her trip."

Jade didn't want to hear voices. She knew that was not a good sign.

"She seems happy that you're a mess. Look at her. Reading her magazine with a smug smile while you sit there shaking, dropping your tea all over the sofa."

Jade looked down. There were spots of herbal tea on her pajama trousers and on the sofa cushions. She glanced at Suni. She did have a smile on her face. Jade tried to work out if it was smug or not. Suni put her magazine down.

"You look washed out. Why don't you go lie down?"

Jade felt exhausted. Maybe if she had a nap she could shake the cotton wool out of her head.

Suni sat beside her. She ran a finger along Jade's cheek. Jade relaxed into Suni's touch.

"Honey, I'm worried about you."

Jade opened her eyes. Suni's brow was creased. Her eyes were soft with concern. "Why do I feel like this?" Jade wanted to cry. She couldn't draw up the tears and didn't have the energy. Why did she feel so sad?

She remembered that someone had died. Who? Maybe Suni knew. "Is Tony…" Jade couldn't bring herself to say the words.

Suni took her hand and held it tightly. "Don't upset yourself. Tony and Maya have gone. You're okay now."

Jade felt sick. Tony *and* Maya? What terrible thing had happened? And why couldn't Jade remember?

❖

Maya heard Tony's key in the door as she was setting out a tray of olives, roasted seeds, and the highly salted, full fat crisps that Tony loved so much.

She had been waiting for Tony to get home from the theater so she could talk to her about Jade. She went through to Tony's sitting room and put the tray on the coffee table next to her wine glass and a bottle of beer. Tony walked into the room with a beaming smile. She looked excited. She wrapped her arms around Maya and pulled her close for a smooch.

Maya lost herself in the kiss, loving the feel and smell of Tony. Tony's tongue slipped between Maya's lips, quickening Maya's pulse. Maya kissed her back, hard. She was deep into the new relationship. Tony had claimed a piece of her heart. *Tony sure is a hot and sexy woman.*

"Shall we just go straight to bed?" Tony mumbled into Maya's lips.

Maya was tempted. Her body definitely wanted to, they hadn't had proper sex for days, but Jade was on Maya's mind.

"Shall we have a drink and a catch up first?" Maya asked.

Tony looked down at her with a quizzical expression. "Okay."

When they were both seated on Tony's sofa, Maya took a moment to let Tony have a swig of beer and a handful of snacks. Maya threaded her fingers through Tony's and opened her mouth to speak.

"I saw Deirdre tonight," Tony said.

Maya collected herself. She rearranged her face. "Oh?"

"Yes. I called *her*. I did it. She said I wasn't shrieking or shouting. She heard me and came. God, Maya, I wish you could see her sometimes. You wouldn't believe the outfit she had on today."

Maya shut her eyes. She wanted to listen to the minutiae of Tony's day, but she couldn't focus on anything but Jade. She'd been waiting to talk to Tony for hours.

"Honey—"

"Just a minute, Maya, that wasn't what I was trying to tell you. Deirdre agrees with me. I knew there was something fishy about that Frankie White case."

Maya blinked. She hadn't a clue what Tony was going on about.

"I thought you'd solved th—"

"I never really felt it was solved," Tony interrupted.

Maya bit her lip. She tried never to interrupt someone. It was the height of rudeness. Tony barged through life like a bull in a china shop. Maya often found the inherent honesty charming, but not when she was trying to have a proper conversation.

"Are you thinking about something else? I'm trying to talk to you here," Tony said sharply.

Maya lifted her hand off Tony's knee and took a bigger gulp of wine than she meant to.

"This stuff's important to me." Tony sounded hurt.

Maya met Tony's eyes. "Yes, I know," she said. "I'm sorry. You're right. I'm not focusing on what you're saying. That's because—"

"Exactly! That's what you go on about all the time. You really should take a dose of your own medicine. Or walk your talk. Or walk a mile in someone else's moccasins."

"How is walking in someone else's moccasins relevant?" Maya snapped.

"I don't know. I've never really understood it, but it's one of those things you say. Anyway, it's not nice, is it? Someone having a go at you when you're just having a thought inside your own head for a minute. And not giving someone one hundred percent attention ALL the time."

Maya stared at Tony while the words settled around her.

"Wow," she said after a few moments. "You think I want you to give me your attention a hundred percent of the time?"

Tony looked down at her fingernails. "I guess that was a bit harsh." Her voice was conciliatory.

"Tony, a lot of people don't listen properly. They think they're listening, but really they're just thinking about what they want to say next. That's what I was doing. You're right to call me on it." Maya took Tony's hand in hers.

"Really?" Tony squeezed back. She smiled tentatively.

"Yeah, really. I was thinking about Jade. I'm really worried about her." It felt good to finally speak her fears. A cloud flashed over Tony's face. "I know what you said the other day," Maya rushed on. "I heard what you said, Tony, and I'm thinking about it. Honestly I am. Maybe I am hypersensitive about mental health issues. But you should have heard Jade today."

"You saw Jade today?"

"No. That's just it. She wouldn't let me in."

Tony's eyebrows knitted together. "What do you mean?"

"I went to the marina. Jade wouldn't let me through the gate."

Tony frowned harder. "You just turned up and she wouldn't let you in?" Tony spoke roughly.

Maya flinched. "Yes," she said more sharply than she meant to. "Like I asked you to do. Days ago."

Tony folded her arms.

There it was, that stone wall that Tony threw up so well. "Don't you want to hear how Jade sounded?" Maya asked. She didn't get why Tony was so unconcerned about someone she called her best friend.

"Will you stop seeing problems everywhere," Tony said through gritted teeth.

"Tony, get your head out of your butt. You can't ignore stuff all the time."

Tony clenched her fists. "What do you mean? Ignore what?" Tony looked haunted.

Maya stared at her. "Tony?"

Tony's eyes filled with tears.

"Tony, what is it?" Maya made her voice as gentle as possible.

Tony was breathing fast. "Jade shouldn't have had to rescue me. It was pathetic," she said.

"What?" Maya was so taken aback she shook her head. "Are you talking about that night, on the council estate?"

Tony nodded. She was trembling.

"What were you supposed to do? There were four of them," Maya said.

"I should have sorted it. I shouldn't need rescuing." Tony folded her arms and pushed out her shoulders.

"You help people all the time. You kept rescuing me, last year, if you remember?" Maya wasn't sure why they were talking about this at all, but she stayed with it.

"That's different."

Maya searched Tony's eyes. "So it's okay for you to rescue people but not for people to help you, is that it?"

Tony shrugged. "Yes. No. Oh, I don't know," she said impatiently. She sounded frustrated. Maya knew Tony sometimes had problems getting her words out.

"What if it had been me? Or Jade? Would you have expected us to get ourselves out of that situation?"

Tony thought about it. "No," she said quickly. "No. But I would have helped you. If Jade had come straight to me, we could have sorted it together. But she didn't. She went to that other boy. She left me there." Tony stopped talking. She stared grimly ahead for a minutes. "She left me there with those bastards."

Tony was rigid. Maya touched her hand gently.

Tony jumped and snatched her hand away.

"Tony, what is it you're not telling me? What happened?" Maya spoke softly. She wanted to pull Tony into her arms but didn't want to touch her in case that made Tony feel worse.

Tony sat absolutely still for several minutes. Maya sat beside her, giving Tony space.

When Tony spoke, her voice was calm and unemotional. "I can feel him breathing into my neck from behind, saying what he was going to do to me."

"Do you want to tell me?"

"No."

"Maybe it would help. Get it out of you," Maya said.

"No. It wasn't just him, though. They all said what they wanted to do. They made it sound like it was going to happen."

"Did anything else happen?"

"Yes. He pressed into me. He was hard. I can still feel that in my back. I don't ever want to feel that again. Ever. He put his hands on me. I want to kill him. I want to beat him and beat him until he falls to the ground, and then I want to stamp on him. I want to grind my boot into his groin."

Maya didn't say anything. She let the words resonate.

A tear ran down Tony's cheek. She snatched it away. Tony's vulnerability was obvious and raw. Maya's heart melted and she felt absolutely awful. She'd been pushing and pushing Tony.

Tony bit her lip. "I feel so stupid."

Maya held her arms out.

Tony came to her then. She was tense for a moment. Then she relaxed. Maya pressed her lips against the top of Tony's head.

"I was scared," Tony whispered.

Tony's body tensed again.

"Don't talk anymore. It's okay." Maya held Tony gently, like a child. "You're safe now, my darling. I'm here."

CHAPTER EIGHT

Tony stretched in bed. For the first time in days, she felt okay. She still felt uncomfortable if she thought about the gang incident, but that was nothing compared to the sick pit of her stomach feeling she'd had before.

Maya was already up and out. Tony turned in bed, enjoying the crisp, fresh feel of the sheets. Maya had changed the bed the night before, while Tony had taken a bath.

Tony felt a surge of love for Maya. The woman was not only wise but wonderful.

It was Tony's day off. She would go and see Jade. Tony felt bad that she had blamed Jade. What had Maya called it? Transference. Whatever, Tony needed to tell Jade what had happened on that night.

Tony doubted there was anything wrong with Jade. She thought Jade was preoccupied with her new relationship. She'd probably been miffed with Tony at first, and then just got distracted. Tony was sure they'd sort everything out, especially when she came clean about why she'd been distant.

Tony wasn't surprised Maya was looking for problems. She'd missed her own uncle's dysfunctional behavior. That would make anyone paranoid.

The air in front of Tony's wardrobe went hazy. Tony pulled the sheet up around her as Deirdre appeared. She was wearing a shapeless blue denim pinafore dress over a dull yellow shirt, and flat brown shoes.

"I may regret asking, but what are you wearing now?" Tony asked.

"I'm dressing appropriately, as you will see. You can come through now," Deirdre called.

The air next to her flickered and slowly became an old white man in a black uniform, white shirt, black tie, and black cap. He stared dispassionately down at Tony.

"Excuse me, Deirdre! What are you thinking of? Bringing a man into my bedroom." Tony wrapped the sheet as closely around her as she could, trying not to think about how naked she was.

"I've seen hundreds of women in bed. Most of them look just like you," the old man said. He had a calm, quiet voice with a London accent. He was medium height, of slight build with a thin face. His gray hair was cut close. His complexion was a dull pink. His uniform was neatly pressed.

"What does that even mean?" Tony squeaked.

"You are so slow sometimes," Deirdre said with haughty disdain. "Haven't you got it yet? Who am I? Come on, you must know."

Tony stared at the unflattering outfit, topped with a shoulder length, wavy, ginger wig. "Princess Fiona from *Shrek*?"

Deirdre pursed her lips. "I won't dignify that with an answer. Clearly, I am Bea Smith from *Prisoner Cell Block H*."

"Really? I've only seen a couple of rerun episodes. Who is Bea Smith?"

"You don't know *Prisoner Cell Block H* and you call yourself a lesbian? Bea Smith is the top dog of the Australian drama set in a woman's prison. It was all the rage among lesbians of my time. They loved the practically all-female cast, and didn't seem to mind the quite frankly frightening costumes."

"I'm too young for *Prisoner Cell Block H*. *Bad Girls* was more my time."

"Oh, I see. Well, you should check it out. Surprisingly good viewing. If you look closely you can see the sets wobble."

"Fine. Is that what you dropped in to tell me, you and your guest?" Tony nodded toward the old man, standing shoulders back. "Oh. Is that what you are, a prison guard?"

He dipped his head in a yes. "The penny had to drop eventually. Just as well we've got nothing but time, eh, Deirdre?"

Deirdre laughed. "Nothing but time. Even so, that's fifteen minutes of my death I'll never get back thanks to you and your slow wits," she said pointedly to Tony.

"Do you have to be so rude? And can you go in the other room? I want to get out of bed."

"Because you're naked?" Deirdre asked.

"Yes, because I'm naked."

"I've seen hundreds of women naked. Hundreds. In the showers. Most of them look like you."

"I don't care," Tony snapped. "And why do you keep saying that they look like me?"

"There's a lot of lesbians in prison; that's what he means," Deirdre said.

Tony thought for a second. "Well, I still don't care. Now go into the next room."

Deirdre started walking to the door. "As if that will make any difference."

"What do you mean?" Tony shouted after her.

"Like we can't see you anyway."

"What? You can't, can you?" Tony was horrified.

Deirdre fell about laughing. The old prison guard had a good laugh as well.

"Of course not. We're not God," Deirdre said, when she could stand up again.

"Is there a god?" Tony asked.

"Classified," Deirdre said between pinched lips.

Still laughing, both ghosts walked straight through the bedroom door, the prison guard standing back to let Deirdre go first.

Tony threw on some jogging bottoms and a fleece and then walked along the hallway to her living room. She walked past the ghosts and into her kitchen, where she put the kettle on.

Deirdre followed her in. "Tony, this is John Smith."

"Is that your real name?" Tony asked.

"Yes. I know it's a common name, but someone's got to be called it." Smith extended a hand toward her.

"I'd like to shake your hand, but I don't think it's going to work, is it?"

"Oh yeah. I suppose not. I'm not used to being around the living." Smith pulled his hand back.

"John was a guard at Holloway Prison. He knew Frankie White," Deirdre said, leaning against the doorjamb.

Tony sat up.

"Ah, Frankie White. Bad business." Smith shook his head. "Bad business."

They looked at him.

"A very bad business," he repeated.

"You can say more than that. In fact, you have to say more than that. That's why we've come to see Tony," Deirdre said.

John Smith looked around as if someone might be listening. "I don't know. He's a bad man. A very bad man."

"He can't hurt you. He's not dead." Deirdre patted the back of her wig.

Tony poured milk into her tea. "Who?"

"I don't know. He's a nasty kettle of fish. And he will be dead one day." Smith clenched his hands together.

"You Brits and your expressions," Deirdre said. "Look, stop worrying about him. He can't do anything to you now. And by the time he dies you'll have moved on."

"Where?" Tony asked.

Deirdre looked round sharply. "I'd forgotten you were there. Now, Tony, because you hang around the dead, you will hear things you shouldn't. So, a lot like gays in the military, don't ask and I won't tell."

Tony stared at her. "It's the other way round, isn't it? And anyway, that policy's been revoked."

"Oh, I'm so pleased for those sea queens. You couldn't move for queer seamen in the New York of my day. Yes, I'm aware of how that sounds. Anyhoo, there was more action on the Staten Island Ferry than at The Saint on a Saturday night," Deirdre said.

Tony and John Smith stared at her blankly.

She sighed. "Staten Island was where the Navy base was. The Saint was *the* New York gay club of the time." She rolled her eyes. "See what I have to work with," she muttered to nobody in particular. "Anyway, let's get back to why we're here. Spill the beans, Smith. Spit out his name."

"Ron Somers," John Smith said quickly, half under his breath.

The name sounded familiar. Tony remembered Frankie's girlfriend

Rose speaking about him. "Was he the officer that was harassing Frankie?" Tony asked.

"Yeah, he had it in for White. She was a royal pain in the backside; I'll give you that. But he went too far. He made her life hell. It isn't hard to make a prisoner's life hell, if you want to."

"How?" Tony asked.

"They're criminals, so no one's going to take an inmate's word over an officer's. He got on her case night and day. He was a piece of work. Most of the other officers were intimidated by him. He liked me for some reason. That made me more scared of him. I didn't want him turning on me."

"So what did he do to Frankie? Did he kill her?"

Smith took a long suck of breath in. "He pushed White around all the time. Called her names. That wasn't unusual; half the women in there were dykes, like Deirdre said. Obviously, you lesbians are a bad lot. Prison's full of your kind."

"I beg your pardon," Tony said crossly. "Yes, there are a lot of lesbians in prison. That's because lesbians are criminalized. You're more likely to be sent down if you're a lesbian. And you're more likely to commit a crime if you're having a hard time."

"Oh, don't give me no hard luck stories. Prison's full of the dregs of society—lesbians, colored people—and you've all got hard luck stories."

"We don't use that term anymore. It's considered racist. I'm not happy about you coming into my home spouting your homophobia, but no way will I tolerate racism." Tony folded her arms. What was Deirdre thinking of? Bringing this guy into her house.

"Why don't you just stick to the story, John?" Deirdre laid a hand on John's arm. "Spare us your opinions."

"But I don't understand," he said. "I thought colored was the polite word."

"Not anymore, mate. We say black now. And there are loads of black people in prison for the same reason there are lots of lesbians there, because the criminal justice system is stacked against us."

Smith's eyes narrowed. He looked like he wanted to say something. Deirdre's grip tightened on his arm. "Anyway, whatever White had done it didn't justify how he treated her. She beat up two blokes in a bar fight, by the way. Broke one guy's nose. Smashed a bottle over the other one's head."

Tony opened her mouth to protest.

"She admitted it," Smith said quickly. "It still didn't justify how he treated her. He called her all kinds of ugly names for dyke."

Tony wasn't enamored of Smith using the word "dyke" so casually, but she forced herself to keep quiet. She wanted to hear what had happened to Frankie.

"He stood at the shower door, staring at her body. That freaked her out. Women officers were supposed to be in the shower block, but that never stopped him. And he roughed her up. Nothing too serious but enough to intimidate her. He took against her. I think it was because she wouldn't be cowed. She had too much spunk. That was her problem."

"So did he beat her up? Is that how she died?"

"Yes and no. He got another prisoner to beat her up, well, to start a fight with her. White was a scrapper. She could hold her own, so the other prisoner must have had to jump her. She wasn't big, you know, White, but she was like one of those little dogs. They don't quit. No one would have started a fight with White unless there was something in it for them, because White would have got her own back. The other inmates left her alone, so this fight was unusual. I was on duty that day, so was Ron. She'd been hit a lot around the face and head. I wanted to send her to the hospital block, but Ron wouldn't have it. He sent the other prisoner there and insisted White was faking it. I tried to persuade him different, but he wouldn't listen, and I didn't stand against him." Smith glanced at Tony guiltily. "She was in a single cell. We put her in there to lie down. We locked her in for her own safety. My shift was about to end. I checked her before I went home, and she spoke to me. She was coherent; she hadn't been sick. I had no reason to worry. Ron said he would look in on her through the night. I believed him."

Smith went quiet. He looked down and shifted from one foot to the other.

"So he let her die. Is that what you're saying?" Tony asked.

Smith looked up. "'Fraid it's worse than that. Ron Somers beat her up again. That same night. He knocked her out and left her on the floor of her cell."

"How do you know?"

"He confessed it. He boasted about it in fact, round my house, two weeks after her death."

"What a shame you're dead. I can't go to the police with hearsay from a dead prison guard." Tony was frustrated. She needed evidence if she wanted to get justice for Frankie.

"Ah, but there's more," Deirdre said mysteriously.

Smith sidled up to her. "You're sure he can't do nothing to me?"

"I'm sure," Deirdre said.

"Okay then, I've got the confession on tape. And it's still in my old attic. My nephew's a lazy bugger. He's never cleared nothing out. I've been dead nearly forty years."

"How did you tape it?" Tony was intrigued.

"Something didn't add up. When Frankie White was found dead, at first I felt really guilty, like it was my fault. But Ron Somers was too cock of the hoop for my liking."

"Cock of the whoisitnow?" Deirdre spluttered.

"Full of himself," Tony explained.

"I got Ron round my house, got him drunk, and he spilled the beans. He thought I would approve. I pretended to. I taped the whole conversation. I was going to go to the governor."

"Did you?"

Smith shook his head. "I wasn't brave enough. I kept the tape as insurance." Smith glanced over at Tony. "Don't look at me like that. You don't know Ron Somers. You don't know what it's like to rat out a fellow officer. My life would have been hell. I would have been finished. And for what? White was dead, and she was a criminal, and no one cared."

"Someone did care." Tony stood up straight. "Someone loved her and cared about her very much. Her name is Rose."

John Smith met her eyes. "Well, you can do something about it now, can't you."

❖

Maya had tossed and turned thinking about what Tony had been going through. At least she'd been able to talk about it. Tony had slept like an angel beside her.

As she'd tried to sleep, Maya's thoughts had turned to Jade's voice on the intercom. And the other voice, supposedly Suni. Maya had only talked to Suni a handful of times, but there was something odd about the cold voice she'd heard the day before.

She'd fallen asleep in the end, but woke at the crack of dawn and decided to go to the clinic early. She intended to get through the batch of postal prescriptions before her first client arrived.

In her practice room, Maya stood with a bunch of prescriptions in her hand. She couldn't get Jade off her mind. Tony had had a breakthrough, thank God, but there was definitely something wrong with Jade. She had said herself that she didn't have family in the country. Jade had other friends. But when Maya thought about it, apart from work, Jade spent most of her time hanging out with Tony. Tony had said that Jade went off the radar when she got with a new woman. Maybe that was all it was.

But Maya kept coming back to Suni. Maya hadn't liked her on first meeting. When Jade had started dating her, Maya had hoped to get to know her better. Sometimes people grew on you. Unfortunately, she hadn't had the chance.

Maya thought that was a bit odd. Why wouldn't Jade want her best friend to meet her new lover? Suni worked different days from Maya, so Maya never saw her at the clinic. Suni had just turned up. None of them had any connections to her.

Oh God. Was Maya doing exactly what Tony accused her of? Was Maya paranoid about everyone and seeing danger everywhere?

Maya hadn't seen how disturbed her own uncle was. He had spent months plotting to kill her. Maya was consumed with anguish as she remembered. It was a pain she had pushed down. There was a chance it was surfacing in her fears about Jade.

Maya didn't know what to think. She was second and triple guessing herself. She was also analyzing herself, something that was notoriously hard to do.

Okay. Maya was not going to leave the situation alone. She was too anxious about Jade. She would never forgive herself if Jade was getting ill and needed help. Or if there was something sinister about Suni.

She had a couple of choices. One was to go and see Jade again.

Maya didn't relish the thought of that, especially as it had only been the day before that Jade had pretty much told her to go away. The other thing she could do was to dig into Suni's past. It was a shame Maya didn't have any links to the ghost of Suni's ex. Maya caught herself for a moment. She couldn't believe she was thinking like that. *This is what happens when you hang around with ghost whispering detectives.* Well, Maya couldn't talk to ghosts, but she could do detective work. Unless Suni was using a false identity, there must be something she could find out about her.

Maya went to the practice kitchen and boiled the kettle. Squeezing lemon juice into a mug, she stared out the window, turning everything she knew about Suni over in her mind.

Maya fired up the computer and brought up a page of multiple search engines. She typed *Sunita Ghosh* into the search box and pressed Enter.

Maya read through entries about Suni as an alternative health practitioner. She clicked on the links and read each website carefully, looking for anything out of the ordinary. She was hoping to find a malpractice claim. Perhaps a complaint from a former client, or a report that she had been fired from a clinic for having inappropriate liaisons on the premises. Maya was still fixated on Suni having sex during a healing session. She Googled all the health centers that Suni had worked at. There were several across the States. Unfortunately for Maya, none of the health centers had any dirt on Suni.

She hit all the links, weeding out other Sunita Ghoshes, and broadened the search to include all of Suni's previous workplaces. It took most of her free time to get through all the pages.

Feeling disappointed, Maya scanned down the last page.

An entry near the bottom caught her eye. It was about a poetry competition in Iowa. The winning poet had dated a Sunita Ghosh. Hopeful that there weren't that many lesbian Suni Ghoshes in the US, Maya clicked on the link.

Under the heading *Iowa Literature Prize Awards Ceremony, local poet wins poetry prize*, there was a photo of a tall African-American woman holding a trophy. Standing next to her in a tuxedo was Suni. In the article, the poet, Telitha Franklin, assigned the inspiration for her poem "SHE Steals the Pain from Me" to her partner Sunita Ghosh.

Maya was starting to see a pattern, at least in Suni's dating habits. Jade, Felicia, and Telitha were all black women. Two were poets, Jade was an actor, so all three were artists.

Maya started a new search: Telitha Franklin, poet.

She quickly pulled up a Facebook profile. The profile picture confirmed the page belonged to the poet that Maya wanted to make contact with.

Maya signed into Facebook and sent a message saying that she wanted to talk to Telitha about her ex.

As the message disappeared into the ether, Maya wondered if she was being paranoid after all.

She might end up having some explaining to do to Jade.

Late afternoon, Maya checked her Facebook messages. She knew it was a long shot that Telitha would have replied. Iowa hadn't been awake long. Maya, however, had been awake for eight hours, had seen three clients, and had checked in with Tony.

Tony was off on a mission. She had been vague about where and why, but Maya hadn't minded. She had sounded so good, so full of life. It had warmed Maya's heart.

Maya hadn't mentioned that she was checking up on Suni. She didn't want to say anything unless she had to. The comment about being paranoid had hit home. Maya wasn't about to give Tony a reason to worry about her.

On her Facebook page, Maya had a little red message notification. Telitha had responded.

Hey, Maya, not sure what I can tell you about Suni. We didn't date long. She moved on after we split up. I think she went South. Or maybe it was to the UK, if that's where you say she is now. Things didn't end well, so if you're hoping for good things, I don't know what to say to you. Are you dating her? That's usually why people ask. If you are, there's some things you should know. Send me a Skype, Tango, or Facetime number. Let's talk.

Maya couldn't type her numbers fast enough. Bad things about Suni were exactly what she wanted to hear. She felt a bit ashamed of herself. Was she just a terrible prude who thought Suni should keep a respectful, professional distance from clients at work, even if she was dating them? Maya reflected that it wasn't just Suni having sex at work that had unsettled her. Maya hadn't taken to her when they'd first met. The only prior connection to Suni that Jade had was a ghost who was tormenting her. And Jade appeared to be becoming increasingly isolated.

The Skype notification flashed up on Maya's laptop.

"Hi, I'm Telitha." A self-assured black woman smiled up at Maya from the monitor. She looked about thirty-five, curvy with broad shoulders, and strong features. "So are you dating Suni Ghosh?"

"I'm not. My best friend is." Jade wasn't strictly Maya's best friend, but she had decided her cover story needed to explain why she was digging into Suni's past relationships.

"I see. Are we talking about the same woman?"

"It is the same Suni. She's the woman standing next to you when you won that poetry prize."

"Ah. Is that how you found me?"

"Sure is. It's great that you agreed to talk to me."

Telitha grinned wryly. "Hmm. Maya, I don't know if you're going to like what you hear."

"Anything you can tell me would be fine."

Telitha looked away for a moment. "Why did you start looking for people that knew Suni?"

Maya decided honesty was the best policy. Leaving aside mention of ghosts and her intuition. "Suni turned up here three months ago. She started working at the same health clinic that I work at. I don't know anybody in England that knows her. My friend and her got together, and now my friend has disappeared off the radar. She's probably all right, but I'm suspicious by nature."

"I get it. Okay, well, I'll tell you my experience of Suni, and you can do what you want with it. I met her in a bar. I was reading from my new poetry collection. Suni raved about my work. You could tell me I'm beautiful, you can tell me I'm sexy, and that won't do it for me. Tell me my words rock your world and you've got my attention. Suni was charming. Something about her drew me in. We started to hook up. We slept together pretty soon and, I don't mind telling you, I was into her. She was all I could think about. It was intense. It was all good for about a month. Then I wanted her to meet some friends of mine. She flat refused. I don't mean she politely made excuses. She said she was interested in me, not in my friends, not in my family, not in my work colleagues. That made me pull back. I think she sensed it because she was suddenly busy for a good six, seven days. She didn't call, didn't text, nothing. When she turned up at my apartment, I was so damn pleased to see her I forgot all about my misgivings. But that was the night we split up.

"In my apartment I have a parking mirror. You know when you live off a busy road and you need to see what's coming around the corner? Someone gave it to me because I have a habit of pulling out of side roads without looking. But I don't have a driveway, so I put it up in my apartment where the hallway turns onto my kitchen. Well, thank God. Suni left the bedroom and went to fix some drinks. I decided to surprise her. As I turned into the kitchen, I peeked up at the mirror and Suni was pouring something from a small bottle into my glass. I knew it was my glass because I like to drink from a special one my friend had hand-painted for me. I went straight in and took the bottle out of her hand. She looked shocked, but she didn't say a word. She marched past me back into the bedroom and started putting her clothes back on.

"I stuffed the bottle in my kitchen drawer and followed Suni. I wanted some kind of explanation. What the stuff was, what she was doing, but she wouldn't talk to me. I've never seen someone get dressed so fast. She hightailed it out of my apartment even though I was practically hanging off her arm at one point. She shook me off and disappeared. I was left sitting on my bed, holding the little bottle of clear liquid up to the light, wondering what it was. I felt like Alice in Wonderland gone wrong." Telitha took a breath. Then she shook her head. Clearly, the memory still disturbed her.

Maya swallowed. She didn't know what she'd expected, but it wasn't that. "Did you get the liquid analyzed?"

"Sure did. GHB."

"No." Maya felt sick.

"Some people take it recreationally. It doesn't automatically mean she was trying to knock me out for some sinister purpose."

"No, I guess not." Maya said the words, but she wasn't convinced. From the way Telitha spoke, it didn't sound like she was sure either.

"The whole episode scared me. Whatever Suni was doing, the way she ran out of my apartment made her look guilty of something."

"Did you try to talk to her again, or call the police?"

Telitha screwed her face up. "Maybe I should have gone to the police, but, well, I'm not a huge fan. I know it's a stereotype, black people and the police, but my brothers have had a lot of shit over the years. And I knew a woman who was sexually assaulted. The police were no help, and they were my local cops so I wasn't going to rush to call them."

"What about Suni?"

"She disappeared. I found a place online to send off the liquid to. I dropped it in the mail the next day on my way over to Suni's place. She'd gone. The apartment owner was kind enough to let me in because I had some stuff there. It was completely cleaned out."

"She'd gone by the next day?"

"I think she went straight home, packed up, and left. I didn't sleep well. It was early, around nine a.m. when I went there. Suni had run out on me about two in the morning."

"Do you think she drugged you at any other time?" Maya asked.

Telitha put her hands over her face. "Oh God. That's what I've been wondering." She thought for a minute. "I don't think so. I never felt weird. I never had lapses in time that I couldn't explain. I never woke up wondering where I was or what had happened to me. Of course it's possible I might not have realized or remembered. That's the thing with GHB apparently, but wouldn't there have been a bunch of hours I couldn't place?"

"I guess." What Maya didn't say was that Telitha might not realize if it happened at nighttime. She might have just thought she was sleeping. "Is there anything else you can tell me?"

Telitha laughed. "Isn't that enough? No, that's about it. She put me off dating for a long while. It was a shock to get your message. Even reading her name made me feel weird."

"Thank you for speaking to me. I'm really lucky I found you and that you got back to me."

"You need to check that your friend is okay."

"I sure do."

Maya stared at the computer screen long after Telitha had gone. She wanted to rush over to Jade's, but she needed to think. She wasn't happy that her instincts were right. She wasn't happy at all.

Chapter Nine

Tony tried to shift the van into third gear. It complained loudly and spat the gear stick into neutral. Tony grunted as the van shuddered. She grabbed the stick more forcefully, pressed her foot down as far as she could, and shoved it hard. The van protested with a shriek before finally accepting the gear change.

"Are you sure you know how to drive this thing?" Deirdre was sitting in the passenger seat, her legs crossed neatly in front of her. She patted the back of her floral headscarf and smoothed down her tight orange sweater. She flicked a bit of fluff off what would have been called Capri pants back in the 1950s. Then she took out a pair of huge tortoiseshell sunglasses from her purse. She popped them on, even though the day was gray and drizzly.

"Yes," Tony grunted, flooring the accelerator. The van responded by moving ever so slightly faster.

Deirdre's foot tapped the dashboard rhythmically. Tony tried not to let Deirdre's pink stiletto distract her eyes from the road.

"I know I'm going to regret asking this, but what outfit have you got on now?"

"Oh, I love it when you notice what I'm wearing." Deirdre beamed. "I put my favorite driving outfit on. No one did outdoors and feminine like the fifties. I love vintage clothes."

"All your clothes are vintage," Tony pointed out.

"So *you* say," Deirdre muttered childishly. Her eyes moved over the interior of the transit van. "I know funds are tight, but did you have to pick the biggest heap of trash on the car lot? Someone needs to go over this with a wet dishcloth and a gallon of disinfectant." She pointed at the cup holder. "What have they been transporting in that? Pig fertilizer? And when I say fertilizer you know I mean sh—"

"Yes. I know what you mean," Tony said quickly. "It's all they had at short notice. And you're right about funds, seeing as I'm paying for this myself. I don't see you or Frankie White coughing up any money any time soon."

"I think people who drive transit vans must be a filthy bunch. I've gone right off *The A-Team*."

"Don't remember a profusion of transit vans in *The A-Team*."

"Well, you get the point. I'm not going to be making eyes at any removal men for a long time after this experience. I don't care how tight their buns are. All I'm going to be thinking about is that crinkly brown splodge next to the half-crushed fly."

Tony didn't say anything. She sometimes wondered what world Deirdre lived in when she wasn't dropping in on Tony's life. She frowned at the sat nav device stuck onto the windscreen. It said they were a few minutes away from their destination.

Tony had called round to Smith's nephew's house that morning, posing as a house clearance agent. To her surprise, the nephew had jumped at the chance of getting rid of stuff from his loft. Keen to act on the information as soon as possible, Tony had arranged to return in the afternoon. She had thought of asking Maya to come with her, but it was one of Maya's clinic days. She had then dropped round at Jade's but got no answer at all. Tony was disappointed but had decided to get on with the job at hand.

"You have reached your destination." The newsreader-type voice of the sat nav announced their arrival.

John Smith's house was a Victorian mid-terrace that would once have looked lovely with red brickwork and sash windows like the house next door. Smith's house had been covered with fake stone cladding, and the original windows replaced with mock leaded UPVC ones.

"Good God. Smith should have been in prison for what he did to that house," Deirdre muttered. "Do I have to come in? It's bad enough being seen in this van, let alone a monstrosity like that."

"I hate to break it to you, but no one's going to see you," Tony said bluntly.

Deirdre sniffed and then fizzed through the van door to the street. Tony walked past a rusty gate hanging off its hinges and then walked carefully across loose tiles to the off-white UPVC front door. She pressed the doorbell.

John Smith's nephew opened the door a few minutes later. He had light gray jogging bottoms on below a stained brown T-shirt. He didn't smell like he washed often. He had stubble that could in no way be described as designer. It emphasized his square jaw and contrasted sharply with his bald head. He was of medium height and paunchy. He nodded at Tony and then turned away without a word of greeting.

Tony followed him along a dim hallway to a flight of stairs covered in carpet that didn't look like it had seen a Hoover for many a decade.

"My God, Tony, hanging out with you is like being in a scene from *Cat on a Hot Tin Roof* only with exceptionally unattractive characters," Deirdre said, two steps behind her. "Your version is *Filthy Cat on a Shabby Tin Roof*."

Smith's nephew paused on the first floor landing. He reached into the side of a cupboard and pulled out a long pole with a hook on the end of it. He used it to twist the latch on a square access door set into the ceiling. It swung down, resting on a long hinge to reveal an opening about half a meter square. Smith's nephew pulled out a stepladder from behind the same cupboard and thrust it toward her.

"There you go," he said brusquely.

Tony deduced that he expected her to climb up into the loft by way of it.

"Don't you have a loft ladder?" she asked, looking up into the dark opening.

"Stepladder's always been good enough for me," Smith's nephew said. "Candle and matches to the left of the trap as you go in."

Tony gawped at him as he left. She pulled her head torch from her back pocket. Thank heavens she'd decided to wear her work black 501s.

She made her way up the rickety stepladder and poked her head into the loft space. The loft wasn't boarded. Here and there sheets of hardboard had been laid over the joists and then boxes sat on them, but all the walkways were across the wooden joists. Great, so Tony would have to stumble about in the light of one head torch and a candle, balancing on beams, and then carry anything she found down a dodgy stepladder.

With a sigh of resignation, she heaved herself up into the dark space.

Specks of daylight shone through ventilation bricks and a couple of places where presumably tiles were missing and the roofing felt below had become damaged. Dust spun in the thin shafts of light. As Tony's eyes adjusted, she started to make out objects in the room. Apart from two narrow pathways, the entire space was full with stuff. Boxes were piled on top of each other, some stacked right up to the sloping roof. Near the access hatch were Christmas decorations. Old-fashioned tinsel dangled over the edge of cardboard boxes that brimmed with multicolored glass baubles and fairy lights. Various lengths of wood were stacked against the wall nearest the hatch. They nestled against old kitchen cupboards, a heap of tiles, and sections of plastic pipe.

On the other straight wall were half a dozen wall heaters, including an ancient gas fire and an electric fire with pretend plastic coal on it. Tony remembered her grandmother having a similar one. The pretend coal lit up when the fire was on.

Spanning the distance between the two walls were more boxes, a wooden clotheshorse, a broken chair, a radio sitting on a tattered armchair, a typewriter, and piles and piles of flattened, empty cardboard boxes that had once held appliances.

It was quiet. The street noise below was faint and muffled. Even Deirdre was unusually silent. Tony half expected to hear the scuttle of mice.

"He's a lazy bugger, that boy."

Tony jumped. She spun her head toward Smith's voice. He was sitting on the armchair. Tony didn't want to mention that he had an old Roberts radio interweaved with his crotch. To be honest, she didn't want to think too hard about his crotch.

"Look at all this rubbish. He should have chucked it out years ago."

"Well, I'm glad you've turned up. Where's the tape and the tape recorder?" Tony asked.

"He may have moved it, I suppose." Smith walked through the bric-a-brac to a dark corner under the eaves. "This was where I put it. Oh, whaddaya know? There it is. There's my old Revox."

Tony picked her way carefully over to Smith. She pulled out several bits of old stair carpet that were cleaner than the one she'd just walked over, until she was staring at a rectangular machine. Tony judged it to be forty centimeters wide by thirty-five centimeters high. Two large dark gray reels sat on two prongs centered about a quarter of the way down from the top edge. The bottom third of the machine was taken up by a steel panel, housing a series of large steel-faced rotary switches for play, volume, balance, and two combined input selection and level switches, one for each of the two tracks. On the extreme right was a chunky on/off power switch. Above the volume and balance controls were a set of rectangular black buttons as thick as Tony's finger, marked Rewind, Forward, Play, and Stop, and a fifth red one for Record. Two analogue meters sat above the recording level switches on the right. The needles rested at the extreme left. The tape recorder was huge and beautiful. Even though it was covered in dust and cobwebs, Tony longed to touch the dials and switches.

"How the hell did you conceal that from Ron Somers? It's not exactly surveillance equipment."

"Actually, MI5 and the FBI used reel-to-reel recorders. They recorded phone conversations with them. I had a microphone setup with a long cord, that's all."

"I see. So that's the machine. Where's the tape with Ron Somers's confession on it?"

"The tapes were next to it. Oh yeah. They still are, in that little trunk."

Tony opened a small gray trunk to reveal a stack of red cardboard cases about twenty-five centimeters square. She lifted the lid off the top one. Inside was a large clear spool of dark, dull brown tape. On the underside of the lid was written: Conversation with Ron, 17 July 1967.

"Bingo," Tony said.

"Great," Deirdre said. "That means we can get out of here. Drag that antique machine across this treacherous pathway and let us be gone."

"Why are you talking like that?" Tony asked.

"It seemed appropriate. We are standing in the middle of a Victorian junkyard aren't we?"

"Hardly, and you're a bit of an antique yourself, these days, luv," Smith muttered.

"I beg your pardon?" Deirdre stormed off in a wafty way in the direction of the access hatch.

"What strange, made-up language was that? And don't even get me started on your attempt at a British accent," Tony said, lifting the tape recorder by a carry handle on the top of it. "Arff! This is heavy."

Deirdre snickered. "Not so butch now, are we?"

Tony panted after her, heaving the recorder above her knee. "I never said I was. This is so much heavier than equipment is now. Jesus."

"That's the trouble with you dykes," Smith growled behind her. "You think you're men, but you ain't."

"I never thought I was a man," Tony grumbled.

"Well, you look like one from where I'm standing," Smith said.

"Heaven help me. Now shut up, both of you. I need to concentrate on getting this thing down that stepladder without breaking my neck." Tony balanced the machine on a beam at the edge of the hatch, maneuvered herself down, and then, balancing on the ladder, pulled the recorder after her.

She went back up for the trunk of tapes and then lugged both things down to the ground floor. She could hear noises of a football match through the sitting room door. She knocked.

Smith's nephew appeared a minute later.

"That was quick," he said, frowning at her.

"Well, this is all I want, really," Tony said.

He frowned harder. Then he ran his eyes over the tape recorder, before taking the trunk out of her hand. He opened the lid, frowned inside, coughed, and sniffed.

"That must be worth a bob or two then," he decided.

"I doubt it."

"What do you want it for then?"

"I collect old audio equipment. It's a hobby of mine."

"I thought you were a house clearance agent."

"I am."

"Well, you're not a very good one. The clue's in the name. *House* clearance, not the odd bit of equipment clearance."

God, is everybody a comedian today? Tony sighed. "I'm prepared to take this off your hands."

"Five thousand pounds," Smith's nephew said.

"What?" Tony nearly dropped the tape recorder. "You're having a laugh, aren't you?"

"One hundred pounds."

Tony thought about telling him not to go to Marrakesh anytime soon, but she stopped herself. She didn't want to have to pay out any more money.

"Five hundred pounds."

"What? You're going back up now. You need to learn how to barter."

"I had my heart set on getting that stuff out of the house. Loft *clearance* you said. I want the loft to look as nice as the rest of the house." He swung the sitting room door open to reveal a ripped sofa covered in empty beer cans. One was half on its side and spilling its contents into swirly purple seat cushions.

"I'm never going to rely on the kindness of strangers ever again," Deirdre moaned softly.

"Look, mate, I won't fit all that stuff in my van. It's only a transit," Tony said.

"That's the deal then. If you want that, whatever it is, you take away a transit's load from my loft." Smith's nephew folded his arms.

"But how am I going to get it all down? That ladder's a death trap. And I'm on my own. Will you help me?"

"No, I will not. What are they thinking of? Sending a boy to do a man's job. What are you, sixteen? I should have known you were full of it when you came to the door."

"He thinks you're a man. Well, he would. He ain't seen dykes like I have. Hundreds of them, I've seen," Smith muttered.

Tony bit her cheeks. She half wished Smith was still alive, so she could punch him. But that would probably be behaving like a man. Sometimes it was hard to know what to do for the best. Well, she wasn't having him think she was a teenage boy.

"Actually, I'm not—"

"Don't tell him you're a dyke," Smith barked in Tony's ear. "Better he thinks you're a boy. He's not open-minded like me. He ain't seen the number of dykes I have. He won't let you have nothing if he thinks you're a dyke."

"Well, what's it to be?" Smith's nephew asked.

"What if I did give you a hundred pounds?" Tony thought she could write off a hundred.

"Five hundred. Seven hundred and fifty, a thousand—"

Tony cut him off. "All right then. I'll take a transit load away, but that's it."

❖

Tony went back up to the loft feeling bamboozled. She'd definitely have got Maya to go with her if she'd have known she had to cart a transit van's load of junk out of an attic on her own. Come to think of it, she would have gone round and insisted Jade leave her love nest for half a day and pitch in too. After all, the whole detective agency thing had been her idea. Tony was mildly concerned that she hadn't managed to make contact with Jade. It was strange she hadn't returned Tony's calls. She always had before. Even when Tony had gone back to Amy for the fifth time and they'd had a row about the way Amy was treating Tony. Tony hadn't liked it at the time, but Jade was proved right in the end.

Maya had half convinced Tony something was wrong, but Tony didn't have a bad feeling in her gut. It was more likely Jade had disappeared into the parallel universe called "being in lust." Tony had seen it before with that woman from Brighton. Mind you, that had only been for a week. This had been…Tony did a quick count. She stopped dead a few feet from the stepladder. It had been three weeks. That was a long time.

Maya was a clever woman. Tony could do worse than to listen to her. She had been right there for Tony the previous night. Tony felt humbled thinking about how sensitive and caring Maya had been.

Right then. As soon as she'd nailed the Frankie White case, again, Tony would camp out at Jade's until she opened the door.

Pulling herself up into the loft, Tony grabbed anything that would fill up the transit fast, and didn't look too heavy. She rejected the armchair but plumped for the broken wooden chair, and the clotheshorse, which she planned to extend once she got it into the van.

"They're not going to fetch much." Deirdre looked down her nose at the offending objects.

Tony scowled at her.

"You're going about this the wrong way," Deirdre went on.

"What do you mean?"

"You've got to cover the costs. You'll go out of business."

Tony couldn't believe it. "What are you telling me that now for? I'm in the middle of this ridiculous situation. I'm on my own. I don't count you two because you're no help whatsoever in the carrying department. And I have to—"

"Yeah, we know," Deirdre said, picking something out of her nail. "Cart a load of old junk out of this attic; down a rickety, rusty ladder; over moldy old carpet; past an unshaven lay about; across a broken driveway; and into a dirty, dingy, and undoubtedly dangerous vehicle."

Tony nodded. "Not how I would have put it, but that pretty much sums it up. Yes."

"And then what are you going to do with the junk?"

"Get rid of it," Tony said crossly.

"And how are you going to do that?" Deirdre had the air of an overly patient, slightly smug schoolteacher.

"Take it to the tip, of course."

"And they're just going to let you do that, are they?"

Tony let out a yell as the realization hit her. "Goddammit. I'm going to have to pay to get rid of this old crap."

She sank down on the armchair. She wanted to help Frankie, but this was getting ridiculous. She couldn't afford to pay for everything. She swallowed back a knot in her throat that felt dangerously like a tear. When she looked up, Smith was laughing.

"What's the matter with you?" Tony snapped. "If you'd done the decent thing in the first place, none of this would be necessary."

"This is how I react to situations like this. I'm resilient. It's what made me so popular in the prison service. They called me Laughing Boy."

Tony had half an idea what the women in Holloway might have called him.

"Don't let him get to you. Use your head, Tony. What's in here that you can sell?"

"I see where you're going. I used to love that program *Cash in the Attic*. What were they always looking out for?" Tony thought for a moment. "Oh yeah—antiques, collectibles, jewelry, and heirlooms."

Tony trailed her eyes over the contents of the loft. "Well, I don't think there's a huge trade in floral carpet scraps and old empty boxes."

She remembered the transistor radio. "This Roberts radio might be worth something." She picked it up and put it near the hatch. "Have you got any jewelry or silver up here?" she asked Smith.

"Most of the stuff in here is old toot, but there is something," Smith said. "Grab that painting."

Tony went over to a crude watercolor of ships in a harbor. "Oh, oh. Is it valuable?" She scrutinized it. "Let me guess. I genned up on all the potential valuables, including fine art in my *Cash in the Attic* viewing days. I recognize the naive brush strokes. Is it an early Lowry?"

"No. My nephew painted it when he was six. Chuck that old rubbish away. Open the box." Smith pointed to a shoebox that had been underneath the painting.

Tony took off the lid. It was stuffed with bank notes. Smith looked pleased with himself. "I put it up here because what burglar goes poking about in the loft? Serves that lazy bugger right if you have it. He should have cleared all this out years ago."

Most of the notes were green. Tony pulled one out. It was a pound note. "I haven't seen one of these for years."

"What do you mean?" Smith asked.

"They're not legal tender. We've had pound coins for ages."

Smith's face fell. "Well, I tried to help you out."

Tony heaved a sigh. She sat on the old armchair.

Smith studied her.

"What you going to do? You going to walk away? Let Ron Somers get away with it?"

Tony thought about how long Rose had fought for justice. She remembered Rose's face when Tony had left. Her thank-you card had sounded everything but thankful.

Tony had a little bit of money put by.

"Okay." She nodded at Smith.

His shoulders lifted. "Thanks for helping me put things right. You're all right, you know, Tony. For a dyke."

❖

Why would someone give GHB to their partner without their consent? That question had been running through Maya's mind since she'd spoken to Telitha. Maya knew the drug's association with sexual abuse, but that was in the context of targeting strangers. She also knew that people used it recreationally. It was basically a rapidly acting central nervous system depressant.

Maya was convinced that Suni was giving Jade drugs. Whether Jade was taking them willingly, Maya didn't know. Maya had no proof, and she realized she would need to get some. She hadn't spoken to Jade, or even Tony yet. Maya wanted to run some ideas first. She kept coming back to the question: what was Suni doing, and why?

Apart from the conversation with Telitha, Maya had no reason to think that Suni was doing anything wrong. It came down to a gut feeling. Maya hadn't liked her when she'd first met her, but that was hardly evidence of any crime. Maya didn't approve of the way Suni was with clients. Well, specifically the way Suni was with Jade as a client. But that also wasn't a crime. Maya needed to be sure she wasn't painting Suni as a villain just because she didn't like her. Tony had said, rather bluntly, that Maya saw dysfunction everywhere. Maya hadn't liked that idea at all. She wasn't going to discuss the situation with Tony until she had something concrete to say.

Jade had been acting strangely before Suni came along. She hadn't been sleeping, which she'd explained was because she was being haunted by an unfriendly ghost. Maya had gotten used to people talking about ghosts, but she still found it odd. That early behavior of Jade's could have been the onset of anxiety, paranoia, or psychosis, and nothing to do with Suni whatsoever.

However, Jade had mentioned dryness and a salty taste in her mouth, and that food tasted different. She had become isolated from Tony, her best friend, which fit with what Telitha had said about Suni trying to keep her from her friends. Maya wished she could talk to the dead ex, Felicia.

Maya realized what she had just thought and laughed. If someone had told her a year previously that she would one day be wishing she could talk to dead people, Maya would have written *severe delusion problems* in the margin of that person's notes.

Maya just knew Suni had something to do with Jade's strange behavior. But what was Suni up to?

In between clients, Maya researched GHB and its effects. She discovered that the average dose took effect in fifteen to thirty minutes and lasted from three to six hours. Low dosages acted as a relaxant, causing low muscle tone and reduced inhibitions. Medium dosages produced feelings of euphoria, increased sex drive, lowered inhibitions, memory lapses, drowsiness, headache, low body temperature, low blood pressure, tremors, nausea, diarrhea, and urinary incontinence. As the dose increased, there was a higher risk of vomiting, sweating, loss of coordination, breathing problems, confusion, agitation, hallucinations, blackouts, seizures, respiratory arrest, and death.

Maya knew that nearly all recreational drugs had potentially serious side effects. People took drugs in small to medium dosages without killing themselves, but she was worried about the damage Jade could be doing to her body. And that was if she knew she was taking the stuff.

Maya thought about the last time she'd seen Jade. She hadn't complained of nausea or headache. She hadn't looked high. She did seem confused and agitated.

Maya was missing something, something that nagged at the edges of her mind.

Assuming that Suni was secretly giving Jade substances that affected her behavior, why?

Maya recalled reading an article on drugs used for mind control. With a twist, she realized she had been sitting in the same chair, looking at the same monitor. She had noticed the article when she'd had to use Suni's computer a couple of months previously. She hadn't even been sharing an office with Suni then.

Maya quickly did a search on the subject until she found the article. Maya zoned in on one of the drugs mentioned in it: scopolamine. It was known as the zombie drug and, like GHB, featured in cases of sexual abuse. What was especially unpleasant about scopolamine, when used for that purpose, was that it made people submissive and zombie-like. When people recovered from the drug, they had no memory of the time they spent under its influence. She read that it was widely used in Colombia by criminals who sprinkled the colorless, odorless powder into food or drink and then carried out theft, kidnapping, and other crimes.

Medical research on the drug showed that it blocked receptors in the brain so that memories couldn't be formed. Common side effects were a dry mouth, redness, and itching of the skin. The article said that the effects of high doses of scopolamine included hallucinations, delirium, delusions, paralysis, and stupor.

Maya didn't know what to think except she was pretty sure Jade was taking drugs or being given them secretly. She needed to talk to Tony.

Tony picked up on the fifth ring.

"Hey, Maya, great to hear from you. Listen, I'm driving."

"Oh. Are you on hands free?"

"No. I'm in a van. I forgot my headset. Can I call you back?"

"I've got a client in a minute. I'll call you. Listen, Tony, I just want to say—"

"Maya, there's a police car behind me." Tony put the phone down abruptly.

Maya sighed out loud. Oh well, she needed to see her two o'clock. Headaches and constipation couldn't wait. *Well, actually, maybe that was the problem.* Maya chuckled at her own joke. And then she reminded herself that her patients' disorders were no laughing matter.

Oh, lighten up. When Maya had been training, she'd often shared little jokes with her fellow students. It was how they coped with the pressures of exams and the rigors on the spirit of becoming a healer. She missed talking to her peers. Getting together at a couple of conferences a year wasn't enough. Maya had hoped that she could talk to Suni in that way. A knock at the door brought her focus sharply back to the present.

"Come in," she called.

As the door swung inward, Maya forced her attention on her two o'clock client.

❖

Ron Somers's confession had lain undisturbed in Smith's attic for the best part of forty years. The magnetic recording tape was in good condition.

At home, Tony plugged the Revox tape machine into a wall socket. Both meters lit up with a yellow light. Tony smiled.

"That means it's got power," Smith said.

With Smith's guidance, Tony then attached the reel recorded in Smith's living room in 1967 onto the left hand spool. She locked it into place, threaded the tape through the tape heads, and slipped the end of the tape into the slot on the right hand spool.

"Okay, press play and cross your fingers," Smith said, leaning back against Tony's favorite armchair.

"Is something exciting going to happen soon?" Deirdre chipped in, stifling a loud and obviously fake yawn. "Quite frankly, the trash at that garbage dump was more interesting than watching you mess about with that thing. Did you see that buff young garbage disposer? I bet he knows how to drive a big rig. I wouldn't be interested, though, even if he was dead. Sordid scenes are so punk rock. I'm more of a glam rock kind of boy. Spitting's very overrated."

Tony looked up from the reel-to-reel recorder. "Shall I press play then?" she asked Smith, who was staring open-mouthed at Deirdre. "Yes, she has that effect on people."

He turned to Tony. "What? Oh yeah, press play."

Tony pushed down the big play button. Both spools began to turn, and the tape moved under the heads, transferring from one spool to the other. The recording came out of the machine's integrated speaker.

There was a click, some shuffling noises that sounded like a chair being moved and then Smith's voice: "What do you want, beer?"

"Is the pope Catholic? Course I want a beer. Got a Double Diamond?" a medium voice with a strong London accent replied. Tony guessed that was Ron Somers.

"The beer the men drink," Somers said.

Both men laughed.

Tony looked quizzically at Smith.

"That was an advert in the sixties," he explained.

"There you go." Smith's voice was nearer. There was the sound of another chair being pushed forward.

Somers started laughing. "They got you good, didn't they?"

"What? Who?" Smith sounded annoyed.

"Jenkins and her gang. 'Don't touch the back garden. That's where I hid the money.' It's one way to get your garden dug over."

"She wrote in her letter that all the money was buried in her mother's garden. I had to report that. Had to," Smith grumbled.

"Jenkins said her mother's always wanted to plant vegetables. Now she can," Somers said. "The Forest Hill constabulary aren't very fond of you, though. Your name's mud with them."

Smith hovered over the reel-to-reel machine. "Fast-forward it," he muttered, looking cross. "The bit where he talks about Frankie White's not for ages yet."

Tony laughed. She pressed the fast-forward button. The tape sped through the heads. A speeded up version of the conversation came through the speaker.

After a few minutes, Smith said, "Try it from there."

Smith was speaking when Tony pressed play. "Have you had your interview with the governor yet?"

"Yeah. All done and dusted. The police have finished with me, and the governor's happy. Frankie White, rest in peace, eh?"

There was the sound of glasses clinking.

"Cheers," Somers said and then laughed.

"What?" Smith asked. "Why you laughing now?"

Somers laughed some more. The laugh was low and sinister, a quiet chuckle that didn't include anyone but himself. After a while, he said, "I hated that woman."

"Yeah, I know," Smith said. "Here, pass your glass."

There was the sound of beer being poured.

"I hate dykes. And she had no shame. She didn't care who knew it," Somers said. "Fucking dykes, I hate 'em."

"There's hundreds of them in there, hundreds," Smith said.

"Filth. Every one of them. White got what was coming to her."

"I suppose so."

"Suppose so? You bloody know so. You hate dykes as well. I know you do."

"I didn't think they were real before I joined the prison service," Smith said.

Somers laughed. "You're so stupid. They're not fairies. That's the men. Ha! Ha!" Somers fell about at his own joke. Then he sniffed and took a long glug of beer. "Fill it up, mate."

Somers's voice came over the sound of more beer being poured. "She needled me, that bitch. But I got her in the end."

"What do you mean? I thought…" Smith tailed off.

"I set that fight up with Marsh. Marsh is brewing up some potato slop in the kitchens. She's going to call it vodka and sell it to the other women. I agreed to turn a blind eye if Marsh and two of her mates jumped White. I took a walk down the corridor so I couldn't be blamed, and so I wouldn't have to stop it. I gave them a good fifteen minutes."

"My God, they could have killed her."

"I was hoping they would."

There was silence for a moment. Then Somers said, "Just pass the bloody keg over here, will you?"

There was the sound of his glass being refilled. "But they didn't, did they?" Somers continued. "White got some blows in. She was a good scrapper. I'll give her that. Then you came along, sticking your beak in."

"I couldn't help it. I was doing my rounds."

"Huh. Bloody jobsworth. Anyway, at least you didn't gripe too much about dumping her in her cell."

"Hmm…we shouldn't have done that, though. Should we?" Smith sounded like he felt bad.

"That's what I don't get. What are you so upset about a dyke for? She was lowlife. All that crap about getting her to the hospital wing."

"She was out cold. You took Marsh to see the doctor."

"I had to get Marsh out of there."

"Well, I didn't know that at the time, did I?"

"I wanted White in her cell because I'd had enough of her. She was making a fool of me. She couldn't shut her mouth. Always had a comeback. No matter how many times I called her a filthy dyke, she never just took it. She knew I was going to slap her around in her cell later. She didn't care."

"You…" Smith stopped talking.

"Don't tell me you've never hit any of them."

There was silence, then Somers's voice again. "What, never? Well, you're an old-timer. You probably don't care anymore. I'm a young man, in my prime. I ain't going to take it. They're criminals. They deserve a slap." Somers sounded like the drink was starting to get to him. "Frankie White was a piece of filth. I wasn't going to put up with that. It was fun. Even though she wasn't a worthy opponent. She was still out of it. I was looking forward to a bit of a scuffle. In the end, it was just me punching her. I didn't have to worry about bruises for once so I concentrated on the head. Then I pulled her off the bed and kicked her a few times. She needed to know who was boss. I lifted her back into bed, pulled the covers over her, and left it till morning."

For a couple of minutes, no one spoke. There was just the sound of a clock ticking. Then Somers's voice again. "What you looking at me like that for? I don't care that I killed her. She should have kept her mouth shut. And you'd better keep your mouth shut an' all."

Smith didn't say anything.

"I mean it, Smith. I shouldn't have told you that, but I'll deny it if you say anything. It'll be your word against mine. No one will believe you. And you'd be ratting out a fellow officer. I'll see to it you're finished. You can't be that far off your pension, mate."

There was a noise of a scraping chair.

"I'm off," Somers said.

After a few seconds, Somers spoke again. His voice was farther away and menacing. "Keep your mouth shut, Smith. I know where you live. You could have a nasty fucking accident, one of these dark nights."

There was a far off door slam and then a fumbling sound. Then the tape went dead.

Smith looked at Tony. If a ghost could look haunted, he did.

"Gawd. It's all there still, then."

Tony nodded slowly. Her mind was racing. The confession was explosive. She had proper evidence. She didn't like only having one copy. She checked the connectors on the reel-to-reel recorder.

"Excellent. I've got just the audio interface I need. It's the same for transferring vinyl or mini disc."

"What's mini disc?" Smith asked.

"A long-forgotten medium," Tony said, going to the kitchen draw where she kept all her leads and techie bits and bobs.

"Not unlike yourself, then." Deirdre hovered in the air by Tony's right shoulder as she fumbled about at the back for the bit of kit she was looking for.

"What?"

"Well, you're forgotten, or at least unheard of, and you're a medium. You're just not long. In fact you're on the short side."

"Recording medium, for God's sake," Tony snapped.

"Who cares, darling? To be honest, I lost interest when you said converter."

Tony plugged two jack to phono leads from the outputs of the reel-to-reel to the inputs of the audio interface, and then inserted its USB output connector into her laptop. She pulled up her recording software and did a quick test.

On playback, the first words of Smith and Somers's conversation came out of her laptop's speaker. The recording was perfect.

Tony checked her notes for the start of the important bit. The counter had been at 1342. She fast-forwarded the tape to the same point. Then she hit record on the laptop, and play on the reel-to-reel.

"What are you doing?" Smith asked.

Tony looked up from monitoring the recording level. "Making an MP3 file of the conversation."

"Christ, I know you lesbians like tongues, but do you have to keep speaking in them?" Deirdre snapped. "What are you saying?"

Tony sighed. It was bad enough she had to work with ghosts. Having to explain modern technology to people that died in the eighties and sixties was ridiculous. "This is a computer," she said, speaking slowly and separating each word.

"She thinks we're stupid," Deirdre said to Smith.

"Look, all I'm doing is making a copy. Once I've got a digital copy I can make as many copies as I want in seconds."

Both ghosts were looking at Tony blankly.

"I can store them in different places. If we lose this"—Tony waved at the reel-to-reel—"we lose the confession, right?"

"Oh, I see," Smith said. "So whatever you're doing, it's like having several copies of the tape, and you're hiding them in different places in case something happens to one of them."

"Yeah. That kind of thing."

"Clever." Smith looked impressed. "I worked with hundreds of dykes like you, hundreds, but none of them had your nous."

"Thanks. I think."

"Now you're acting like a proper detective," Deirdre said, clapping her hands.

The recording had finished. Tony checked it. It was as clear as the original taped version, and, more importantly, it was all there.

Tony's mobile went off. It was Rose Henderson.

"Hello, is that Tony?"

"Rose. Yes, it is. How amazing that you've called me now."

"I just wanted to make sure you got my letter. I sent it to your theater, as I didn't have an address for you. I think I was a bit rude, dear."

"Not at all. Rose, I've just found something that is going to change everything for Frankie's case."

"What? You have?" Rose sounded confused.

"Rose, don't ask me how I got it, but you were right. Ron Somers was responsible for Frankie's death."

There was a sharp intake of breath on the other end of the phone. "How do you know that?"

"I've got a confession. On tape. I'll email you a copy now. Rose, you may want someone with you when you listen to it."

"Oh, Tony. You're not messing about, are you?" Rose said with a sob in her voice.

"No, Rose. You've been right, all these years."

"I'll look out for your email. Thank you, Tony. Oh, thank you so much."

Tony quickly composed an email to Rose and attached the MP3 file. Feeling satisfied, she sat back in the chair.

"So, what now, Superdick?" Deirdre asked.

"Aww. You haven't called me that for ages," Tony said. "Go to the police?"

"What about Ron Somers? Why don't you trace him? Oh, and don't forget to take the van back."

"You'd make a great secretary," Tony told Deirdre.

"Yes, I would. And I could wear glasses, and a long dark wig... or should I be blond? I'd definitely need a pair of those black stockings with the line up the back."

Tony didn't answer. Her attention was entirely on the screen in front of her as she searched the Web for any mention of Ron Somers.

❖

By the end of the day, Maya was exhausted. All her appointment slots had been taken, which meant Maya keeping on top of each person's allotted time. When she had first qualified, she had found it very hard to rush people when they needed to talk. Her initial appointments had stretched from one hour to two or more as she had taken very detailed case histories. She knew that a strong element of the healing process was to be heard, and she had wanted to be the kind of healer who made plenty of time for her clients. Unfortunately, she also had a policy of charging as fair and affordable a fee as she could. Those two factors meant Maya couldn't earn enough to pay her own bills. So she compromised. She allowed one and a half hours for the first visit, kept follow-ups to forty-five minutes, and she charged less than many other herbalists in the area.

Her final patient left, clutching his new sleep mix. Maya had to make up the stack of repeat prescriptions that she hadn't got to that morning.

Maya lined up her set of measuring vials and retrieved the plastic jug from the basin filled with sterilizing solution.

The first script was for hay fever, and included ephedra, a restricted herb. Maya opened the locked cupboard that she shared with Suni. Her hand went quickly to the square liter bottle of ephedra, but her eyes rested on Suni's section. This was the perfect opportunity to snoop through Suni's stuff.

She started by noting down the names of all the tinctures and dried herbs. Maya had been researching drugs, but she knew that some plants had strong enough properties to be used as recreational drugs. Cannabis sativa was a good example. Scopolamine was in fact a plant-based drug, derived from the nightshade family.

In a few minutes, Maya had a list of Ayurvedic herbs and preparations to research. She could do that later, but it occurred to her that a locked cupboard of herbs was a good place to hide illicit substances. Suni could have drugs hidden behind or amongst the legal stuff.

She wasn't sure whether to touch Suni's bottles and jars or not. Maya was a very honorable person. She respected other people's space, and she hadn't messed with Suni's area, unless she'd had to dust it, or mop up a spill near one of Suni's items. Surely Suni would notice if Maya started pulling things out. There was no way Maya would be able to place them back exactly. The question was did Maya care about upsetting Suni? It would be pretty awful if it turned out that Suni was completely innocent and had been helping Jade all along.

Yes, but why wouldn't she contact Jade's friends? If Jade was ill and needed help, why wouldn't a new lover get her as much help as she could?

Maya pushed her reservations aside. She picked up the brown jars and bottles one by one. She examined them, glanced at the contents, and looked behind them. Unable to help herself, Maya dusted and cleaned as she went along the rows. She told herself that would be her cover story if Suni asked.

She got to the final row without finding anything unusual. She supposed she could take a sample of each of the capsules and send them off for analysis. It would be very easy to put any kind of powder into capsules. Maya had a capsule making machine herself.

Maya sighed. She wished she'd studied Ayurvedic medicine. Then she might know if any of the capsules had been replaced. She opened one of the jars and sniffed. Then she shut the lid back on quickly. That was a really stupid thing to do, considering what she'd read about scopolamine. She could have knocked herself out.

She waited a minute, watching for signs of dizziness or light-headedness.

Nothing happened. Maya sighed with relief.

More cautiously, Maya picked up the next jar. It was lighter than the others. The label said Rasayana. Unlike the other jars, this one was opaque and Maya couldn't see the contents. She turned the lid. It was fixed shut.

Maya turned the jar upside down. There was a rim where the bottom met the side. There was something weird about it.

Maya held the bottom and twisted.

It opened.

There was a hidden cavity accessed from underneath. Maya shook out the contents. It was a small rectangle of blotter paper divided into squares less than a centimeter wide. A cartoon image of different fruits was printed onto each square. Along the bottom in tiny letters was the legend: *one of your five a day*.

Maya put the blotter paper back in the jar and put the jar in her pocket. She would definitely get it analyzed. She was almost certain it was LSD. Her roommate at college had experimented with different drugs. Maya hadn't been tempted. Her father's behavior on or off his medication was enough to make Maya want to keep sober. Her roommate had had a very similar piece of perforated blotting paper that she'd said was "trip."

Maya put everything else back and then got on with preparing her patients' prescriptions. She tried not to rush them, as it was important to be accurate with the measurements and to label the directions correctly and legibly. It was getting late, and she wanted to go and see Jade. She deliberated about calling Tony again. Tony was obviously busy. Was it worth talking to her? Maya wasn't even sure what she'd found. It would be better if she managed to see Jade first.

It *was* important to share things and be open, but Maya was absurdly sensitive about Tony's opinion of her. Tony's suggestion that Maya was paranoid had hit a nerve. More importantly, Maya didn't want to bother Tony now that she knew what Tony had been going through. She didn't want to bring any of this stuff up unless she had some proof.

Maya had been wrong about people before. She had thought they were kind or damaged or loving, when in fact they'd been trying to hurt her. Maya knew the only way she could put her past behind her was to face her fears.

And she was terribly afraid about Suni.

❖

The strangest thing about the room was how bright orange it was. Jade got a rush that started in her toes and swept upward through her body. Her toes tingled. Suddenly, she understood what the expression meant. She liked the idea that she had experienced a genuine toe tingle.

She closed her eyes. The inside of her eyelids was orange too. No wonder Tony liked lighting. How lovely to be able to paint everything in beautiful colors.

Suni came down the steps from the kitchen carrying a little rocket. She was floating on a cloud of white wood. Jade vaguely remembered the steps were painted white, but they looked fluffy like clouds. Maybe they were made of dry ice like in the theater. Jade was born to be on the stage. As soon as she stopped sitting in her living room, she must get a job.

Suni floated across another white cloud that lay across the floor. In the orange light, Suni's skin was intensely brown. Her lips were crimson. She looked like she'd been eating plums. She held the little rocket toward Jade. "I've brought you a present."

Jade tried to work out how she could fit inside the purple and silver spaceship.

Suni flipped a switch and it turned into a beautiful light. It cast a purple glow across the muffled surface of the white leather sofa. It looked liquid. Jade immersed her fingers in it. The liquid light swam between her fingers like tiny shrimps tickling her skin with their antennas.

"How are you feeling, honey?"

Jade tore her eyes away from the light. Suni was sitting next to her. She began to stroke Jade's knee. Each stroke was like an embrace. It was distracting, but Jade was more interested in the big red blobs spinning slowly on the periphery of her vision.

She turned toward the little rocket and tripped out. It was alive with light. Huge scarlet swirls danced within the glass. One blossomed like a mushroom cloud. It flowed out of the rocket ship and floated toward her. Just before it reached her it split into a hundred strands.

The glass radiated strand after strand. They pulsed and hummed, riding on an invisible current.

Jade went to them and then tried to trace their path across the room with her hands. She danced with them for a while. They blended with her skin. Jade knew her skin was dark brown, but it wasn't really. It was hundreds of colors and shades. Brown was far too small a word for all that Jade's skin was.

Suni laughed. The sound tumbled over Jade's right ear, warming her lobes as if Suni herself were stroking them. Jade sensed that Suni wanted her attention, but the strands were very important. She rode with them again.

The most beautiful music began to play. Strings and piano filled the room. Jade sighed and closed her eyes as a sweet voice poured exquisite sadness into Jade's ears. The sound trickled gently to her heart. The woman wanted her to love her. Jade breathed out a harmony of her own, blending her voice with the singer. Everyone wanted her to love them lately. She had forgotten about the voices, but here was one again.

"Jade, something is really wrong here."

Jade didn't want to listen to *that* voice. She wanted that voice to go away. She tried to reach the singer again, or even the other voice, the voice that whispered behind the singer. She thought she liked the whispering voice, but she couldn't remember.

"You need to listen to me, girl. Suni is messing with your head."

Jade looked over at Suni. She was sitting very still, staring at her laptop.

"Drink this." She pressed a glass of water to Jade's lips. The water was cool and lemony and very wet. It ran across Jade's tongue. She felt it slipping over the inside of her throat. She felt it going all the way down past her chest and into her stomach. Wow. It was amazing. There was a chalky disc on Jade's tongue. It dissolved into bitterness. Jade shuddered, but the lemony water was running through her mouth again and the bitterness melted away.

Tony swam in front of Jade's eyes. She was in a tiny square frame. The frame receded as Tony walked away. Then she came toward Jade again. It was Tony from their trip to Provincetown.

Jade had a sudden rush. She went with it. There was a black arm holding the tiny, square Tony. Nobody's skin was that color. The hand was a black glove. It sprung out from beneath a black cloak. The cloak flapped up and down. A hood rose to a point above the face of death.

Jade remembered that Tony was dead.

She tried to feel sad, but nothing happened. Everyone died in the end. Jade accepted her place in the universe. She was a drop of water flowing in a river.

Suni looked up from her laptop and smiled. "Checking Facebook," she said.

Jade giggled at the idea. She wanted to say to Suni, "Why don't you just see your friends?" She wondered if Suni even had any friends. Oh but, of course, she'd only been in the country for...

Jade couldn't remember when Suni had come to the UK. She wasn't sure it mattered anyway.

"Oh, my God. You'll never guess who's gotten in touch," Suni said. She was staring back at the screen. Purple light flickered on the raised lid of her computer. It was very dancey. The lid snapped shut.

Jade jumped.

The purple light ran across Suni's body. Jade watched it.

"Well, that's a damned nuisance." Suni folded her arms. Jade wondered why there was so much she didn't understand. She didn't know what her own face looked like anymore. There were no mirrors anywhere. Where were the mirrors?

"Goddammit! We can't risk it. We're just going to have to move things up."

She got up and went toward the bedroom. Jade followed her.

Suni turned.

"If you can't help, don't hinder."

Jade flew through the air. She landed on the couch. The purple light washed over her body. She dived into the spinning bubbles and began to swim.

❖

Tony yawned and stretched. She glanced out the window. The sun was starting to drop on the horizon, sending a warm glow across the sky. *How many Web searches can I do before I drill a hole in my own head?* The World Wide Web couldn't care less about Ron Somers.

Deirdre coughed. "Honey, you've been twiddling about with your bony and badly manicured digits for hours. How long does it take one barely sentient lesbian to look up an address in the phone book?"

"He's not listed, Deirdre. That's the first thing I tried. You need to be patient. Detective work takes time."

Deirdre yawned pointedly and then tapped an imaginary watch. Tony wondered why she bothered. Couldn't she conjure up a ghostly one for the effect? Did ghosts have to dress in ghostly attire the same as the living? Did Deirdre have a ghostly wardrobe somewhere?

"I'm afraid she's already with a client. You'll have to wait."

Tony looked over at Deirdre. She was talking to fresh air. Smith was staring at the same spot of nothingness.

"What's going on?" Tony asked.

"Another ghost wants you. You're getting popular with spirits in need," Deirdre said.

Tony smiled.

"It's because they haven't met you yet." Deirdre smiled in a patronizing way. "No, not you. I'm talking about Tony. Actually, she's not half bad," she added in a stage whisper. "All the same, you'll have to come back later. I'm afraid you're in a queue. Just take a number and someone will get back to you shortly."

Tony ignored Deirdre and tried to think of a new set of words to type into the search engine.

Smith sidled up to Deirdre. "Didn't like the look of her. Troubled. Desperate. Wild eyes. She's one of her lot, an' all. I should know. Seen hundreds of them, I have. Hundreds."

Tony clenched her jaw. She tried "prison guard suspected of killing Frankie White moves."

The search result was very unhelpful.

"Excuse me. No pushing!" Deirdre cried.

"Help me, Tony," a familiar voice murmured in Tony's ear.

She looked up, startled.

A faint version of Rose Henderson swayed next to Deirdre.

"I'm at home, Tony, and in terrible trouble. Help me."

Jade opened her eyes. The room was intensely bright. She flinched. She'd always hated the overhead light and never put it on. Tony had been promising to fit something more ambient for ages.

Jade sat up slowly. There was a lava lamp on her coffee table she didn't recognize. She shook her head. She didn't understand what was going on. Weird stuff kept happening, things she only had sketchy memories about.

There was a horrible noise droning on and on. It was like a needle bumping against a record. Except she didn't have a record player. Or any vinyl.

Jade shuffled over to the MP3 player and switched the iPod off. The track info said it was a sound effect.

There were bags and cases sitting by the bottom step. Jade recognized her suitcase. She didn't remember packing it.

Suni came through the bedroom door with another bag. "You're up. Good."

Was Suni moving in or moving out? It was possible they were already living together. Everything was very hazy in Jade's mind.

"Stay there a moment."

Jade didn't think she could move anyway. Her body was heavy. She wanted to go back to sleep. She turned her head toward the sofa. Her cupboard doors were all open. The cupboards were empty. Good God, was she moving out?

"Look at me."

Jade turned to Suni. Dust blew into her eyes. She sniffed sharply at the same time as taking a step back. Her eyes streamed for a minute and she couldn't see, and then she felt intensely calm.

"Come with me." Suni stretched out her hand.

Jade took it. Suni's hand was very cold. "Your hand is freezing," Jade said.

"Hmm?" Suni walked Jade up the steps to the kitchen. "Oh yeah, I have cold hands, I guess."

Suni led the way to the front door of the boat. "Wait here," she said. Jade was completely happy to wait. Suni stuck her head outside.

A minute later, she took Jade's hand again. "This is the perfect time. Actually, it's better to go now, less people about. Right, Jade, keep next to me. If we bump into anyone on the way to the car, let me do the talking, okay?"

Jade nodded. She wanted to please Suni.

They stepped outside, walked across the deck of Jade's boat, and onto the walkway. The marina lights threw an amber light onto the boardwalk and across the black water. There were faint sounds from the other boats of people cooking and the quiet chatter of TV sets.

They passed no one on the way to the gate. Suni hit the release button.

"Wait here." She dropped Jade's hand and opened the gate. Jade glanced up at a streetlight. There was a halo around the lamp.

Suni took her hand again and pulled her through the gate and onto the street. They walked quickly to a car Jade had never seen before. Suni opened the back door.

"Get in and lie on the backseat," she said quietly.

Jade scrambled in and stretched out across the cloth seats. Suni laid a blanket over her.

"I'm going to pull this over your head. You'll be able to breathe just fine. I've got to get some more stuff so just lie here quietly. In fact, you must be tired. Why don't you go to sleep?"

The car door shut. Jade felt a wave of tiredness wash over her. She shut her eyes and felt the rise and fall of her chest. She counted the breaths, and then she slipped away, into a dream.

❖

Tony rang Rose's intercom.

There was no reply.

She pressed her hand against the door.

It opened.

Tony hesitated.

Listening for any noises, she stepped inside.

It was dark.

She fumbled until she found a light switch. It didn't work.

Deirdre and Smith had disappeared just after she'd left the Tube station. Tony had decided to continue to Rose's flat anyway. She needed to reassure herself that Rose was okay. As her eyes adjusted to the dark, Tony made out the stairs leading up to Rose's flat.

She started walking up them.

Light spilled out onto the upstairs hallway. Rose's flimsy door had been kicked in and was ajar.

"Rose," Tony called.

As she walked quickly into Rose's flat, an old man came out of her sitting room.

"Oh, someone's come to help. Thank God," he said.

The short, broad-shouldered elderly man peered at her with an anxious expression. He had a square jaw, a small nose, large ears, and a good head of white hair. The same white hair came out of his ears and nose in clumps. His shoulders bent forward giving him a stoop.

"Where's Rose?" Tony asked.

"They've taken her to hospital."

"Why? What happened?"

The old man looked at her doubtfully. "I thought someone had told you. Some toe rag broke in. Rose went for him. You know what she's like, but she came off worse, I'm afraid."

"Oh, no! Which hospital? I'll go and see her," Tony said. She was too late. She felt awful.

"There's nothing you can do for her there, love. But there is something you can do here. Her place is a mess, and we need to secure her front door."

"Okay," she said, happy to help. She followed the old man into Rose's sitting room.

The room had been ransacked. Books had been tipped from the bookcase and strewn across the carpet. The drawer from the little side table was upturned on top of the books. Cushions from the chaise were scattered next to it. The framed photos and posters had been ripped off the wall and thrown to the floor. Most of the frames were smashed. There was glass everywhere. A big cupboard near the armchair was open and empty. Its contents lay tumbled and broken at its feet.

The old man went through the sitting room and into Rose's kitchen. The kitchen had been torn apart in a similar way.

"Hey, love, do you know where Rose's laptop is? She'll want it in hospital," he asked.

Tony shook her head. "I don't know, sorry. But if you can't find it, the burglar probably took it, right?"

The old man frowned. "No. He ran off, just after Rose collapsed. That's when I came. I scared him off. He ran past me, but he was too quick." The old man looked ashamed that he hadn't managed to catch the thief. "He didn't have a bag, and nothing in his arms. Think. Where have you seen her with it? You know how attached Rose is to that thing. She was mumbling for it when they took her away."

Tony peered at the old guy. "I don't know where she kept her iPad, sorry. How do you know Rose? You didn't say, Mr.?"

The old man pulled his head back out from a kitchen cupboard. "Jones. We go back years. Where's her tools then?"

"I don't know. I don't know Rose that well. We're acquaintances really."

Mr. Jones straightened up. "I see. Have a look in those cupboards."

Tony opened one of the few cupboards that hadn't been disturbed. There was a small metal case in one corner. She pulled it out and blew off a layer of dust. There were several old tools inside.

"Found them," Tony said.

"Good. Take them to the front door. There's some boards along the passage, leaning against a wall. Go get them, will you? We can use them to fix the door. I'll meet you there," Mr. Jones said. He walked over to her, bent down, and began looking through the cupboard where she'd found the toolbox. "We need nails," he grunted.

Tony found the boards where Mr. Jones had described. When she brought them to the door, Mr. Jones was already there with a box of nails.

"Right, hold one across here." He indicated one of the split panels. "I'll tap the nails in."

Tony knelt in front of Rose's sorry-looking door. It had been weak to start with. At least they'd leave her with a stronger door. She held the board up against the bottom half of it.

Deirdre appeared on the inside of Rose's flat. "Sorry, Tony, I got called away," she said.

Tony glanced at her. She was concentrating on holding the board.

"Smith's too scared to come out, but he says that's Ron Somers."

"What?" Tony looked behind her.

The old man was bent over the toolbox. "Didn't say nothing," he grunted.

"Tony, you need to be careful." Deirdre peered through the doorway. Her eyes widened in horror. "For Christ's sake, Tony, watch out!"

Tony turned.

Somers was two steps from her, his arm raised, his fingers wrapped around a hammer.

The hammer crashed toward Tony's head.

❖

Maya came out of the subway, crossed the road, and walked along Aspen's Way until she came to the turnoff to Poplar Marina. She knew she had no evidence or any real reason to think that Suni was the evil villain that Maya had decided she was. But Maya was not going to be able to rest until she'd seen Jade.

About a hundred meters away, she hung back as Suni came through the gate, carrying a box. Maya tucked herself into a shop doorway. She wasn't ready to confront Suni. If Suni was on her way out somewhere, it would be a perfect opportunity to talk to Jade on her own.

Suni put the box into the boot of her car and then turned back to the gate. She let herself through it with a key and disappeared inside.

Once the gate had closed, Maya walked quickly up to the car. There was nobody in the passenger seat. Maya peered in the back.

The whole backseat was taken up with stuff covered in a blanket. Maya's curiosity was piqued. Maybe it was valuable items that Suni didn't want anyone breaking in for. Maya could see some bags at the foot of the passenger seat now that she was up close. Suni looked like she was moving a lot of stuff.

The car beeped and its headlights flashed.

"Hey, Maya. Can I help you?"

Suni was right behind her.

Maya straightened up. Suni was holding a box of groceries. How had she got back to the car so quickly? Maya's mind raced as she tried to make sense of Suni catching her by surprise. Maybe she'd left that box on the boardwalk rather than make the trip all the way back to the boat.

"I just dropped in to see Jade," Maya said.

Suni looked good. She had the same confident, bordering on arrogant, air as always. She didn't respond to Maya's comment. Instead, she strolled up to her boot, balanced the box on the edge of it, flipped it open, and slotted the box inside. Maya spotted bedding, towels, and a suitcase before Suni shut the lid again.

Suni walked over to Maya. She looked Maya's body up and down.

"Been working out?" Suni asked. "You've got great definition." She squeezed the top of Maya's bare arms with both hands. Maya shivered. Suni's touch was icy.

"God, you've got cold hands," Maya said.

"Why is everyone obsessed with that?" Suni muttered.

"Isn't it a professional disadvantage, what with you being a masseuse?" Maya said.

"Some people like it," Suni said tersely. "It's good I ran into you. It gives me the chance to say good-bye."

"Good-bye?"

"Yes. Things are coming to the end with me and Jade."

"Oh." Maya tried not to sound too delighted. "Well, relationships are hard." She didn't know why she felt the need to make a banal comment. "But you said good-bye? I'll see you at the clinic, won't I?"

Suni shook her head. "I'm moving on. I'm done with London.

To be honest, the UK's such an insignificant little island. I don't know how you stop yourself from going stir-crazy." Suni took a step closer to Maya and dropped her voice. "Don't you feel like someone is always looking over your shoulder?"

Suni stared hard into Maya's eyes. Maya stood her ground, though she wanted to pull away. "So you're leaving the whole of the UK?"

Suni nodded.

"You're leaving? Just like that?"

Suni shrugged. "I'm impetuous that way." She smiled without no trace of warmth.

Maya took a step back. She felt they understood each other. She was burning to say something, but she didn't dare. Not until she knew Jade was safe.

"Well, good-bye then. I'm going to see Jade." Maya turned away.

She walked to the gate and pressed the buzzer to Jade's houseboat. She glanced over to Suni's car. She was sitting in the driver's seat, texting.

Maya pressed the buzzer again. There was no reply.

Maya had a thought. She walked quickly up to Suni's car.

Suni put her window down a crack.

"Can you let me through the gate?"

Suni shook her head. "No can do. That would be an invasion of Jade's privacy. If she wants to see you, she'll let you in."

Maya clenched her jaw. "Is she there?"

"She was there fifteen minutes ago. Maybe she's gone to see a neighbor. Why don't you try the buzzer again?"

Suni shut her window, buckled up, adjusted her rearview mirror, and drove off.

Maya memorized the number plate. She had a strong feeling Suni was playing with her. She jotted the number down on her phone.

She rang the buzzer another time. There was no reply. She tried calling Tony. It went straight to voice mail. Maya's stomach tightened. She wasn't going to feel okay until she'd spoken to Jade. And now she urgently needed to talk to Tony.

❖

Tony instinctively raised her arms to protect her head.

Bam! The hammer smashed into her right elbow. White-hot pain shot up her arm. She went for the tool, trying to grab it as Somers took another swing.

The hammer glanced off Tony's cheek. She darted through into the flat and tried to close the door.

The door crashed into her. The force of it shot her along the hallway.

Somers came at her again. She reached for the hammerhead, wrapped her fingers around it, and held on.

Somers pushed back. He was a hell of a lot stronger than he'd been playing. Gone was the frail old man, replaced by a strong, snarling thug. Sheer terror helped Tony hold her ground.

Like some sick tug-of-war, Somers began to gain control of the hammer. Tony clenched her jaw and held on to the hammerhead for dear life.

Suddenly, Somers stopped pulling.

Tony fell to the ground. She fell by an open bedroom doorway. She glanced inside.

Rose was crumpled on the floor.

Tony froze as the hammer came down.

At the last moment, she put both hands over her head.

The hammer smashed into her hands.

Agony. Tony was in agony.

The hammer crashed down again, and again.

Desperate now, she forced herself to her knees, and up.

She went for Somers, not caring what he did with the hammer. She clenched her right hand and punched as hard as she could.

Somers reeled back. He looked shocked. For a second, the hammer dangled from his arm. He rubbed his jaw.

Then rage filled his eyes and he swung the hammer again.

Tony was dimly aware of crashing noises and people shouting, but all she cared about was Somers. She rushed him.

He fell.

People thundered into the flat. Her arms were wrenched behind her back, and she was forced to the ground.

Face flat against the carpet, Tony took ragged breaths. Her heart thumped in her throat. Dizzy and nauseous, Tony barely made sense of a male voice growling in her right ear. "I'm arresting you on suspicion of grievous bodily harm. You do not have to say anything, but it may harm your defense if you do not mention when questioned something which you later rely on in court. Anything you do say may be given in evidence. Do you understand?"

Tony didn't understand. She didn't understand at all. How were the police there? Could she even be sure it was the police?

She was hauled to her feet, her arms were pulled together in front of her, and handcuffs were snapped on each wrist.

Tony panted and blinked. She counted four policemen in the tiny hallway. Two were on either side of her, one was bending over Somers, and the other hovered near the doorway.

Ron Somers had reverted to frail old man. He was lying on the ground, breathing heavily.

"Oh, oh," he groaned. "My hip hurts. Help me up, mate. I need to get to my friend, Rose. She's in the bedroom."

"No, no. Stay there." The policeman's voice was soft with concern. "The ambulance is on its way." He turned to his colleagues flanking Tony. He glared up at her with disgust. "Get that piece of crap out of my sight."

Tony was jerked toward the door. She walked stiffly with her hands in cuffs. The policemen marched her down the stairs and out the main door.

Police cars were parked haphazardly on the street, their blue lights silently flashing in the dark.

"I hate scum like you," the constable on her right mouthed in Tony's ear as they walked. "Attacking old people in their own homes. You make me sick." He pulled her sharply toward the nearest vehicle.

A small crowd of onlookers had gathered near the cars. Tony kept her eyes facing front. She was horribly worried about Rose. She needed to figure out what had happened and how she was going to sort it all out with the police.

A hand bent her head down. She was pushed into the backseat, and the door slammed behind her. She closed her eyes and concentrated on not throwing up, as the police car pulled away.

CHAPTER TEN

N ame?"

The desk sergeant was probably a dyke. At least she looked to Tony like a dyke. Tony wondered if she'd be the best person to talk to.

"Tony Carson."

"Address?" The sergeant barely looked at Tony as she gave her address. If she felt any solidarity, it wasn't apparent. The arresting officer's eyes were boring into Tony's back, however. She glanced at him. He stared at her coldly.

"Date of birth?"

"Fifteenth of March, 1973."

The arresting officer fell about laughing. "What a joker. If you want to give false information, give a false address, fool. What's that? Your mother's date of birth?"

Tony and the desk sergeant frowned at him.

He ignored Tony, but sobered up when he saw his sergeant's expression. "What? You don't find that funny? He thinks we're going to think he's..." The constable tailed off as he did the maths. "Forty-two," he said a good three minutes later.

The sergeant's eyes flicked to Tony. They flicked away before any real contact could be made. "She's a woman," she said quietly.

The constable pulled Tony round to face him and then dragged her under a light. He scrutinized her face for a couple of minutes. "Why didn't you say you were a woman?" he said sharply, as if it was her fault. "Take off your belt."

Pain shot through Tony's hands as she fumbled with her belt. Eventually, she handed it to the officer.

"Empty your pockets." The sergeant waved toward a container on the desk. She was looking at Tony sharply.

Tony tried to appeal to her: "Look, it isn't just my gender you've got wrong. Let me explain."

"You'll get your chance to explain. Just empty your pockets." The sergeant clearly wasn't giving Tony any special concessions for being on the same team. Maybe she wasn't a lesbian anyway.

Tony plonked her wallet, keys, mobile phone, and loose change into the container.

A female constable stepped up to her. "Arms out to the side." She patted her down and then ran a metal detector down her torso and legs. Tony had been searched at the airport when she'd walked through the detector with keys in her pocket. It felt more degrading somehow at the police station.

"You've got it all wrong," she said.

"You have the right to free and independent legal advice, be it in person or on the telephone," the desk sergeant said.

"I don't think I need it. Let me tell you what happened."

The sergeant took a breath. "Save it for the interview," she said firmly. "You need to listen to your rights."

Tony looked at her. Her head hurt.

"You can have someone informed of your detention. You can consult the codes of practice book which informs you about your rights whilst detained. Have you drunk alcohol or taken drugs in the last twenty-four hours?"

Tony shook her head.

"Do you have any medical conditions? Do you consent to samples being taken? Are you feeling unwell? Have you got any injuries?"

Tony half tuned out of the series of questions the sergeant fired at her, nodding or shaking her head appropriately. She considered telling them her hands and head hurt, but she just wanted to get to the interview and explain.

"Hold your hands out like this." The arresting officer stretched his hands out, separating his fingers.

Tony copied his actions stiffly. He swabbed her hands and then put the swab in a clear plastic bag.

"Move it," he said.

He walked Tony into a small room and gestured toward a chair.

She sat down and rested her fingertips on the wood-colored Formica tabletop in front of her. There was nothing on the table but a piece of paper with her rights on it, and a square black tape recorder. The rest of the room was bare. There were no notices on the scuffed, pale green walls and no other furniture apart for the table and three hard, gray plastic chairs. In the center of one wall was a large window that Tony guessed, from watching cop shows on TV, was a one-way mirror. She looked toward it and then quickly away. She doubted she was a high profile enough arrest to have anyone behind it observing her, but you never knew.

The door opened. A white, middle-aged man in a charcoal suit came into the room. His graying, sandy hair was cut close. He had dark circles under his eyes, a ruddy complexion, and he needed a shave. He was carrying a buff folder. He sat in the third chair and unwrapped a blank disc. He took it out of its case and put it into the tape recorder. He inserted two more discs and then switched on the machine.

"For the benefit of the recording, my name is Detective Sergeant Paul Ashton. This is ten p.m. on the fifteenth of July, 2014, at Belsize Police Station. You do not have to say anything. But it may harm your defense if you do not mention when questioned something which you may later rely on in court. Anything you say may be given in evidence. You are currently under arrest on suspicion of aggravated burglary. You may seek legal advice at any time. Do you understand?"

Tony nodded. She hadn't asked for a lawyer yet. She was sure she could get it all straightened out by explaining what had really happened.

"Say it aloud, please."

"Yes," Tony said. Her voice sounded weird.

"Do you want legal advice?" Ashton asked her.

"No."

"Do you have any reasons for not wanting it?"

Tony was confused. "Why? Do you think I need it?"

"That's up to you. Do you want it?"

Tony sighed and shook her head. "No."

"State your name, date of birth, and address for the recording."

Tony recited her details again.

Detective Ashton looked at her briefly before reading a sheet inside the folder. "So what's a forty-two-year-old woman doing breaking into old people's houses? Looking for cash, were you? Got a habit?"

"No," Tony said, trying to sit up straight. Something about the chair and the light and the bare room made her want to curl over and avoid their eyes. She knew she hadn't done anything wrong, but she felt guilty anyway. "You've got it wrong. I didn't break into Rose's flat."

"You know her then?"

"Yes, I know Rose Henderson. Well, I know her a bit. I didn't break in. I—"

"So she let you in because she knew you," Detective Ashton interrupted her. "Technically, it's not breaking and entering; it's entering by deception. Doesn't make much difference. It's still attempted burglary, but that isn't the worst thing anyway. The thing you're going to do time for is attacking those frail old people."

"Frail! He's not frail."

Ashton looked at her with disgust. "You're a real piece of work, aren't you?"

The constable pulled his chair closer to her. "That old man's at the hospital right now. It's touch-and-go."

Tony pulled back and shut her mouth. What was going on? She remembered launching herself at Somers. God. Had she really hurt him? Did he hit his head on the way down? She remembered a look of triumph in his cunning old eyes just before she was marched out of the hallway. Maybe he'd collapsed after she'd left. She glanced at both the policemen. They were looking at her like she was evil.

She swallowed. "How is Rose?"

The policemen exchanged a look.

"You take the biscuit, mate," the constable said.

"No, that's actually good," Ashton said. "She's feeling guilty." He leaned across the table. "How do you think she is, after what you did to her?"

Tony blanched.

"I don't think she's going to make it," Ashton said.

"Look, I didn't attack Rose. Please listen to me. I'm sure this is all to do with a crime Ron Somers committed when he was working in Holloway."

"What?" Ashton sat back. He glanced at the officer next to Tony.

"He killed a prisoner called Frankie White. Or at least he let her die."

Ashton folded his arms and clenched his jaw. "What a pile of crap. Ron Somers worked with my dad. He was a straight-up bloke. No way he'd do something like that." He put his hands on the tabletop and bent across until his face was inches away from Tony's. "They got me out of bed to take this case on account my dad worked with Somers. Somers asked for me specially when he called it in. That was when he heard you ransacking the place and beating up that old lady." He stabbed a finger toward Tony's face. "And just before you turned on him."

Tony had a bad feeling it wasn't going to get sorted out quickly at all.

"I want a lawyer," she said. She sat back in her chair, trying to look confident.

The policemen exchanged a look.

"Solicitor. You're not in America." Ashton slammed the buff folder shut and snatched it off the table. "Take her to a cell," he growled.

❖

The legal aid solicitor, Daniel Solomon, sat next to Tony. He looked like he had talked to a lot of criminals in his time. Tony wondered if he had been full of youthful exuberance and lofty ideals when he started out. Impossibly, he looked more tired than Detective Ashton. They faced off against each other across the table like two old bears. Tony supposed that made her the bit of salmon lying on the forest floor.

Tony's hands hurt and her face smarted. She had no idea what time it was, but guessed it was sometime in the early hours of the morning. She'd asked, but no one had told her how Rose was. She hadn't appeared to Tony again, which she hoped was a good sign.

Daniel Solomon cleared his throat. "My client has explained to me that she went to see"—he glanced at the sheet of paper in front of him—"Rose Henderson and was attacked by Ron Somers there."

"That's a load of rubbish. Remind your client that Mr. Somers is sixty-five years old."

"He's very strong," Tony said.

Dan Solomon turned to her. "You don't have to reply. In fact, it's sometimes better to think before replying."

"All this has got to do with his confession. I just know it has," Tony said.

"I've spoken to Ron Somers about that alleged confession. He doesn't know anything about it. He says you're lying."

"Well, of course he would. That doesn't matter. I have the confession as a sound file," Tony said.

Ashton scanned his eyes over the custody record sheet. "You can play it to me. Is it on your phone? There's no MP3 player or memory stick here."

"It's at home, on my laptop."

"So how did Mr. Somers know about it then?" Ashton asked.

"I don't know. I didn't tell him. I didn't know who he was until..." Tony realized she couldn't say how she knew he was Somers. "Later," she finished.

Ashton flicked his eyes toward the arresting officer who was sitting apart from them on a fourth chair pressed up against the wall. "It's a load of old cobblers, isn't it? You're making it all up. Ron Somers has an exemplary service record. I don't believe he would have had anything to do with the death of a prisoner. Why have you got it in for him? How do you even know him?"

"I was asked to look into the death of Frankie White. She was a prisoner in Holloway."

Dan Solomon sat upright. "Okay, I see, so when did Ms. White die?"

"Nineteen sixty-seven."

The policemen looked at her for a second then they both burst into laughter. Even Solomon looked doubtfully at Tony. "That's a long time ago."

"Yes. It's like a, what is it called, a cold case," Tony said.

"It's not a cold case. It's not a cold case at all. We haven't got any open case on, what's her name?" Ashton said quickly.

Solomon looked at his notes. "Frankie White. Maybe you should check."

Ashton didn't look happy. "Well, you know what? That's not what I'm here for. I'm here to find out why she"—he pointed at Tony—"why she broke into an old lady's flat and beat two old people up."

"I didn't break in. Somers was already there."

"That's a lie. He disturbed you trashing the place, after you'd beaten up the old lady. That's when he called us." Ashton glared at her.

Somers must have called the police while he said he was looking for nails. Tony was tired and frustrated. "I wish you'd just let me explain. Ron Somers is the subject of the case I'm on."

"Case? What do you mean case?"

"Are you an investigator?" Dan Solomon asked.

"Yes, I am," Tony said.

"And you hadn't established this?" Dan Solomon said to Ashton.

His eyes narrowed. "What are you, ex-prison service?" Ashton asked.

Tony shook her head.

"You're not police. You don't know anything. Ex-military?"

Tony shook her head again.

Ashton folded his arms. "Oh God, don't tell me you're a bloody amateur detective. Have you got a license?"

"No."

"Well, you're going to need one soon. Shame I can't nick you for that right now. Amateur bloody detectives. If there's one thing I hate more than ex-forces playing private detective, it's bloody amateurs. No wonder you cocked this up. Right. Still doesn't explain why you attacked the old lady, but I'm guessing you were after Somers. Trying to lean on him, were you? Got a bit heavy?"

"Let's talk about the alleged assault on Ron Somers, and come back to the alleged assault on Rose Henderson," Dan Solomon interjected. He had an unemotional voice. Tony found it very soothing. "First of all, what is the health status of Ron Somers? You said you've spoken to him. So he's conscious, and able to talk?"

Ashton glanced quickly at the arresting officer. "He's currently on an observation ward," the officer said.

Solomon turned to him. "What's he being observed for?"

"Signs of ill health," the officer said defensively.

Ashton groaned.

"So, he's not currently showing *any* signs of ill health?" Solomon pressed him.

The officer looked at Ashton.

"What was he admitted for?" Solomon asked.

"He said he had chest pains, and his hip hurt, and he was feeling dizzy and weak. He's sixty-five." The officer shot Tony a look.

"So, what did they find on examination?"

The officer looked at Ashton again. Ashton coughed. "It's unclear at this time what the extent of Ron Somers's injuries are."

"I was defending myself. He attacked me," Tony said.

"With a hammer? It was just lying around at Miss Henderson's was it?" Ashton said.

"It was in a toolbox, in a kitchen cupboard."

The officers laughed.

"It was. He was there when I got there. He said someone had broken in and attacked Rose, and she had gone to hospital. He asked me to help him fix her front door."

"Fix the front door. You got the gift of the gab, all right." Ashton sniggered.

"I had my back turned to him, holding a board up to the door when he came at me with the hammer."

"Come on, he's a frail old man. What reason did he have to attack you? Admit it. You didn't have anything on him. There is no *confession*. You were trying to get him to admit to something he didn't do. Probably trying to record that with your phone. So you got a bit worked up. Did you just mean to frighten him with the hammer, is that it?"

"I didn't have the hammer. He had the hammer. He hit *me* with the hammer!"

"Wait a minute. He hit you? Where?" Daniel Solomon ran his eyes over Tony's head, face, and neck.

"My hands mostly." Tony pulled her hands up from her lap, resting them on the table. Dark bruises were visible. Tony looked at them with fascination. They hadn't been there the last time she'd looked.

Solomon's eyes widened. "Has this bruising and swelling been seen by the doctor?" he asked sharply. He flicked through a couple of sheets of paper in the file in front of him. "I don't have a doctor's report here."

Ashton frowned. He turned to the arresting officer. The officer got up and came to look at Tony's hands. He looked worried.

"She never mentioned nothing about her hands," he said to Ashton. "She was asked the welfare questions. Sergeant Lewis asked her. I was there."

Ashton gave him a warning look. "This has just come to our attention now. Ms. Carson did not inform us that she was injured."

Solomon straightened up. "Now that I'm looking for it, I can see an enormous bruise on her left cheek. Was that bruise there when you arrested my client?"

The arresting officer swallowed. "Must have been." He looked anxiously at Ashton. "It didn't happen when we arrested her."

A small wave of relief flowed through Tony.

"She needs to be medically examined. We can resume this interview after we know the extent of my client's injuries." Solomon shut the folder and stood.

For a second, Ashton remained seated. He frowned at Tony's hands and then at her cheek. Finally, he nodded at the other policeman, and Tony was helped to her feet.

❖

Maya hadn't slept a wink. Tony's cell wasn't even taking messages anymore. Around two a.m. after tossing and turning in her own bed for a couple of hours, Maya had caught a night bus across the next borough to Tony's apartment.

Maya's heart had sunk when she'd found the apartment empty. Maya had phoned all the London hospitals. Tony hadn't been admitted into any of them. Finally, she'd got into Tony's bed and tossed and turned there until daylight glowed behind Tony's bedroom blinds.

The theater wouldn't be open for hours. She called Tony's dad. He hadn't seen Tony, but promised to call her if he did. The only other place Maya could think to look was Jade's boat.

At eight a.m., she stood outside the gate at Poplar Marina. It was going to be a hot day. The sun was pale lemon in a bleached, cloudless sky. The skyscrapers of Canary Wharf stretched into the expanse of space above them. A few cars drove past, but traffic was light. The gentle sound of lapping water drifted over the gate.

Maya pressed Jade's buzzer several times but didn't get any answer. Jade's cell was unavailable. It looked like the number had gone out of service. Maya was worried about Jade, and now about Tony as well. She was banking on them being together, having experienced some bizarre accident that affected both their cell phones.

Maya stared at the line of buzzers in frustration. She knew where Jade kept the spare key, if only she could get through the damn gate. A man walked past with his dog. He narrowed his eyes at her. Maya realized she must look suspicious, glaring at the intercom system. She took a sip of her espresso and smiled at him. He looked away.

Maya started pressing buzzers. She knew it was still early, but she was getting impatient. She prioritized the buttons nearest Jade's, hoping they corresponded to the boats' positions as well.

"Yes?" A terse female voice came out of the speaker underneath the buzzer buttons.

"Hi, I'm a friend of Jade's—"

"Bell eight."

"Yes, I know, she's not answering. Listen, I've been trying to reach Jade for days. Her cell's dead. I'm really worried about her. Can you buzz me through so I can check whether she's in the boat or not?" Maya decided not to complicate things by bringing Tony into the conversation.

There was silence. Then a long breath. "We're not allowed to let anyone through if we don't know them."

"Maybe you do know me. I'm a very good friend of Jade's. Are you one of her neighbors?"

"Ah-ha."

"Are you from the Dutch barge with the lovely window boxes?" Maya thought flattery was in order. She was pretty sure the voice was the barge owner's high maintenance girlfriend. They were moored next to Jade's barge.

"Ah-ha." She didn't sound very flattered.

"Look, I think we've met. I'm the American with long, dark hair. I've stayed over on Jade's boat a few times."

There was another long pause.

"Wait there."

Maya wasn't sure what that meant. She hoped it was something good.

The gate opened a crack. Maya made out a scowling face. The woman's face relaxed a millimeter when she saw Maya. Maya recognized the petite, brown haired, blue-eyed girlfriend of the barge owner. Maya supposed she was quite pretty, or she would be, if her face wasn't permanently set into a frown. The woman opened the gate cautiously and then peered over Maya's shoulder. She looked left and right and up the street. Finally, she turned back to Maya.

"I thought it was you. I haven't seen you for ages."

"I have been trying to see Jade for a while. There's a problem with her phone. I wonder if her bell works."

"Oh, the bloody bell works. It's been getting on my nerves, buzzing away. I don't think she's there, though."

"Really? Where would she go?"

"How would I know?" The girlfriend shrugged.

"Her girlfriend's gone," Maya said.

"What, the Indian girl?"

Maya nodded.

"What, for good?" the girlfriend asked.

"I think so."

"Thank God for that. Jade's well shut of that one."

Interested in what the barge owner's girlfriend had to say about Suni, Maya took a step toward her. The woman waved Maya through the gate and then shut it behind her. "Why do you say that?"

The barge owner's girlfriend looked like she didn't want to say why. Maya leaned in, confidentially. "I don't like her."

"I don't like her either," the girlfriend said, shaking her head. "There's something slimy about her. She hit on me once. Jade had only gone out for a paper."

Maya pursed her lips.

"So they've broken up now?"

"Yep."

The barge owner's girlfriend studied Maya. "So is she with you now?"

Maya didn't understand the mental jump. She was about to say no, but then she thought it might work in her favor if the woman thought she and Jade were together.

"Well…" Maya deliberately left the end of her sentence hanging, as if she and Jade were on the brink of something.

"That's explains why you're so anxious to see her that you'd disturb people at this hour in the morning," the girlfriend said to herself. "I'm not surprised you got rid of that awful woman."

"What woman?"

"The one that looks like a boy."

"Oh, you mean Tony."

Maya was about to ask the barge owner's girlfriend if she'd seen Tony, but she narrowed her eyes at the mention of Tony's name. She lowered her voice. "She tried to drown me once. I even sent a letter to the marina manager, but they didn't do anything."

Maya bit her lip. The way she'd heard it, the barge owner's girlfriend had been drunk and fallen in the water. Tony had bravely dived in to pull her out, only to be berated for her efforts. Tony and Jade had laughed about it later. Maya felt a stab of pain at the memory.

"She's just like a man, that friend of Jade's, your ex," the girlfriend said.

"No, she's not," Maya said shortly. Every time the woman said Tony's name it pulled at her heart. She was desperate to go and see if Tony and Jade were in the boat.

"Well, I think she behaves like a man, and she certainly looks like one. Or a teenage boy. Why would you want to go out with a teenage boy?"

Maya bit back her anger. She wanted to lecture the woman about her obsession with gender, and about all the ways that a butch was different from a man. Unfortunately, she couldn't risk antagonizing her and getting kicked off the marina. Not that Tony even identified as a butch.

"Are you even listening to me?" the barge owner's girlfriend broke through Maya's musing.

"Sorry, I was thinking about something else for a minute."

"God, are all lesbians like men? Anyway, I was saying, you and Jade are much better off with each other. You're both quite normal. At least Jade used to be."

"What do you mean?"

"I used to like Jade. She plays reggae too loud sometimes, but mostly she's chilled."

Maya resisted rolling her eyes and telling the woman that Jade pretty much exclusively played soca not reggae.

"She'll lend you anything. But she's been dead weird lately," the girlfriend continued.

"Weird, how?"

"She's been withdrawn. You know how she's usually up on the deck a lot, even in winter. Any little bit of sun, Jade's out there. I saw her lying out on a sun lounger one Christmas day, in a ski suit. She didn't care, as long as she got some sun on her face. But not lately. In fact, she's hardly left the boat at all. The few times we've seen her, she's ignored us. Not even said hello. Vince, my boyfriend, thought he'd upset her, or I had. He always thinks he's done something wrong. I knew it was nothing to do with us. She looked sad. I wondered if someone had died. Oh yeah, and that awful, bloody, droning voice."

"What voice?" Vince's girlfriend had Maya's full attention.

"A male voice droning on and on, and some kind of God-awful screechy music. Self-help CDs is my guess. All hours of the day and night. It was a real pain when we sat on our deck. I could hear it even inside our boat. Vince said he couldn't. I wanted to complain, but Vince said to give Jade some slack. Especially if she was grieving."

"What was the voice saying?"

"I couldn't hear. It was loud enough to bother me but not loud enough to make out the words. Anyway, I started wearing earphones on our deck. Thank God that's stopped now. Yeah, now I think about it, it's been really quiet since yesterday morning."

"Okay, well, thanks for that. I'm going to check on Jade now."

Vince's girlfriend watched Maya from the towpath to her barge. Maya resolved to come back when everything was sorted out and have a good conversation with Vince's girlfriend about concepts of binary gender.

Maya walked onto the deck of Jade's boat. She knocked on the bright red front door. There wasn't a sound from within.

Maya knocked again.

There was no answer. Maya turned the handle and pushed the door. It opened inward. Maya glanced back. Vince's girlfriend was still watching her. Maya stepped inside the boat, straight into the galley kitchen.

The sink was full of unwashed cups and plates. Open cereal boxes sat on the counter. The two-ring hob was filthy. Jade wasn't the tidiest person in the world, but she kept a clean kitchen, and she put everything away because there was so little space.

"Jade," Maya called out. "Tony?"

The only sound was water lapping against the hull of the boat and the throaty quacks of a nearby duck.

She walked down into the dim living area. All of the blinds were drawn. Maya looked at her watch. It was eight thirty, still early, so that wasn't totally unusual. Maybe Jade was sleeping. She felt a flicker of hope. It wasn't unusual for Tony and Jade to share a platonic bed.

Maya went straight to the bedroom at the other end of the boat. She walked past piles of things pulled out of cupboards.

Maya knocked on the bedroom door.

Again, silence.

Cautiously, Maya opened the door.

The room was dark. It was in the same state of disarray, and there was no sign of Jade. Or Tony.

Her heart sank.

Maya stepped inside, flipped the light switch on, and sat on the edge of the bed.

She picked up one of Jade's sweaters that was lying across the duvet. It smelled of Jade's perfume. She held the sweater just under her nose. *Jade, where are you?* She might not have supernatural powers, but Maya knew something was terribly wrong.

She called Tony's cell again.

It just cut her off.

Her eyes traveled to Jade's shelves. Where were the African carvings?

Maya began opening drawers and looking inside the wardrobe. Whole drawers of Jade's stuff were gone.

Maya went back into the living space and opened all the blinds up.

There were white mug rings on Jade's prized mahogany coffee table, and food stains on her fluffy white cushions. There was a big dark stain across her designer Robin Day sofa, and a bright red splash across Jade's white sheepskin rug. All of Jade's framed photos were missing. In fact, almost anything personal to Jade was missing: books, CDs, her laptop, her e-book reader, and the painting that had hung on the wall over the sofa. There had been a few clothes in the bedroom but no carvings or other knickknacks, no jewelry and no accessories. Where were all the thick wooden bangles that Jade always had weighing down her arms?

The bathroom was filthy and there were no cosmetics or toiletries in there at all. There wasn't even a roll of toilet paper.

Maya was shocked. It was very, very odd.

Had Suni stolen all of Jade's stuff? But why? And where was Jade then?

Maya decided to have a look around the outside of the boat.

She walked up the steps, past the galley kitchen, and stepped out onto the deck. Vince's girlfriend had disappeared.

There was nothing out of place in the front deck area. Mind you, there was usually nothing on the deck to be moved except Jade's plants.

They were gone.

Maya walked around the boat to the small storage area behind it. Jade kept her sun loungers under a little porch. They were there propped against the side of the boat as usual, but in front of them was a collection of debris. Maya went in for a closer look.

Inside a plastic crate were Jade's carvings. The elephant's trunk was broken clean off. Unbelievably, Jade's tablet and e-reader were there. Maya's stomach tensed. There was no way Jade was staying somewhere else. Not unless she'd been committed to a psychiatric hospital.

Maya pulled out the tablet. It powered up briefly and then went dead. Maya glanced back to the crate. Underneath where the tablet had been, and in pieces, was Jade's cell phone. Maya picked up the leopard print skin Jade had bought at Camden Lock market. It had the little rip in the top right corner that had appeared two weeks after Jade had bought it.

Maya went through the rest of the items in the crate. They were all personal things that Jade loved. There were pieces of jewelry, photos of Tony and Jade's family, signed copies of novels from her writer friends, and CDs from the musicals she'd been in, some where the sleeve had been signed by the entire cast. There was no way Jade would leave this stuff outside in a crate. She was either really ill or...

Maya's mind flashed to the blanket on the backseat of Suni's car. It had taken up the entire backseat. Oh God, was it possible that had been a person, lying on the seat?

Had that been Jade?

Maya's mind raced. Even if it was Jade, where was Tony?

Tony was already missing when Maya had seen Suni leaving. Was there any possibility Suni had abducted both of them?

Maya thought quickly. Why on earth would Suni do that?

But why the hell would Suni drug her former lover?

The stuff covered in a blanket had been pretty bulky. It could have been two unconscious people.

There were a couple of sheets of paper at the bottom of the crate. Maya pulled them out. The top sheet was a printout of the advert Maya remembered seeing weeks back for a cabin in Scotland. Clipped to it was a receipt. Two days previously, Suni had booked the cabin for the same week. At the bottom of the receipt was a phone number and an address for Glenford Rentals.

Maya dialed the number.

Someone picked up on the second ring.

"Glenford Rentals, can I help you?"

"Yes, please. My name is Suni Ghosh. I've rented one of your cabins and I've stupidly mislaid the address."

"Ah, yes," the cheerful Scottish voice said, "I see you're on a mobile phone. Can I text that information to you, pet? You'd best have a satellite navigation reference. It's right in the middle of the forest. Very peaceful."

"Thank you so much."

Maya grabbed the crate of Jade's stuff and set off, almost at a run. She needed to move fast. Suni had a day on her. Maya still didn't have any real reason to think that Suni was going to harm Jade, or that Tony was with them, but Maya wasn't going to take the chance.

Maya needed to get home, pack, and get on a plane to Scotland.

Tony felt like crap. Despite being given painkillers, her head and hands still hurt, and she felt nauseous. She wanted to sleep, but she was too wound up. She was in one hell of a predicament with the police. And overriding all of that, she was terrified for Rose. What if Rose died? Tony kept seeing her lying on the floor. She hadn't looked good.

Why had Somers attacked Rose? How did he even know where she lived? He had some game going with the police. God, he was a slippery bastard.

Tony was sure hours had passed. She had been examined and then returned to her cell. The police had told her she would have to wait until Somers had been seen by a consultant at the hospital. Dan Solomon had said they were entitled to do that if they wanted to. He thought there was no point in pushing them.

Tony had tried sleeping, but the concrete bed was the most uncomfortable piece of furniture she had ever lain on, and that included the ground when camping. She thought a bed of nails would be more comfortable. The tiled cell walls were bare except for the odd stain that Tony didn't want to get too close to. She was sitting on a blue plastic mat stuck on top of the bed area. There was a toilet near the bed. Tony hadn't fancied using it, as someone could look into the cell through the small hatch on the cell door at any time.

The air in front of the wall to the left of the cell door began to flicker. From past experience, Tony knew a ghost was coming through. A few seconds later, the distorted air turned into a thin black woman. Tony recognized her from Jade's headshot.

Felicia screwed her eyes up and looked disparagingly around the cell.

"Oh no. You're not going to be any use to me at all. This is too sordid a scene, man. I need someone clean. Someone upright."

Tony didn't say anything. Things were bad enough. She wasn't going to make excuses to a ghost she hadn't even properly met.

Felicia took a few slow steps over to the bed. She ran her eyes over the toilet area and turned up her nose. "You a player? A pimp?" She looked at Tony doubtfully. "A ho?"

Deirdre fizzed up in exactly the same place Felicia had materialized. Tony wondered if there were such things as portals for ghosts.

"She's more of a ho, ho, ho," Deirdre said. "But none of us are laughing right now, are we, Tony?"

Tony shook her head.

"Take me to somebody else," Felicia commanded. "She can't help me from in here. And she can't help her friend, either."

"What friend?" Tony asked.

"Jade. At one time she was your best friend, so Deirdre tells me." Felicia sounded angry. Tony remembered Jade saying the woman was angry, but it seemed like she was angry at Tony, not just angry in general.

"What do you mean?"

"Now, Tony…" Deirdre took a step toward the bed.

"She's in trouble. I got it wrong. Boy, did I get it wrong."

Tony stood up. She kept half an eye on the cell door. It wouldn't help her at all if the police caught her talking to herself. They had the power to section her. "Wrong about what?"

"I didn't want to talk to you because you're white. I don't trust white people. Nothing personal. It's just I haven't had good experiences, if you know what I mean." She looked from Tony to Deirdre. "Well, why would you, you're both white. But anyway, I should have come to you. You're not Suni's type at all."

Tony frowned and turned to Deirdre. "Translate?"

"Get to the point, Felicia," Deirdre said sharply. She looked anxious.

"Suni wouldn't have fancied you, and then Jade wouldn't be in danger. Just saying."

"Jade's in danger? How?"

"Suni's taken her somewhere. Jade's all drugged up. I think Suni did that. Can't be sure. It was hard to get through. Takes a lot of energy, doesn't it?" she said to Deirdre.

Deirdre nodded. "Sure does. You're new at this. There's training courses you can go on. I can hook you up with a good instructor."

"Deirdre! Surely you can talk about that later. Felicia, why is Jade in danger?"

"Suni's on a trip. I couldn't see that, when we were together. She gets off on controlling people. I'm damn sure now that she drove me to suicide."

Tony stared at Felicia. "What do you mean?"

"She messed with my head till I believed I was worthless. People whispered in my ear. I thought I was hearing voices, but it must have been Suni. I bet she drugged me up, like that poor, crazy, confused child."

"What child? Do you mean Jade?" Tony asked.

Felicia nodded.

Tony felt sick. Oh God, Maya was right. Only she had thought Jade was going mad. It looked like Suni had been trying to drive Jade crazy. Tony walked quickly to the cell door. "I need to get out of here."

"Calm down, Tony." Deirdre walked to her side.

Tony rounded on her. "Why didn't you tell me?"

Deirdre looked apologetic. "Well, I didn't exactly know. And it's not my job."

Tony was shocked. She was about to say something choice to Deirdre when the hatch flew open.

"Stand away from the door. Sit on the bed." The arresting officer was the other side of the cell door.

Tony sat back down. The ghosts disappeared. The door swung open and the constable came into the cell.

"The report's in on Somers, and there's news on Rose Henderson. Come with me."

❖

Maya rang Tony's cell phone again. It was still going straight to voice mail. Maya buckled up her seat belt and tucked her carry-on bag under the seat in front of her. She kept thinking of the shape under the blanket in Suni's car. She had convinced herself that it was two drugged people. It was possible. Jade was petite, and Tony wasn't exactly huge.

On the other hand, Suni could have been picking Jade up en route, and Tony could be somewhere else entirely. Maya didn't know what to think. Maybe Tony was out of town and something had happened to her cell phone. She hoped Tony hadn't gone away with that Beth woman. She'd always been into Tony.

Maya looked out the plane window to the runway. Drops of rain were collecting on the thick double glazing. What was wrong with her? She had no reason to think Tony was being unfaithful. The mind played tricks when a person didn't know what was going on. She was filling in the blanks with her fears. Maya had left her number with Tony's dad, and with all the hospitals. No one had called.

An air steward came down the aisle checking seat belts. Maya knew she'd have to switch her phone off soon. If Tony wasn't in Suni's car, Maya needed to let her know where she was going.

She quickly wrote a text: *Honey, where are you? Call me as soon as you get this message. I love you, you're funny and sweet, and I feel more for you than I have let myself feel for anyone. Jade and Suni have gone to Scotland, and I'm on my way there now. I have a hunch something is terribly wrong. If that's not true I will walk in on a hot scene, and eventually they'll forgive me. I need to talk to you. More than that, I need to see you. Call me as soon as you see this. Xxx*

She tried to busy her mind with logistics. She would rent a car at Glasgow airport. The drive was around three hours. She didn't really care if she made a fool of herself tearing after the couple. Suni had lied to her. Unless she had already booked the cabin and forgotten to cancel it. There was a chance Suni was going to the cabin just by herself. In which case, Maya would just back off and come home. She made a note to make sure she had lots of gas in the car. As soon as her phone could be switched back on she'd research a motel near the cabin, just in case.

As the plane began to taxi along the runway, Maya began to feel more than a little foolish. The state of Jade's boat was strange, but really, was Maya allowing her imagination to completely carry her away? That lump in the back of Suni's car could have been anything. Maybe it had looked people-shaped in Maya's memory. She was aware of how the memory could play tricks. She'd studied the reliability of witness testimony as part of her psychology degree. Descriptions of perpetrators were notoriously unreliable, especially if taken some time after the event.

Oh well, Maya was on her way. If worst came to worst, she would just be out of pocket for the expensive plane ticket and the cost of the rental car. Oh, and the huge dent to her pride.

❖

Ashton sat across the table from Tony, looking as rough as she felt.

"Luckily for you, Mr. Somers has been discharged from hospital and Miss Henderson is stable. We've still got enough to charge you for assault. And that poor old lady isn't out of the woods yet, so I suggest you get it all off your chest. What went wrong? Why did you hurt the old girl?"

Tony felt like she was in the film *Groundhog Day*.

"Somers must have beaten Rose up. But I've no idea why, or even what he was doing at her home."

"He was her friend. Why shouldn't he be there?" Ashton said.

She laughed. "No way was he her friend. You don't know who she is, do you?"

Ashton glared at her. He didn't say anything.

For the first time in hours, Tony felt a small spark of power. "Rose Henderson was Frankie White's girlfriend. She founded the Justice for Frankie campaign. She hates Ron Somers. He was the man who killed Frankie."

Ashton blinked. "That's rubbish. They were friends," he insisted.

Dan Solomon lent forward. "Why do you say that, Detective Ashton?"

Ashton shuffled. He glanced at the arresting officer and then dropped his eyes to the table.

"Did Ron Somers tell you he was friends with Rose Henderson?" Dan Solomon asked.

Ashton's eyes widened.

"If they weren't friends, how did Ron Somers know Ms. Henderson's address, I wonder?" Dan Solomon said.

Ashton looked decidedly shifty. Tony would have bet money Somers had somehow convinced Ashton to give out Rose's address. From the look on his face, he had no idea of the Frankie White connection.

"I need to hear that sound file you say you've got," Ashton said to Tony.

He stood, his face grim.

Dan Solomon smiled reassuringly as Tony followed Ashton out of the interview room.

❖

Jade stared at the neat lines of pills on the rough wooden table in front of her and felt nothing. Her head ached dully. The room spun on its axis and then settled. The pills were supposed to provide some kind of answer, but Jade couldn't remember what the question was.

She shifted on the chair. She didn't know where she was. The walls were made of strips of pine. The floor was wooden. The ceiling was wooden. The cupboards in the kitchen beyond the archway were wooden. That was a lot of pine. Jade had never been fond of the orangey tone of antique pine. She guessed she was either in a cabin or a tree house. She could go and look. There were blinds drawn low over windows to her left. But it didn't seem to matter.

Jade searched inside herself for a feeling. She was numb. All she knew was that everyone was gone.

She bent her head into her hands and wept.

It helped a little.

She wiped the tears from her face with cold fingers. A photo pushed to the edge of the table caught her eye. She picked it up. The photo was Tony, in Provincetown.

A spark flickered inside her. Jade recalled the holiday. It had been exciting and dangerous. They'd been chased across sand dunes by two thugs. Jade remembered the hard knot of rope in her mouth when she'd lain on the floor of the cabin on Maya's uncle's boat. She'd been there for hours with her arms and legs tied. She'd stared death in the face and never given up hope.

Jade reached down but couldn't feel anything resembling hope.

Jade had no strength left. All she wanted was peace.

She slumped forward on the table and closed her eyes to sleep.

Nothing.

The room was quiet as a grave. Jade felt suspended in time, as if she was hovering on the edge of an important action.

She felt the overpowering need to make everything stop. To just stop.

Jade opened her eyes, and there were the pills: little white, shiny, round pills. They were laid out in groups of ten. Four neat lines, ten pills wide. Beside them was a plain glass tumbler, full of water.

Jade's lips were dry. She reached for the glass. It felt cool and smooth in her hand. She took a sip.

The water slipped down.

The pills had their own particular beauty. Jade thought they must be sleeping pills.

She picked one up. A memory clicked into place. She'd held this pill between her thumb and forefinger before. Its satiny softness was familiar. She popped it into her mouth. The sweetness of its shiny coating dissolved on her tongue. Jade took a sip of water and swallowed them both down.

She knew what she had to do. She swept the rest of the first line of pills into the palm of her hand. She brought her hand toward her mouth.

CHAPTER ELEVEN

The cabin stood out from the pitch-black forest around it. After three hours of driving, Maya had squinted along a small, unlit track that led to the isolated cabin. She couldn't even be truly sure that she was at the right cabin, but this was where the sat nav had led her.

She sat in the car outside the cabin and checked her phone again. There was still no word from Tony.

The cabin was quiet. It was the early hours of the morning. Maya had considered checking into a motel, but she would never have been able to sleep. If all was well, Jade would forgive her. Eventually.

The cabin was boarded with slats of dark pine and topped with a steeply sloping roof. A steel chimney pointed into the sky. Maya made out a small front porch. Windows overlooking the porch and the front glowed from within. Curtains were drawn across them. Around the corner from the porch was a pale yellow door.

Maya slammed the car door shut.

Steps and a ramp led from the path to the door. The sharp tang of wood smoke hung in the air. The cabin was surrounded by pine trees in all directions. They stood tall and immobile, bearing silent witness. A moon, shrunken to a sliver, reclined above the trees in a deep blue sky, pinpricked with stars. In the distance, Maya heard the gentle gurgle of running water. It was a beautiful spot.

Maya made her way carefully to the front steps. She realized she hadn't given Tony the address. She was now almost certain she was about to make a monumental fool of herself. On the outside chance that her fears were justified, Maya needed someone else to know where she was.

She pulled out her phone and texted: *Hey, gorgeous, I forgot to give you the address: Wildwood Cabin, Fort Augustus, PH32 7BN.*

A rustle nearby reminded Maya she was in the middle of a forest. It was probably a wood mouse or something, but it was a good idea to go on into the cabin. God, she hoped it was the right place.

She walked quickly to the front door. There was no bell or knocker so she rapped on the wood with her fist.

It was so quiet she heard the footsteps within as someone came to the door.

It opened inward to reveal Suni.

Maya sighed with relief. She was at the right place then. She smiled.

Suni smiled back.

"Your phone, please," she said.

Maya was confused. "Huh? I—"

Suni nodded toward Maya's jacket pocket. "Give me your phone."

There was a click behind her. The barrel of a gun pressed into her back. Maya stiffened. She started to turn.

"Stay where you are," a voice said behind her. It sounded just like Suni.

"Well, you wanted to come in, didn't you? Be my guest." Suni swept her hand toward the interior of the cabin. She was being perfectly polite and charming.

Fear snaked through Maya as the gun pressed harder into her back.

"Get a move on. It's bloody cold out here," the voice behind her complained. A hand shoved her forward.

Maya was pushed into a sitting area with sofas and a table lamp. The door slammed and was bolted. Maya turned.

She stared at the woman laughing at her with the front door key in one hand and a pistol in the other. It was Suni.

Maya shook her head and looked back at the woman who had answered the door. The identical woman also laughed.

"Do you think she's got it yet?" the woman with the gun said.

The woman who'd answered the door stepped forward. "We've met before. I'm Suni, Sunita." She stretched out her hand. Maya didn't take it.

"And we've met before as well, my name's Anita." The woman with the gun crossed in front of Maya and stood next to Suni.

"You're identical twins." Maya bit her lip.

"Give the woman a cigar, only don't because this is a non-smoking cabin. This little backwater doesn't allow smoking in the privacy of your own rental home," Anita said casually.

Maya stared at them both. She searched for a way of telling them apart.

"We were half expecting you, but you've come at a very annoying time," Suni said.

Anita waved the pistol in the direction of an archway. "Get through there."

Maya walked past the sofas into a small dining area.

Jade was sitting at a wooden dining table. As Maya walked toward her, she scooped up a handful of little white pills.

Maya didn't give a damn if they shot her. She ran to Jade and knocked the pills out of her hand.

Jade blinked at Maya. She had dark shadows under her eyes. She'd lost weight. Her skin was drawn and pale. Her eyes were red, and her hair was wild. Jade normally wore her hair in short locks. It was all over the place.

Maya hugged her. Jade didn't resist, but she didn't hug Maya back.

"It's Maya," Maya said.

Jade looked at her. She was obviously confused. She yawned and rubbed her eyes.

"What are these, sleeping pills?" Maya asked the twins.

They nodded simultaneously. Anita was still pointing the gun at her.

"How many did you take?" Maya asked Jade.

Jade yawned again but didn't answer. She looked about to fall asleep. Maya thought quickly. What emetics could she find in a forest? She knew that Polygala senega grew in forests in North America. Maybe it grew in Scotland too? She might be able to find something that would make Jade vomit. That's if she could persuade or get past the twins.

Suni walked to the table and counted the pills. She swept them into a Ziploc bag, then she picked up the pills Maya had knocked to the floor. "One," she said to Maya. She patted Jade's head. "Just one little pill," she said in a baby voice. "Never mind, honey. You'll do better next time."

Maya hated her. She hated her with a vengeance.

Jade rested her head on her arms and closed her eyes. Maya reached under and pressed down on Jade's carotid artery. Her pulse was strong and steady. Maya glanced at her watch, counting.

Jade's heart rate was slightly slower than it usually was, but within the normal range. Her breathing was regular. Maya didn't think she could trust the twins to tell her the truth, but Jade seemed okay, for the moment. Maya stroked her hair. Jade made a little "Mmm," sound in her sleep.

"Let's have a private conversation," Suni said.

Maya glanced up. Suni was looking at Anita.

"Okay." Anita tipped her head toward Maya and Jade. "Bedroom?"

Suni nodded. She put her hands under Jade's right arm. "Get the other side of her. We'll carry her between us," she said to Maya.

Anita raised the pistol, aiming it at Maya's chest.

Maya helped lift Jade to a standing position. They walked her back through the living area, past the front door, and into another room with twin beds in it. It was empty. Maya's mind raced. What the hell was going on, and where was Tony?

Suni laid Jade down on one of the beds and then walked to the window. She pulled the curtains aside and checked that the window wouldn't open. Then she walked into the en suite bathroom and did the same thing.

Finally, she stood in the doorway. "I'm looking forward to spending some time with you at last, Maya," she said pleasantly.

"Wait a moment," Maya called out. "Where's Tony?"

Suni smiled. "Misplaced your girlfriend, have you? How careless."

The door shut and a lock was turned.

Maya went to Jade and tried to rouse her. Jade mumbled in her sleep. Her body was completely heavy.

Maya sank down onto the other single bed. They'd taken her phone and her car keys. She was in the middle of nowhere, and even if she managed to break them out, she'd have to carry Jade. She couldn't rely on Tony or anyone else coming to help.

What the hell was she going to do?

❖

Tony sat at a computer terminal in an office-type room at the police station, trying to remember how to access her Dropbox account remotely. Dozens of pairs of eyes bored into her back. She didn't understand the problem. On *Cagney and Lacey*, people came into the squad room all the time. It had been made clear she wasn't welcome in that part of the police station by the blatant stares of anyone she'd passed when Ashton had walked her into the room.

Well, it was their own fault. They should get into the digital age and have computers for the public to use when they were assisting with inquiries. Bristling, Tony sat up straight in the office chair. She wanted to raise it a touch higher but knew that if she misjudged it and shot to the ground the embarrassment could just finish her off.

Tony was in knots, trying to get out of the police station to go and see Jade, but Ashton wouldn't release her until he'd heard the MP3 file.

Ashton had finally conceded that Tony hadn't been responsible for the assault on Rose. He had also reluctantly dropped the assault charge on Ron Somers. Apparently, Somers was as fit as a flea, and had come through the incident entirely unscathed. That meant that Tony's punches had been ineffectual, but under the circumstances that was just as well.

Tony did a Web search for "how to access Dropbox files remotely." Ashton shifted beside her.

"I'm watching you. Don't think you can grab any old sound file and pass it off as something."

"You can see what I'm doing," Tony said. "I just use Dropbox to send large files to people, and I don't do that very often. It's just luck that all my sound files are stored in it."

"Hmm, luck," Ashton said darkly.

Tony logged on to her account and quickly accessed her sound file folder. "Here you are. What do you want me to do, play it?"

"Yes, I want you to play it." Ashton separated the words like Tony needed things explained to her slowly.

Tony double-clicked on the file.

A hush came over the room as officers stopped what they were doing to listen.

Ashton's face changed from suspicious to miserable as the recorded conversation played its course.

When it had finished, he sat, staring into space. Tony forced herself not to say anything, but she was aware of time ticking by. Who knew what state Jade was in? She wanted to talk to Felicia again.

"How did you get that recording?" Ashton asked eventually.

"My client got it from another guard's family. The original is on reel-to-reel tape. I have the tape."

Ashton stood up. "Come on," he said, walking ahead.

He stopped in front of the custody desk. "This one's being released. No charges," he muttered, half under his breath. Then he walked away without a backward glance.

The same custody sergeant was on duty. She looked a lot more tired than when Tony had last seen her. She produced Tony's belongings.

"Check you've got everything on this list, and then sign it at the bottom please," she said in a friendly way. It was the friendliest Tony had heard anyone be since she'd been arrested. She realized, as she scrawled her name on the signature line, that the sergeant wasn't actually being friendly. It was just she was speaking to Tony like she was a normal person.

Before she had even left the police station, Tony clicked her phone on. The screen stayed dark. She held the power button down. There was no response. Tony groaned. Her phone was dead.

She walked back to the custody desk.

"I'm sorry to bother you, but this is urgent. Do you have an iPhone charger I can borrow by any chance?" Tony knew she was relying on lesbian solidarity, of which the sergeant might feel none.

The sergeant flicked her eyes left and right. "We don't usually do this, but, well, you've been here all night, and you look like you've had a rough time of it." She glanced down at Tony's hands. "Are you pressing charges about those bruises?"

Tony flexed her palms and grimaced. "What, against Somers, you mean?"

"Is that the old guy?"

Tony nodded, and then shrugged. She didn't know if she wanted to or not.

"Well, it's up to you. Here." The sergeant pulled the end of a charger out from under the desk. Tony pushed the connector into her phone. The sergeant took Tony's phone and put it under the desk. "In case anybody else comes by," she said quietly.

"I hope Somers is going to be charged for the assault on Rose," Tony said.

"So do I," the sergeant said. "As soon as the old lady's able to talk, we'll be interviewing her about the incident." She shuffled some papers around and then glanced back to Tony. "So. Amateur detective, eh?" She looked like she was mocking Tony, but in a different way from the other police officers. The sergeant was teasing rather than trying to humiliate her.

Tony smiled shyly. She felt insanely grateful that someone was being nice to her. The events of the previous twelve hours had taken their toll.

"We don't really fraternize with PIs, but hey, if you fancy a coffee sometime." The sergeant scribbled something down on a piece of paper and pressed it into Tony's hand. Tony glanced at it. It was a phone number. There was nothing about the night that was going to surprise Tony.

"Um, thanks," she mumbled. She didn't bother to say she already had a girlfriend. She had no intention of calling the sergeant. She slipped the number into her back pocket.

The sergeant disappeared through a doorway into another small room and sat at her computer. Tony read the notices telling her what to do if she needed a solicitor or an interpreter. She was warned that CCTV cameras were in operation. She saw that the police station was having an open day. She was mildly interested in the possibility of seeing police horses and vintage police cars but felt she would give the tour of police cells a miss.

Anxiously, she looked at the clock above the desk again.

"Excuse me, would it be possible to get my phone?" Tony called to the desk sergeant.

She handed it to Tony with a smile.

Tony had a whole heap of messages and texts. The most recent text was from Maya. It gave an address in Scotland.

Tony scanned Maya's previous messages.

She saw with horror that Maya thought Jade had been abducted. Tony pushed through the main entrance doors. She had to get to Scotland, and fast.

CHAPTER TWELVE

Maya groaned and rubbed her eyes. She must have fallen asleep. She'd been awake most of the night trying to think of solutions. She hadn't had much sleep the night before. No wonder she'd dozed off.

She got off the bed and pulled back the curtains.

It was morning. Rows of pine trees stretched out in front of her. Their gray-brown trunks huddled tightly together. Mossy green branches spread out laterally just above head level. The forest floor was a tangle of brambles, ferns, and the occasional fallen tree. A bank rose steeply in the distance. The air was misty with rain that streamed down the window.

Maya tried the window catches. They were firmly shut. She examined the lock. It was a single bolt type. She could get it open, but she'd need a thin bit of wire like a paper clip or a bobby pin and an Allen wrench or something similar. It didn't look expensive. It might even open with a pair of scissors or a screwdriver.

Jade turned. Maya had slipped Jade's shoes off and put the duvet over her during the night. It might be the middle of July, but in Scotland it was cold.

"Jade." Maya bent next to the bed and whispered as loudly as she dared.

Jade mumbled something and turned away from her.

"Jade." Maya tried again.

This time, Jade's eyes flicked open. She stared dully at Maya.

"Where's Tony?" Maya whispered urgently.

Jade's eyes softened. "Dead. I think," she croaked out.

Maya's stomach turned to ice.

Jade's eyes fluttered shut, and within a few seconds, she had fallen into a deep sleep. She didn't respond to Maya gently shaking her.

Maya refused to believe Tony was dead. She wouldn't let herself believe it until she had concrete proof. She went into the bathroom. There was one small window above the sink. Maya could squeeze through it if she had to. Carefully, she clambered up onto the sink to have a look.

The lock was the same type as in the bedroom. The glass was obscured so Maya couldn't see what was outside.

The bedroom door lock clicked as it was turned.

She jumped down and ran some water.

Suni, or at least Maya thought it was Suni, appeared in the en suite doorway.

"Oh. And there was I hoping you'd be just in a towel," Suni said.

Maya wiped her hands.

"I'd love to have a little chat with you, if you can spare the time." Suni smiled in the charming, creepy way that had made Maya uncomfortable from the start. The pistol dangled from her right hand. Maya wondered if she would use it. She tacked that on to her list of things to find out.

In the living room the curtains had been drawn back. Misty light floated in through wooden casement windows, brightening the small room. There was a roaring log fire in a black stove in the corner. The strips of pine boarding the walls, ceiling, and floor looked lighter in daylight.

The other twin was sprawled across the oatmeal sofa sorting supplies. She stuffed some rope and a roll of black plastic bin liners into a rucksack. She looked up but didn't say anything.

Maya sat on the edge of one of the armchairs. She needed to find out if Tony was still alive, and what the twins had planned for them all. Maya decided engaging them in conversation was the best approach.

"Is there any way to tell you two apart?" she asked bluntly.

A look flicked between them.

"Would it comfort you to be able to tell us apart?" the twin Maya thought was Suni asked.

Maya felt a stab of fear. She knew when she was being played with. "I just wondered, that's all," she said, trying to sound like she couldn't care less.

"Come and sit between us," Suni said, patting the sofa.

Maya tensed. The last thing she wanted to do was to get close to either of them.

"The only way to find out what you want to know is to come here," Suni said slowly. She pursed her lips and patted the sofa again.

Maya got up. She was damned if she'd let them know how scared she was.

"Hold my hand." Suni dropped her voice, taking Maya's hand in hers. Maya glared at her. Then she stiffened as an icy hand grasped her left wrist. She remembered the cold touch. "That was you, packing the car," she said to the other twin.

"Yes. I'm Anita." Anita pronounced her name with a soft *tha* at the end, in the Indian way.

"You have cold hands. She hasn't? That's the only way to tell you two apart?" Maya asked.

"That's right, except not just cold hands. I have cold skin pretty much everywhere. You're welcome to check." Anita's voice had the same melodic tone and sweet low pitch that Suni's had.

"No, thanks." Maya stood and returned to the armchair. Their eyes followed her. "What do you want?"

"From you? Nothing," Suni said. "We're just going to have a bit of a chat, some fun, before…" She trailed off.

"Before we go our separate ways," Anita said.

"We'll be moving on, and you and Jade will be going to a very special place. One we all have to go to sometime." Suni's hushed voice was kind.

Maya felt sick. "You're going to kill us."

Suni grinned. "You're so blunt. I like that. It's refreshing."

"Where's Tony?" Maya asked.

Suni's eyebrows flicked upward. Anita stared back at her coolly. Neither answered her.

Maya clenched her jaw. "Why are you doing this?" She tried to subtly look around the room to see what might be useful.

"That's an interesting question," Suni said.

"Aren't we going to drug her?" Anita asked with a sigh.

"Oh, I don't want to. I'm so over all that controlling with drugs thing."

Anita frowned at her sister. "You want her to remain conscious and alert?"

"She's not that alert. She hasn't had much sleep. She's not a physical threat anyway. There are two of us, in case you've forgotten, and we have weapons." She turned to Maya. "If you were thinking of making a rush for the kitchen drawers, don't bother. We cleaned everything out while you were sleeping."

Maya swallowed.

"At least put the handcuffs on her."

"Plenty of time for that later. Lighten up, Anita." Suni smiled at Maya. "You want to know why we've been messing with your friend's head, don't you?"

Maya nodded.

Suni lowered her voice. "Would you like me to tell you?"

Maya nodded again. Suni's voice was so quiet she had to lean forward to hear her.

"Would you like us to share our deepest, darkest secrets?"

Maya frowned.

"You have to say yes," Suni said. "Think of it like a game. Like twenty questions."

Forced to play along, Maya said, "Yes."

"We've messed with Jade till all she wants to do is die," Suni said.

Maya flinched. "Why?"

"Because we can." Suni's matter-of-fact tone was chilling.

"And it's enjoyable," Anita added.

"Jade is poised in that moment where all she wants to do is let go. We've brought her to the edge of a cliff. She craves peace. She feels worthless. She's one step away from death." Suni spoke like a detached social worker discussing a case. Maya bit her lip. Suni's mindset scared her.

"Are you interested in death?" Maya asked her.

Suni's eyes glittered. "She's trying to analyze me," she said to Anita.

Anita stared coldly at Maya. "I don't like therapists."

"Oh? Why's that?" Maya asked, sounding very much like a therapist.

"She didn't like the diagnosis our psychiatrist gave us," Suni said. "He didn't have a clue, to be honest."

"What was his diagnosis?"

"Narcissist. He said we were a narcissist."

Maya noted that Suni referred to herself and her twin as if they were one entity.

"When was that?" she asked.

"We were nine," Suni said.

"I'm getting bored, Suni." Anita shifted on the couch. She looked at her watch.

Maya sensed the conversation was hitting a nerve. She longed to ask why the twins were referred to a therapist at nine years old, but they might shut down if she pushed it. It was important to keep them talking.

"How did you get Jade into the state she is now?" Maya asked quietly.

"So sweet of you to show an interest," Suni said. "Oh, for God's sake, throw some more logs on that fire, Anita. It's freezing in here. I wanted to go to Cornwall. I've heard it's beautiful and there are some very sharp rocks."

Anita rolled her eyes. "Not nearly isolated enough." She got up, stretched, and walked to the stove.

"What were we talking about? Oh yes, how to bring someone to the brink of suicide. Have you ever wondered how you could make someone think they're going crazy?" Suni asked.

"Funnily enough, no, I haven't," Maya said sarcastically.

Suni looked pleased. Maya regretted letting herself be provoked.

Anita had perked up too. She opened the stove door and shuffled the logs inside with a poker.

"To control someone properly you need to isolate them." Suni was sitting neatly on the couch. Everything about her was precise. She watched Maya's face carefully as she spoke. "That's easy in the first stages of lust. We're blessed with magnetism. It draws women to us. The next step is to start doctoring the subject's food and drink. Different drugs are useful for different purposes. Hallucinogens are invaluable, but so too are amphetamines because they quickly deplete the body and deprive your subject of sleep. Sleep deprivation and drug combinations are the fastest way to confuse and disorientate someone. It's important that your ability to control the subject isn't disturbed. Jade was perfect because she's unemployed, she's got no family here, and she has the worst best friend in the world."

Maya's flesh crawled. Suni was talking about Jade like she was a lab rat.

Anita shut the wood stove door and got up.

"Jade was an interesting subject," Suni said. "She was stable when we started. It took a bit of digging to find her weaknesses. She's trusting, and she's suggestible. And of course, like everyone, she had ancient pain we could unleash." Suni sat forward. "You don't want to do that too early, Maya. It can work against you. You need to work on the confusion until your subject's reality is distorted. If you do it right, she won't know if it's night or day."

Anita walked to Maya's chair and sat on the arm. "It's not hard."

"I love how everyone thinks technology's their friend," Suni said. "Tell me this, Maya, what's Tony's cell number?"

Maya frowned. She didn't know.

"You wouldn't be able to tell if I went in and edited your contacts, would you? Poor Jade was so disappointed that Tony never replied to her. And she was driven mad by all the texts and calls from people she didn't know. She smashed her own phone in the end."

"I still don't understand why you're doing this," Maya said.

Anita leaned in. "I love the dark recesses of the mind. Some people enjoy physical torture, but it doesn't interest me. I like to see all the twists and turns. I love seeing how uncomfortable you are right now. I love that you're trying to hide it."

"We've made a study of the human psyche under pressure," Suni said.

Anita smiled at Maya. "Where's Tony?" she asked.

Maya tensed.

"You don't know, do you?" Anita laughed in a way that chilled Maya to the bone.

Suni reached down beside the sofa. "We read your texts. Before we did this to your phone." She held up the remnants of a cell phone. She tossed the pieces into Maya's lap.

Maya stared down at them. The phone had been smashed into so many pieces it was hard to tell if it was hers or not. The case, or what was left of it, looked familiar.

"Is it kinder to leave someone with a ray of hope?" Suni asked her sister.

Anita watched Maya's face carefully. "No, Suni, I don't think so. Maya, you can stop worrying about your miserable excuse for a girlfriend. Tony isn't coming to rescue you anytime soon."

The words hit Maya like a blow to the chest.

Anita stood up. "I'll put this with the other contraband," she said, brandishing the poker at Suni.

Maya palmed several pieces of her phone and then let her arms go slack. She wanted the twins to think she was overcome by despair. She didn't have to act that hard. Despair threatened to overwhelm her.

"You see that, right there. That's your vulnerability, Maya, your terrible fear about what's happened to Tony." Suni wet her lips with the tip of her tongue. "That's currency to us."

Maya clenched her teeth. "Where are your moral boundaries? Do you have any empathy?"

"Now you're thinking like a scientist, Maya." Suni looked at her coldly. "Or to be more precise, like a psychiatrist. Next you'll be asking if we're a sociopath." She shared a smile with her sister. "You single people are very *single* minded. That's your limitation."

"I'm not single. I'm with Tony." *Or I was. God, make Tony still be alive.*

"Not single like that," Suni said. "I mean you single unit people. You people that don't have a twin. You irrelevant people. You arrogantly treat us like *we're* the strange ones. I never wanted to have a bond with any of you, except for mamaji, our mother. Tell me, when did you stop caring about your dolls' feelings?"

Maya blinked in confusion. "I…I can't remember."

"When you realized your dolls were unimportant. When our mother passed away we lost interest in you people altogether. Except for studying you. Your feelings are interesting but insignificant. They're nothing compared to what we can achieve with our bond, are they, Anita?"

Anita pursed her lips. "If you say so, Suni."

"But isn't it all about our bond? About us, separate from the world?" Suni asked.

"If you like," Anita said quietly.

"We need to talk later. We're coming back to this conversation," Suni said. Then she turned to Maya. "You disappoint me. I'd hoped for more from you, what with your degree in psychology."

"How do you know about that?" Maya asked.

Suni and Anita laughed. "We checked you out, all of you. We checked everyone out at that sad little clinic. As soon as I met Jade, we checked her out too, and Tony. How long did it take you to look into my background, Maya? Two months?" Suni said.

Maya didn't say anything.

"I'd completely forgotten about that award Telitha won," Anita grumbled from the corner.

"Yeah, but hurray for Facebook. Thank God she got cold feet about maligning my good name." Suni grinned at Maya. "She sent me the sweetest message. Gave us just enough time to leave before you caught up with us. You found the address then?"

Maya stared at her.

"It was a bit of a risk, getting you to come up here." Anita stood up.

"But less of a risk than leaving you in London, armed with information," Suni said.

"But I don't have much information," Maya said. "I don't really know anything. Listen, why don't you both just go? We're miles from anywhere. By the time someone found us, you could have completely disappeared."

The twins stared at her.

"Surely that's the easiest way out," Maya said quietly.

Suni looked like she was considering the idea.

"Yeah, but what would be the fun in that?" she said.

Anita shook her head again. "That was sad. See, Sunita, she's not that interesting. We might as well drug her."

"I don't want to drug her," Suni said sharply. "I'm enjoying the conversation. I want to talk about her uncle." Suni watched for Maya's reaction.

Anita sighed. She went through into the kitchen area. There was the sound of a kettle boiling.

A shuffling noise came from the other side of the room.

Suni and Maya turned toward the bedroom. Jade was swaying in the doorway.

Suni leapt up.

It was just the distraction Maya needed. She slipped all the pieces of plastic and metal in her hand into the front pocket of her jeans.

Anita rushed through from the kitchen. "For God's sake, Suni. I told you to cuff her."

"I didn't think I needed to. I'm amazed she can stand, let alone walk," Suni snapped.

Maya quickly felt along the sides of the chair.

"I need some water," Jade said. Her voice was rough.

Suni steered Jade back into the bedroom.

Maya's fingers wrapped around a slim object under the seat cushion. She shoved it into her jeans pocket quickly.

Anita turned back.

Maya prayed she hadn't seen her hand move.

Anita pointed the pistol at her. "Get in there with Jade."

Maya walked cautiously past Anita and then into the bedroom.

Jade was lying back down on the bed. Suni was fastening a pair of handcuffs onto her wrists.

Anita waved the gun at the second single bed. "If you don't mind," she said tersely.

Maya went to the bed.

"We need to speed this up," Anita muttered to Suni.

Suni clipped another set of handcuffs over Maya's wrists.

Maya stared coldly at her.

"Why don't you relax? We won't keep you long," Suni said, then she followed her sister out of the door.

The door shut.

The key was turned.

❖

Tony floored the accelerator. The small hire car responded briskly. Tony drove as fast as she dared in the rainy conditions. Misty purple mountains rose in the far distance. Forested hills flanked either side of the two-lane Scottish A-road. The scenery was a blur of green and gray through steady drizzle that fell from the blanketed sky. The car had inbuilt satellite navigation, so Tony didn't have to think about which route to take. Unfortunately, that left her plenty of headspace to worry herself sick.

Felicia buzzed into the front passenger seat. "I think I've just helped your girlfriend."

"Maya?" Tony asked.

"If that's her name. Jade isn't coherent. I can't get a proper handle on what's going on in the cabin."

"You can't see for yourself?"

"That's what I just said, didn't I?"

Deirdre shifted in the backseat. "Jade can't see ghosts, so most ghosts that connect through her won't get any visuals, just sounds."

Tony glared at her in the rearview mirror. She was annoyed with her spirit guide.

"How did you help Maya? What's going on at the cabin?" Tony asked Felicia.

"I nagged at Jade until she went and interrupted Suni. That bought Maya a few minutes to stick her hands down the chair cushions."

Tony frowned. "How does that help exactly?"

"There's a tiny screwdriver there. It fell out of a cracker last Christmas."

Tony grunted. "How on earth do you know that?" she asked.

Felicia shrugged. "I think I'm psychic now that I'm dead. I didn't used to be."

"Our connections with the world of the living are random," Deirdre chipped in. "You never know what you're going to get. I wanted to be assigned to a cultured Simon Templar kind of medium. Instead I get Bruce Willis in a vest, but with less muscles."

The rain was coming down harder. Tony flipped the headlights on.

"Why does she need a little screwdriver?" Tony said. Sometimes talking to ghosts was like pulling teeth.

"I'm not sure exactly. I think Suni has a gun, though."

Tony tensed. She didn't bother asking what use a tiny screwdriver would be against a gun; she was too busy keeping herself from screaming. "I'll never forgive myself if something happens to them. I can't believe I let my phone battery run down. Why didn't I go see

Jade? I'm so damn selfish. I should have listened to Maya. She tried to tell me."

Deirdre took a deep breath. "Calm down, Toots. You were off saving Rose. She'd probably be sitting next to me in the back of this sardine can if you hadn't rushed off to help her."

Tony narrowed her eyes at Deirdre. "Thanks, but I'm still cross with you."

Deirdre screwed up her forehead. "Why?"

"You didn't warn me about Jade."

"I didn't know. I wouldn't let anything happen to Jade. Well, not if I was allowed to intervene."

"What does that mean?"

"Never you mind. Anyway, I'm a spirit guide not an angel. You need to take charge of your own destiny." Deirdre's voice was as matter-of-fact as usual, but there was a slight edge to it. Tony suspected Deirdre was worried.

Tony filed the spirit guide not angel comment away to think about later. "Are you sure Suni has a gun?" she asked Felicia.

"No," Felicia said casually. She was avidly watching the road ahead. "I've never seen such a cold, wet place. Everything they said about England is true."

"This is Scotland. And sometimes it's sunny in Scotland," Tony muttered.

Felicia didn't look like she believed Tony for a minute. "I've got a strong feeling there's a gun, that's all. It's foggy back there."

"God, really? That won't help. The rain's bad enough."

"She means the connection's foggy. She can't see, remember? Just hear." Deirdre spoke up over the sat nav's spoken commands. It was indicating a turnoff onto another A-road, one mile ahead.

"It's like a bad phone connection. Drifts in and out. Jade's doped up. I had to shout and shout in your girlfriend's direction so she would find the screwdriver."

Tony took a deep breath. She was frantic, and ridiculous talk about stupid objects wasn't helping. "What if I don't get there in time? I don't know whether to phone the police or not." She peered at the mile counter on the sat nav. "I'm still thirty miles away."

"Why don't you phone Sergeant Pepper-Spray? She bats for the Sapphic All-Stars, didn't you say?"

Tony thought for a minute. "That's not a bad idea. She'll think even less of me, but that doesn't matter. Deirdre, can you read the number? It's on a screwed up piece of paper in my back pocket."

A second later, Tony felt a tingle in the pocket area.

"Carol Lewis: 06849 338461," Deirdre said in a muffled voice.

Tony didn't want to think about Deirdre's muffled voice too hard. Instead, she activated her Bluetooth voice command and recited the number. There was a ringing tone before the call was picked up.

"Is that Sergeant Carol? I mean is that Sergeant Lewis?"

"Who is this?"

"Tony Carson, the private investigator. We met last night. Well, this morning really. I was the—"

"I know who you are. I didn't expect to hear from you so quickly. Are you driving?"

"Yes."

The sat nav interrupted with a command. "Left turn ahead onto the A811."

"Are you on a hands-free phone?" Sergeant Lewis asked.

"Yes, Sergeant. A Bluetooth one." Tony felt like she was talking to her school headmistress. She remembered Mrs. Tennyson fondly. She was attractive in a strict kind of way.

"Okay. It's better not to talk on the phone at all when driving. Can you pull over?"

"Um. I've got an emergency situation. That's why I'm calling."

"What's wrong?"

"My girlfriend and my best friend might be in danger," Tony said.

"In danger how?"

"They're in a wood cabin in Scotland, well, Jade is. That's my best friend. She went there with her girlfriend. Or she may have been abducted there. My girlfriend Maya thinks Jade's been taken there against her will. Maya's gone to help her, but I haven't heard from her, and I'm getting unobtainable from her phone now."

There was silence from the other end of the line. Then Sergeant Lewis cleared her throat. "But why do you think they're in danger?"

"Suni might have a gun."

"So why haven't you dialed 999?"

"Because…I'm not sure." Tony realized she couldn't tell Sergeant

Lewis how she knew about the possible gun. "Maya got one last text out before her phone went dead. She said she thought Suni had a gun."

"Is she unstable?"

"Maya? No. She had a nasty shock earlier in the year, and she's been a bit quiet lately, but she's all right—"

"I meant this Suni woman. Who is she anyway?"

"Jade's girlfriend. A very new girlfriend that none of us know. Her last girlfriend committed suicide so she probably is unstable, and she was caught trying to slip drugs into another girlfriend's drink."

"How do you know this?"

God, why did she have to ask so many questions? "Maya found out," Tony said. She had listened to all the messages Maya had left on her phone, detailing the very worrying information about Suni. Tony slowed to take the left turn. She glanced quickly at the sign to make sure it was the right road, even though the sat nav was telling her to turn.

"Is she in your detective agency?" Sergeant Lewis asked.

"Maya?" Tony thought for a moment. Maya wasn't, but she should be. "Yes."

The line went quiet. Presumably Sergeant Lewis was thinking. The rain picked up. Tony flipped the wipers to the faster setting. She was driving along a densely forested area. The rain and the closed space either side of the road made visibility poor.

"Okay, I see your dilemma about bringing the proper authorities into the situation at present," Sergeant Lewis said. "What is the location?"

Tony gave her the address.

"What's Suni's last name?"

Tony thought. "I don't know. She's an acupuncturist and a masseuse. She works at the Blue Water Clinic in Stoke Newington."

"Okay. Description?"

"It's a small building just off Church Street."

Sergeant Lewis grunted. "Of the woman, Tony. I need a description of Suni, and as there may be a firearm involved you'd better describe your friend and girlfriend as well."

"I've never met Suni."

"Oh for God's sake."

Tony thought that Sergeant Lewis could use a bit more patience. "Well, Jade's only just met her. And she went off the radar. I should have made more effort to see her. I can't help feeling this is all my fault."

"There's no time for your self-indulgent guilt. You're supposed to be a private investigator. Pull yourself together and think."

Tony swallowed. "She's Indian, she's got short hair. She's gorgeous, apparently. She's boyish or soft butch, or at least she must be if Jade fancies her."

Sergeant Lewis made an exasperated sound. "Not sure what I can do with a description like that, but it's better than nothing I suppose. There may be a photo of her on the clinic website. I'll look. What about your friends?"

As Tony described Maya and Jade, she eased out a deep breath. Giving the information to Sergeant Lewis was reassuring. Tony felt much better with someone else, someone living, involved. And someone who could really help if it all went horribly wrong.

"Right. Leave this with me. I've got a mate in the Scottish Police. I'll run this past her. Meantime you go to the cabin and assess the situation. Hopefully, you'll get there and they'll all be sitting on the porch, having a chat and a cup of tea."

A deer leapt out of nowhere in front of the car.

Tony hit the brakes.

There was a horrible screech. The car slid on the wet road.

Tony took her foot off the brake and swerved hard.

The deer bounded off.

"What's happening?" Sergeant Lewis sounded worried.

"A deer jumped in front of the car. It's all right, though. I avoided it." Tony's heart hammered in her chest.

"Are you okay?"

"Yes," Tony said, breathing hard.

"Get off the phone then. And slow down. You'll be no help to your friends if you wreck the car. Drive carefully. Let me know what's happening as soon as you get there. Don't you dare forget."

Tony dropped her speed. She kept her eyes fixed on the road ahead, glancing to each side occasionally to check for kamikaze deer. "I won't. Thank you so much, Sergeant Lewis."

"Carol. For God's sake call me Carol."

Tony glanced at the two ghosts. They were both staring wide-eyed ahead, mouths open, their bodies tense as boards.

"What are you two scared of?" Tony asked. "It's not like anything can happen to you."

Deirdre snorted. "My life flashed before my eyes then. I hate it when that happens. Mind you, I did get a glimpse of a hot scene in the St. Mark's bathhouse that I wouldn't mind reliving." She sighed deeply. "Oh well, those days and that particular position will probably never come again."

❖

Maya brought both cuffed hands up to her front right jeans pocket until she could get her fingers inside. She pulled out all the bits of the phone and tossed them onto the bed. She shuffled around until she was in a position to search through the pieces. She was looking for anything she could use as a shim.

With the tips of her fingers, she worked a rectangular bit of thin metal off a chunk of circuit board.

It was her bad luck that the solder was good and the bit of metal was practically welded to the PCB.

Ignoring the pain in her wrists, she worked away until finally she pried it loose.

She lined the shim over the locking mechanism of the handcuffs, resting the top edge against the first knuckle of her right thumb. She pressed the shim down between the lock and the teeth.

With the tip of her thumb, she tightened the cuff one notch.

She pushed the shim down further and heard the satisfying click of the lock opening.

She slipped her right hand out of the cuff and then shimmed the left cuff open.

Glancing at the door, Maya eased out her cramped wrists and flexed her fingers. At that moment she was insanely pleased that Suni and Anita's modus operandi was to isolate their girlfriends. If Maya had had more contact with them, they might have known about Maya's escapology skills.

Jade was lying flat out on the other bed. Her eyes were open.

Not daring to speak, Maya stood up. She put a finger to her own lips and walked into Jade's line of vision.

Jade's eyes widened, but she didn't say a word. Her eyes traveled down Maya's body. When she saw her free hands, Jade's eyes widened again and her chest swelled with a deep breath.

Maya sat on the edge of Jade's bed. She slipped the shim into the lock mechanism on each of Jade's handcuffs and unlocked them.

Jade sat up, gingerly rubbing her wrists.

"We have to get out of here," Maya whispered. "How do you feel? Can you walk?"

Jade blinked. "Walk?"

Maya sighed. Jade looked confused. She was staring at Maya like Maya was speaking in a language she didn't understand. "We're going to have to climb out of the window. I need to pick the lock first," Maya said.

Jade slowly turned her head toward the window and peered at it.

Maya grabbed the tiny screwdriver she'd pulled out of the side of the armchair.

At the window, she pushed the small flat blade into the lock. She jiggled it, then twisted it.

Nothing happened.

It wasn't as cheap a lock as she'd thought. Maya wanted to jam the screwdriver into the lock and try to force it open, but she knew she could break the blade. If her lock-picking tutor had taught her anything it was that patience won the day.

She tried pushing and turning.

Then she bent the blade at forty-five degrees to the lock. She twisted it again.

Click. The lock barrel withdrew.

Maya let out her breath.

She looked out the window and couldn't see anything except trees and driving rain.

Maya's jacket was in her rental car. The twins had emptied her pockets and taken the car keys.

"Do you have a coat?" she whispered to Jade.

Jade stared back at her. "I don't think so."

"Jesus. Well, we've got no choice. We're going to have to go out in that weather like this. We're lucky they didn't take our shoes."

Cautiously, Maya pushed up the bottom sash window.

There was nobody around.

She beckoned to Jade to come stand beside her.

Jade didn't move.

Maya grabbed her and pulled her to the window.

"You go first. Head up that slope, straight ahead. Get behind the trees. I'll be right behind you. If I'm not, keep going. Get help."

Jade looked at Maya, then she looked out the window. Maya was just thinking she'd have to push Jade out the window when Jade nodded grimly. Maya helped her onto the ledge.

Jade swayed for a moment in the open window.

Then she jumped.

She landed like a cat on the stone path outside.

As Maya heaved herself up, she heard voices outside the bedroom door.

Jade inhaled sharply. Maybe the rain hitting her face woke her up because she began to move slowly away from the house, up the slope.

Maya practically vaulted through the window, then closed it behind her in the hope of hiding which way they went.

Rain soaked her to the skin as she pushed uphill. She grabbed Jade's hand as she caught up to her, forcing Jade to run.

Maya half dragged Jade behind her as she headed for a thick pine tree at the top of the slope.

❖

The wood was dense with no clear paths, and it continued uphill as far into the distance as Maya could see. The forest floor was a knotted mass of tree roots and blackberry bushes. Maya's lungs were exploding in her chest.

Jade went down.

Wrenched backward, Maya fell too.

She stumbled to her knees, panting.

Jade sat up on the ground looking dazed. She pulled her ankle free from a blackberry stem that had snaked around her ankle. She winced.

"Have you hurt your foot?" Maya was desperate for Jade to say she was okay.

Jade bit her lip. "It hurts. Yes. Why are we running? Where are we?" she asked.

Maya wanted to sob. "Jade, think. Is there another route? Can you remember anything from the journey?"

Jade looked blankly at her.

There was no way they could keep going uphill through the dense woods.

"What's wrong with me? I feel weird. Am I ill?"

Maya pulled her attention back to Jade. "Those bastards have pumped you full of drugs. That's why you feel so odd."

"What bastards? Do you mean the two Sunis?"

"Yeah. The two bitches from hell," Maya muttered. Maybe the trail was clearer in the opposite direction. They'd have to skirt the cabin. Maya stood up, putting a hand out to Jade.

"They are kinda bitches." Jade took her hand and pulled herself stiffly to her feet.

"Let's try this way." Maya turned.

She led them down the slope. Jade limped beside her. Even though it was downhill, their progress was slower than before.

Maya scrutinized the forest for any other signs of movement. Apart from the steady drip of rain, it was quiet. At least the dense foliage was keeping them relatively dry.

Jade's skin looked sallow in the weird gray-green light that filtered through the trees. Even though Jade struggling, Maya needed to ask the thing she dreaded most. "Jade, did they kill Tony? Is she dead?"

Jade froze. She looked terrified. "Do you think that too?"

Maya bit back a wave of nausea. Her mind couldn't grasp the idea that Tony had been murdered. The only thing she could do was keep going. She pulled Jade forward.

At the bottom of the slope, the trees began to thin out. Maya branched out to the right, keeping well away from the cabin.

The canopy opened up, throwing more light and more rain at them.

They pushed through a line of trees and came face-to-face with a—

A huge lake.

It was massive. There was no way across, and no boats within view.

Jade stared out over the water. Her eyelids drooped like she was struggling to stay awake.

Maya took a breath and thought. She looked left. A way off was the cabin, and the road. The twins had taken her keys. She couldn't hot-wire the rental car because it was too new. The immobilizer would kick in if she tried.

"Maybe if we can get to that road..." Maya thought aloud.

Jade followed her gaze. "We can be spotted from a road."

"Shit. You're damn right. They've got a vehicle. They could easily pick us off on the road. In fact, it's probably the first place they'll look. We need to stay away from it." Maya checked out the route beyond Jade. It looked like the forest gave way a few meters ahead. She nodded in that direction. "That way, then."

Gently but firmly pulling Jade, Maya picked her way over the sodden ground between the loch and the forest. Their shoes were quickly caked in mud. Rain soaked through Maya's sweater right to the skin. Her jeans were wet and getting heavier by the minute. Jade was panting hard. She was still limping and looked to be in pain. The wind near the water's edge was strong. Maya was so bitterly cold it hurt.

They rounded a corner and saw a track ahead cutting through the forest. On the other side of the track, the forest sloped downward.

By the time they reached the track, Maya could see the slope was more of a ravine. It was a steep drop to a raging stream running parallel with the track. The stream was about six meters wide, and white with fast-running foamy water. The track was their only option.

Keeping away from the ravine, Maya led them forward. Maya walked as quickly as she could, checking that Jade was okay with the pace. They needed to keep moving to keep warm.

Maya thought back to her journey. It had been nighttime. She'd felt like she'd been driving for ages in the middle of nowhere. She racked her brains to remember any buildings she'd passed close to the cabin. She hadn't taken much notice. She'd kept her eyes on the dark, badly lit road. She thought she'd maybe passed an inn just before she'd turned onto the forest road. She hoped to hell the track was running in the same direction as the road. That way they'd be walking vaguely in the direction of the inn.

"Hey, girls. You're going the wrong way."

Maya turned.

One of the twins was four steps behind them, a gun trained on Maya's chest.

"This is Suni's damn mess. I'd like to shoot you both here, but I can't. Any fool could come by and see your bodies." Anita took two steps closer and raised the gun to Maya's head. "Turn around. Get in front of me. Keep walking till you hit a lake."

❖

Finally, Tony was on the small road to Pine Lodge cabin. The rain was coming down hard. Tony had her headlights on full beam and she still had to crouch over the windscreen to see the road ahead.

She passed a warm and dry looking building called the Lochside Inn. Both ghosts were still with her. Neither had said anything for ages. Tony wondered if that was why people thought ghosts were spooky. Then she remembered, most people couldn't see them.

A mile after the Lochside Inn, the road turned into two rough tracks. Tony ground to a halt. The sat nav was as silent as the ghosts beside her.

She stared left and right, not knowing which way to go. She wound down her window and got drenched but couldn't see any signs for the cabin.

She thought that the left fork looked like the straightest route. She started toward it.

"No, go to the right." Deirdre sprang to life in the backseat.

"Are you sure?" Tony frowned. The left fork looked a lot more likely.

"Yes, I'm sure. Go right."

Tony didn't want to waste time. Deirdre hadn't let her down so far. She took the right fork.

The sat nav woke up from searching for a signal. "Turn around when possible," it declared.

"I told you," Tony said.

She stopped again and prepared to do a U-turn.

"This is the right way." Deirdre leaned over from the back. Tony couldn't feel Deirdre's body any closer, but her voice was louder. "You definitely need to go up this road. Trust me."

Tony released the clutch and continued up the track.

The track carried on straight for about two hundred meters, traveling along the edge of a forest. Then it bent round to the left, running into the heart of the forest. A dark, dense network of pine trees fanned out on either side. The only area of light was over the track itself.

Tony saw some figures on the horizon ahead.

"Pull over," Deirdre said.

"What?" Tony.

"No time to explain. You need to tuck the car away. Drive onto that open bit, just off the road. Then head through the trees as quietly as you can until you're nearly on them. Make sure they don't see you."

Tony peered into the tangle of pine trees and bracken. Then she stole a look at the sky above. Rain was pouring out of it. "Why?" she asked.

"Just do it. You'll see why." Deirdre's voice was urgent.

Tony pulled the car off the road and jumped out.

"Grab the tire iron from the boot. You'll need it." Deirdre padded to her side.

Tony didn't argue. She opened the boot, pulled off the carpet matting, and prised the tire iron out of the mini spare wheel kit.

Deirdre had said *Make sure they don't see you.* Keeping an eye on the track, she headed into the forest slightly and then walked parallel to the road.

The thick overhang kept the rain off, but it was dark in the woods. She stumbled over a branch.

She slowed down. As she walked on, she glimpsed a huddle of people on the track. She stopped.

They were walking slowly. Two in line and one behind. Tony crept nearer.

It was Maya and Jade. Relief flooded through her as she realized they were both still alive.

Then she saw the gun in the hand of the Indian woman walking behind them. That had to be Suni. Now Tony understood Deirdre's instructions. She needed to stay behind Suni.

Stepping lightly, she threaded between a group of oak trees.

Snap! A twig broke underfoot.

Tony froze.

She leaned into the girth of the nearest tree, praying she couldn't be seen from the track. She heard the murmur of voices. The group kept walking. Cautiously, she took a step out from behind the oak tree.

Suni was just a few meters away. Gripping the tire iron, Tony edged closer. As she took a step onto the track, Felicia floated past her, slipped through Suni's body, and whispered something in Jade's ear.

Jade turned and saw Tony. She looked shocked but spoke to Suni. "Felicia said to say hi," she said.

"What?" Suni stopped. Her shoulders tensed.

Maya turned. Her eyes darted to Tony. Her jaw dropped. Tony took three steps and smashed the tire iron onto Suni's head. She went down.

Maya grabbed the gun.

"Christ! I thought you were a ghost till you hit her," she said.

Jade stared at her with big bleary eyes. "Are you alive?" she asked.

What was wrong with them? "Yes," Tony said impatiently. "Point that gun at her. I'm going to get the car. Wait here." She tossed her mobile at Jade. "Call this person—Sergeant Lewis. Tell her what's happened."

Tony ran back to the car and reversed it.

"I was tempted to run her over," she muttered as she got out. "Let's get her into the backseat."

For some reason, Maya was talking on the mobile phone and Jade was staring down at Suni.

Maya cupped her hand over the phone. "Jade's drugged. She's confused."

"Okay. Tell Carol we'll meet the police at the proper road, where it forks into the two tracks."

Maya nodded. Jade walked to the car, limping, and got in. Tony grabbed hold of Suni and shoved her into the back of the car. Maya got in next to her with the pistol in her hand.

"I don't want you to sit there," Tony said. "You drive."

"Don't even go there, Tony. Have you fired a gun?"

Tony shook her head.

"Well, then." Maya didn't wait for an answer. "Let's go," she said.

Tony drove as fast as she dared. She wouldn't be able to relax until the would-be murderer was in custody.

Maya was talking to Carol Lewis. There was a groaning noise from the back.

Tony looked in the rear view mirror. Suni was stirring. Maya pointed the pistol at her. She tossed the phone down, looking grim. Tony floored the pedal. The fork was just ahead.

A woman stepped out of the woods onto the track ahead and stood right in the middle of the road. Tony screeched to a halt.

She blinked. She couldn't believe her eyes. The woman was Suni. She had a gun pointed straight at the car.

"What the hell?"

"There are two of them. Twins," Maya shouted as Tony dived out of the driver's door.

The pistol exploded. The noise rang sharply through the forest. The windscreen shattered.

Tony ran at the other Suni. She was staring into the barrel of her gun and then Suni went down as Jade ramrodded her from the other side.

Suddenly, Maya was standing over the other Suni with the other gun. "On your knees, bitch," she said.

"Who the hell is that?" Tony asked.

"Suni," Jade said grimly.

"Well, who's the other one?" Tony stabbed her thumb in the direction of the hire car.

"Her sister, Anita."

The track ahead was ablaze with lights and sirens. Armed police ran toward them.

Tony saw Maya drop the gun and raise her hands, and then she was face first on the ground surrounded by policemen, for the second time in as many days.

❖

Tony sat at the foot of a double bed with a black-and-white bedspread on it, drying her hair with a towel.

They'd been interviewed by the police for several hours and Jade had been seen at the local hospital. The consultant had insisted on keeping her in overnight for observation. Jade had flatly refused. Once her vital signs were confirmed as stable she was allowed to leave.

They'd headed straight for the Lochside Shopping Centre to buy dry clothes. From there, they'd checked into the nearest hotel. It was a chain. As long as Tony could get dry, get a shower, and get a meal, she didn't care.

They were all exhausted. Jade had declined dinner and gone straight to her room.

A wave of tiredness hit Tony. It competed for her attention with the hunger nagging at her belly.

Maya stepped through the bathroom door, fanning steam into the room. Her long dark hair dripped water down her naked back. She had a white towel rather modestly draped around her waist. Tony couldn't keep her eyes off her.

Maya dipped her eyes and smiled a sexy smile. She lay on the bed next to Tony and rested her head on Tony's knees. Tony stroked Maya's cheek. Looking down at her, Tony swallowed. She couldn't bear to think what had nearly happened.

"I could have lost you," she murmured.

Maya opened her eyes. "I thought I had lost you." She stretched and sat up. "I thought they'd murdered you. I imagined all sorts."

Tony shook her head. "What a sick pair they are." Her stomach tightened. Suni was in custody. She was the twin that had shot up the windscreen. But in the confusion when the police arrived, Anita had escaped.

"Do you think they'll tell us if they catch Anita?" Maya asked.

"Sergeant Lewis will," Tony said.

"They scared me," Maya murmured.

"Of course they did."

"No, I mean, on a deep level. I asked them why they were drugging and controlling Jade. Their explanation was that they enjoyed it."

Tony swallowed. "Do you think there's ever an explanation for behavior like that?"

Maya bit her lip. "They played with me. It was a game to them. When I didn't know where you were, they jumped on that and used it. They were completely in sync. One sociopath is frightening enough, but two, working together..." She shuddered.

"If we don't know why people do stuff like that, it is terrifying. How do you help someone like that? We can't even really punish them," Tony said.

Maya's eyes widened. "Tony Carson, that is very thoughtful."

Tony smiled. "And if you don't mind me saying so, that's why you're drawn to psychology. I have no idea what your childhood felt like, but I do know you need to understand why your father was how he was. And you need to make sense of your mother, for that matter."

Maya exhaled. "Well, that would have been more empowering if you'd coached me to come to that conclusion myself. But, basically, you're not wrong."

Tony came in for a nuzzle. "All that communication and analysis must be rubbing off on me," she mouthed into Maya's lips.

Maya snuggled right into Tony. Then she started kissing Tony's hair, breathing warm air into Tony's ear.

Tony's body responded with a vengeance. They hadn't been intimate since the gang incident. Tony wanted Maya badly.

She kissed her hard. Maya opened to her, pulling her down onto the bed.

"Suddenly, I couldn't care less about dinner," Maya said against Tony's lips.

"Me neither," Tony said.

There was a knock on the door. Tony wanted to ignore it. She wanted whoever it was to go away. The knocking came again.

Maya pulled back. She was breathing hard. "Maybe it's important."

There was another tentative knock. Tony grabbed a robe.

Jade stood in the corridor, smiling weakly at Tony. Tony waved her in.

"I know how ridiculous this sounds," she said. She looked lucid but still worse for wear. She swallowed. "Tony, I'm scared. That woman is still out there somewhere."

"You want to sleep in here, with us?" Tony asked.

Jade nodded.

"Of course," Maya said, getting up. The towel slipped right off her.

Jade looked startled. "I don't think I'm quite up to a threesome," she joked, smiling weakly again.

Maya quickly put a robe on.

"Do you want any dinner?" Tony asked.

Jade shook her head. "I just want to sleep. If I can."

"Well, this is a family room. And you are family. There's that single bed, or you can sleep in the double with Maya?"

"Or with Tony," Maya said quickly.

"Such an obliging couple. Always quick to offer each other up to anyone who comes knocking," Jade said. She was joking like she always did, but her eyes were flat. "I'll be fine over there, guys. Thank you."

Jade went over to the single bed, got in, and pulled the covers up.

Maya sat on the edge of Jade's bed. She stroked Jade's arm. Jade's breathing slowed, and her face relaxed.

Tony's tummy rumbled.

"Room service?" she whispered to Maya.

Maya nodded.

❖

When Tony and Maya woke, Jade had already got up. She wasn't at breakfast.

Tony found her in the grounds of the hotel, sitting on a bench, her face up to the sun. The rain of the previous day had melted away. It was clear and bright, and warm enough to sit comfortably in a T-shirt. Jade was wrapped up in a tight-fitting fleece, zipped up to the neck.

"I wondered where you were. Did you go to breakfast early?" Tony asked. She sat next to Jade on the bench. It looked out to green rolling fields, where shaggy brown cows chewed lush grass.

Jade smiled. The smile didn't chase the sadness from her eyes. "I'm not hungry. I feel weird." She spoke quietly, like she had no energy.

"I'm not surprised. Maya said they've been pumping you full of all kinds of drugs."

Jade's eyelids flipped shut for a second. "I can't think straight. My brain can't handle much." Jade's lip trembled.

"Jade, I really screwed up," Tony said. "I wasn't there for you."

Jade shrugged. "Maya said they changed my phone details and hid my tablet."

"Yeah, they did. That didn't help. But I should have come to see you." Tony swallowed. "Jade, something happened the night we saved Repo."

Jade held her gaze.

"They threatened me, those boys. They threatened to rape me." Tony spoke low. She stumbled over the words. "They didn't. Well, one of them groped me, my breasts, my…groin area." She wanted to find the youth all over again and beat him senseless. "Bastard."

Jade looked at Tony with horror. "I didn't know, Tony…" She trailed off, her voice choked with tears.

Tony took her hand. "I know you didn't. I couldn't tell you. That night I was ashamed. And then, oh, Jade, I can't explain it, but I shut down. And this is awful, I blamed you somehow."

"Me?" Jade sounded like a child.

"I'm sorry. I'm so sorry. I know it wasn't your fault. Of course it wasn't, but when I knew you were there at the time, talking to Repo, maybe watching…" Tony couldn't carry on speaking. Nausea rose in her throat.

Jade squeezed her hand. "I wanted to come to you straight away. I knew I should have." She was angry. "I believed that ghost boy. He said the gang wouldn't listen to me; they'd only listen to Repo. That's why I didn't come to you. And I didn't see anything, not when I was on the walkway. I would have come down there and kicked their arses, man."

Tony smiled. "That's what *I* should have done," she said quietly.

"Tony, you did what you could. You kept yourself safe, didn't you?"

Tony shrugged. "I suppose so, but you had to rescue me. I shouldn't have gone there on my own. I was stupid."

Jade blew air through her lips. "You've been stupid for a long time," she joked, then she caught Tony's eye. "You want to talk stupid? How about trusting a woman who turns out to be an evil twin, whose twin is just as evil? You weren't stupid. Reckless, maybe."

Tony nodded. "Yeah. Well, that's something for me to think about. And how I closed down to you. You're family. You're everything to me, Jade."

Jade pulled Tony to her. Jade's body was trembling. Tony wasn't scared of that bitch Anita. If she came anywhere near Maya or Jade, Tony would act first, answer to the police later.

"It's lovely to be hugged so tight, but your grip is ridiculously strong, and I think my ribs are starting to bruise," Jade mumbled into Tony's shoulder.

Tony pulled back. "Sorry."

Jade sat back and cast an eye over the rolling hills. "Back home then?"

"Yep." Tony nodded once. She stood.

As Tony started walking back to the hotel, Jade slipped her arm through Tony's.

❖

Rose Henderson had been put in a side room off the main ward. She was sitting in the armchair next to her bed, leafing through a women's magazine.

She looked up when Tony came through the door and smiled.

Rose's face was shocking. It was a swollen mass of cuts and bruises. One eye was half shut. Both cheekbones and eye sockets were deeply bruised. The bruises were turning from dark purple to yellow. Her lips were cut and a dark bruise ran around her jawline.

"How are you feeling?" Tony asked in a hushed voice.

Rose rolled her eyes. "I *was* feeling fine until you rocked up and gave me the fragile treatment. This magazine is boring as hell, though. Do tell me you've brought a book of juicy lesbian stories. You know, the kind where they get down and dirty."

Tony laughed. "No, sorry."

Rose patted the bed. "Well, at least sit down and tell me a juicy lesbian story. I'm going out of my mind here. Everyone's very nice, they're treating me like royalty actually, but I just want to go home now. I'm going to discharge myself." She stared at Tony thoughtfully. "They won't let me go home by myself, even in a cab, but they might release me into your custody. Will you tell them you're going to look after me?"

"Sure, but don't you need someone to, I don't know, make sure you don't..."

"What? Have a fall and break my hip? Die in the night from the terrible shock of it all? Suddenly collapse from complications they didn't know about?"

"Well, yes," Tony said. "Any of the above."

Rose took a breath. "I'm fine, Tony. I bloody well hurt everywhere. That bastard got some kicks and punches in. He took me completely by surprise."

Tony sat on the bed. "What happened?" she asked.

Rose looked sheepish. "It was partly my own fault. I couldn't resist calling him, could I?"

Tony frowned. "You have his number?"

Rose grinned. "Yes. I've been calling him for years. I never say anything, just leave this heavy silence on the line. Drives him mad."

"You're a hoax caller," Tony said.

"Non-violent direct action, it was called in my time," Rose said.

Tony loved Rose's power. Even bruised and beaten, she was a gutsy woman.

"I couldn't resist telling him about the confession. I didn't think he could do anything. I had no idea he knew my address. That evening, I was watching the telly when I heard someone kicking the front door in. I ran out to the passage, and there he was, glaring at me. 'I've come to talk to you about that confession,' he said. 'I want it. Where is it?'

"That's when I knew he was Somers. 'It's in my bedroom,' I said. Of course it wasn't, but that's where my mobile phone was and I wanted to call the police. I bent to get it off the bedside table when he hit me from behind. He caught me off guard. All I remember as I went down, and the blows kept coming, was him saying, 'This is how your precious Frankie died, just like this. You can go and join her now, you bitch.'"

Tony swallowed. "That's horrible. Did you tell the police that?"

Rose shrugged. "I did. But I don't think they'll do anything."

"They might. I've got a contact in the police; she's in our gang," Tony said.

Rose raised her eyebrows. "What, in both our gang, yours and my gang?"

"She's a lesbian, yes. Anyway, she told me they've charged Somers with assault, and the Crown Prosecution Service is looking into the confession."

"Well, that's something. I'd love to see him get what's coming to him," Rose said, sinking back into the chair. "How did you get hold of that confession, anyway?"

Tony had devised an updated cover story. "I'm a private investigator. Somers worked with another guard, John Smith."

Rose looked thoughtful. "I remember that name from the early days of the campaign."

"His family found the letter addressed to you when they were clearing out Smith's house. They phoned my agency because they were worried about contacting you directly. Subsequently, they found the confession."

"So you lied to me, you naughty thing." Rose pretended to be annoyed. "I'm finding it hard to understand why Frankie said she'd made it up about Somers, when clearly she hadn't."

"Me too," Tony said. "I can only think she didn't want you to worry."

Rose looked sad for a moment. "Maybe. I suppose it doesn't matter now. What's really important is that we got justice for her, in the end." She shifted in the chair. "Right, dear. Do you think we can go see that cute nurse on reception and try to get my parole sorted out?"

❖

It was a glorious day. Tony sat on Jade's deck, lazily watching a pair of ducks paddle between the houseboats. Every so often, their heads disappeared under the dappled green water for insects and weeds. The sky was the pale blue of a baby's blanket and wispy with cloud. A warm breeze stirred the air.

Tony stretched. Her hands and shoulders were still sore, and she hadn't quite caught up on sleep, but life was starting to feel good again. She'd had a long talk with Maya. In the wake of all the miscommunication, Tony could see why Maya banged on about listening skills. Tony didn't know how quickly she could change a lifetime of ignoring what was right in front of her, but she was committed to having a go.

Jade and Maya had stepped out for croissants and pastries. They had spent the previous few days clearing, cleaning, painting, and repairing the damage on the houseboat. Jade's pagan friend had done a cleansing ritual. Tony had no idea what it entailed, but the whole boat smelled of sage.

Tony glanced at her phone. She had a new email notification.

She opened her email app and clicked on a message from Amy, her ex-girlfriend and the other mother of Tony's child, Louise.

Tony's mouth dropped open as she read that Amy was bringing Louise back to London.

Whoa. That's going to change things.

Tony couldn't be happier for her daughter to come back home, but Amy?

A movement to her left made Tony turn her head. Frankie White was leaning casually against the cabin. She tapped two fingers to her forehead and gave Tony a little salute. Deirdre dropped in beside Frankie and then strolled across to an empty deck chair. She perched herself on it.

"You didn't give up. I appreciate that," Frankie said.

Tony responded with a nod. "Why did you say you'd lied about Ron Somers harassing you?"

Frankie sighed. "I needed Rose to move on. I couldn't take it anymore."

Tony turned to Deirdre with a frown.

Deirdre pushed huge round sunglasses further up her nose. "Being pulled to Rose all the time was hurting Frankie. It's disturbing for a spirit to be haunted like that by the living. What could she do? She couldn't talk to her. She couldn't be with her. It's nice when people think of you fondly. But when they won't let go of their grief, especially intense grief, it hurts. All that pain, thrown at a spirit, it's not cool. We expect it, initially, but if it goes on and on, it ties us to the living and it's painful."

"I just couldn't take it anymore. Plus, I got to thinking I was wrong about Somers. I don't remember him beating me up that night. It's all confused in my mind. I didn't know for sure that Somers let me die till now. She told me." Frankie pointed to Deirdre, who reclined gracefully into the deck chair. "I suspected, but I didn't know he set up the fight. If I'd known all that, and if I'd known about the confession, I'd have asked you to go after him." She shrugged. "But you did, anyway."

"Something was keeping you here. You probably knew on some level that you needed justice," Deirdre said.

"But being here was driving me nuts. I needed Rose to let go, and

I thought my way was best," Frankie said. "It turns out your way was better. Thanks, mate." Frankie ran a comb through her hair and smiled openly at Tony. She looked carefree and relaxed, like she did in the photo of her on the motorbike. With a final nod to Tony she vanished.

"Forgiven me yet?" Deirdre asked. She bit her lip tentatively.

Tony smiled at her. "Yes. Some people would say I'm lucky to have you. I'm not saying that. I'm just saying that some people would."

"Hmmph!" Deirdre snorted. "Oh, and sign Maya up for the agency. You never know when you might need some actual detecting."

"Jade and I were talking about that..." Tony said, but Deirdre disappeared too, just as Maya and Jade stepped onto the boat and tossed a bag of warm croissants in Tony's direction.

Jade's appetite was back. Her skin looked vibrant, and the dull look in her eyes had almost disappeared. She was halfway through a pain au chocolat, letting the molten chocolate dribble over her fingers.

Tony's mobile rang. The caller ID said Carol Lewis. Tony spoke to her while Maya made coffee and Jade started on another croissant.

Sergeant Lewis didn't talk for long. Tony relayed the information. "Jade, Sergeant Lewis thinks Anita got out of the country. Her name was on a passenger list on a flight to the US three days ago."

Jade froze.

"The US officials have been informed, so there's a chance she'll be picked up."

Jade and Maya exchanged a look.

"But there's some good news. The CPS is taking up the case against Ron Somers."

"Good," Maya said. She was sipping her espresso from a pure white espresso cup that Tony didn't remember Jade having. She suspected Maya had bought Jade a set.

Tony turned to her. "Jade and I have a proposition for you."

Maya smiled. "I don't care how many times you ask me, I'm not going to do my trapeze act in my skimpy, body-hugging costume."

Tony gulped. "I haven't ever asked you that, but I will now."

Jade's face relaxed. She broke into a smile. "That I got to see. But that wasn't the proposition. We'd like you to join the agency."

Maya raised her eyebrows. "Really?" She thought. "What would my role be?"

"Detecting," Tony said. "You're obviously good at it. And you can do all that other stuff, breaking into places, getting out of handcuffs..." The words resonated. Tony glanced at Jade.

She flinched. Then she caught Tony's eye. "Don't tiptoe round me, Tony. It's going to take some time, but I will heal from this. You can help by not acting guilty. It doesn't suit you, my friend."

"Learn from the situation and move on," Maya said. "We're all governed by our pasts. The trick is to be open to looking at that. I can trust my instincts again. A few months ago, I didn't know that, which is why I was so obsessed with making sure Jade was all right."

"Thank God you were," Jade murmured. She looked up from her new laptop to give Maya a sweet smile.

"I have to admit, this communication stuff of yours might actually be the tiniest bit useful," Tony said. She wanted to lean over and kiss Maya.

Jade cleared her throat. "I've been doing the accounts. They're in a dire state. The last cases have been expensive ones. We can't afford to run at a loss."

Tony sighed. "Yeah, we need to think about that."

"There is some good news." Jade clicked up a spreadsheet. "I've been researching the value of the stuff you kept from Smith's loft. The Revox is worth around two hundred pounds, and those tapes are about twenty-five pounds each. There were twenty of those. He had two hundred pound notes, and the going rate for an old pound note today is three pounds fifty. With the other stuff you brought out, all in all, we made approximately a thousand pounds from your attic clearance."

"Hey, that's not bad. The van only cost me forty," Tony said.

"Yeah, well, we had a lot of other expenses—hotel rooms, plane flights. We'll be lucky if we break even."

The barge owner's girlfriend stepped off the towpath onto her boat. She scowled at Tony, smiled at Maya, and beamed at Jade. Jade gave her a wave.

"So what do you say, Maya? You didn't give us an answer. Do you want to join our fun but costly detective agency?" Tony said.

Maya pursed her lips. Then she grinned wryly. "Why not? How dangerous can it be, right?"

Tony raised her coffee mug. "To the Supernatural Detective Agency," she said.

They leaned in for a clink of cup against mug.

The barge owner's girlfriend screwed her eyes up suspiciously at them and then swung the door closed with a slam.

"The Supernatural Detective Agency," they said in chorus.

About the Author

Crin Claxton is the author of the vampire novel *Scarlet Thirst* and the ghost mystery *The Supernatural Detective*. Short stories have been published by Diva Books, Bella Books, Bold Strokes Books, *Diva* magazine and *Carve* webzine. S/he has recipes in *The Butch Cook Book*. Poems have been published by Onlywomen Press and La Pluma. *The Supernatural Detective* won honorable mention in the Foreword Indie Fab book of the year awards (2013, Gay & Lesbian section) and was nominated for the American Library Association Over the Rainbow booklist (2013).

Crin is a lighting designer and technician for theater. S/he is a qualified medical herbalist. S/he was Festival Director for the York Lesbian Arts Festival 2007–2009. S/he lives in London with hir wife and son.